About the Novel

Like her native Cuba, Graciela Altamira is beautiful, defiant, passionate, and constantly threatened with some kind of trouble.

Far from her tropical home, toiling in a New Jersey doll factory, Graciela longs for the same happy ending that always seems to come in her beloved *telenovelas* — a kiss powerful enough to erase the sins of her past and the haunting memory of her homeland.

But how can she forget when she lives among the ghosts of that little Cuban town? With Caridad and Imperio — two women Graciela has known since girlhood — by her side in the factory, it seems she'll never be free of her past, never truly able to pursue the possibility of love she finds quite unexpectedly in the cold, gray New Jersey winter.

Tomorrow They Will Kiss is a tale of love pursued at any cost, of how friendship and history unite us for better or worse, and of the hope for that redemptive kiss capable of reconciling estranged lovers and countries.

"Eduardo Santiago has captured the voice of Cuban womanhood in all its whimsical, musical beauty. This is a compelling and compassionate story."

—Charles Fleming,
author of *After Havana* and *The Ivory Coast*

Ibarionex Perello

EDUARDO SANTIAGO was born in Cuba and grew up in Los Angeles and Miami. He was a 2004 PEN Emerging Voice Rosenthal Fellow, and his writings have appeared in *Zyzzyva*, *The Caribbean Writer*, *Slow Trains*, the *Los Angeles Times*, *Square Peg Magazine*, and *I.F.P. Magazine*. He holds a BFA in Film and Television from California Institue of the Arts and is a former writer-producer on several Telemundo sitcoms. He has also worked as an event organizer at independent bookstores. He currently writes for CBS2 News in Los Angeles, where he lives with his dog, Lyon.

TOMORROW THEY WILL KISS

Tomorrow They Will Kiss

A NOVEL

EDUARDO SANTIAGO

BACK BAY BOOKS

LITTLE, BROWN AND COMPANY

NEW YORK   BOSTON

Back Bay Books / Little, Brown and Company
Time Warner Book Group
1271 Avenue of the Americas, New York, NY 10020
Visit our Web site at www.twbookmark.com

First Edition: July 2006

The characters and events in this book are fictitious. Any similarity to real
persons, living or dead, is coincidental and not intended by the author.

CIP or LOC no. TK

10 9 8 7 6 5 4 3 2 1

BINDER'S CODE TK

Printed in the United States of America

DEDICATION TO COME

A single Cuban can manage to gain anything in this world except for the applause of another Cuban.

— Luis Aguilar Leon

TOMORROW THEY WILL KISS

Chapter 1

GRACIELA

Telenovelas can be cruel with that first kiss. I sat in front of my television set and waited for the protagonists to finally find true love the way farmers waited for the first rains of spring.

"Don't worry, Graciela. Tomorrow they will kiss," I sighed to myself with complete certainty as the night's episode ended. I always watched as the names of the actors rolled across the screen while the romantic theme song played. This was my time. This was when, inspired by the music and the drama I had just watched, I allowed my mind and my heart to merge, just for a blissful moment, just until a screeching commercial message shook me out of my daydream. Used Cars! Used Appliances! Easy Credit! It was 1967 and everything offered to Latinos on the Spanish-language channel was just as used.

I turned off the set and went into the bedroom to check on my two boys. Ernestico, who was nine years old, slept curled up in a ball, his long legs tucked under like a cricket. Manolito, one year younger, slept on his back, his chubby self open to the ceiling, fearless.

I returned to the living room, unfolded the sofa into the uncomfortable bed it became every night, and lie down.

Alone, as usual.

But as always, with a little prayer to every saint and virgin I had ever heard about. Even the ones I didn't believe in.

"Send me the right man," I prayed, "or take away my desire to find true love."

Early the next morning, I waited downstairs in the cold, narrow lobby and that strange loneliness came over me again. I thought how warm and comforting it would be to have a man's arms around me. My breath made a cloud on the glass door and I drew a heart in it with my finger. For a second, I imagined the face of Mr. O'Reilly, the foreman at the factory, in the middle of the heart.

"Estás loca," I said to myself. You're crazy. And using the same finger, I quickly drew an arrow through it.

A familiar car horn cut through the frozen darkness. I tightened my overcoat and rushed out into the wintry New Jersey wind, across the stretch of icy sidewalk to the idling van.

Six of us rode with Leticia to the toy factory every morning. Imperio and Caridad were already there, as usual. They were always the first to be picked up and the last to be dropped off.

Caridad was sitting in the front passenger seat and Imperio sat in the back, behind Leticia. When I slid open the door, a gust of cold blew into the overheated van that always smelled like raw pork. Particularly in winter, when the windows had to be shut tight against the cold.

"Por Dios, Graciela, close the door," Imperio said before I

had a chance to sit down. It was as if she expected me to get in without disturbing the temperature.

Imperio had a sharp tongue that she tried to soften by constantly referring to God. *"Por Dios,"* she'd say, or *"Dios Mio"* or *"Santa Madre de Dios."* But there was venom behind her benedictions. She was a short and skinny person and had always had, as long as I could remember, a nasty disposition, a tendency to complain and to order people around. Which was odd coming from such a tiny person. Even after she reached maturity she was built like a ten-year old boy. Her dark skin had a reddish tint to it that became even more noticeable whenever her anger flared, which was frequently. She did not have any children of her own. Maybe this was because of her impossibly narrow hips and flat chest, or her sour spirit, or because she once saw a dog take his last breath. Or maybe because sometimes the saints really were paying attention.

"Santa Madre de Dios, I can't stand this cold wind one more minute," Imperio said. "I'll never get used to waking up while it's still dark out and spending the rest of the day in dusk until nightfall. It's inhuman."

"Imagínate," Caridad said with a delicate shiver, "they say it's going to drop below zero again tonight."

Caridad was thick of build, but not fat. She looked luxuriously stuffed and upholstered, like an expensive sofa. Her skin was very pale, and she carried herself with an elegance that, as a girl, I had admired from a distance. Her big brown eyes were always in a state of surprise or discovery. She wasn't stupid. She just wanted everyone to believe that she was as innocent and sheltered as a society debutante. That she was the type of person who had never been touched by the cruelties of the real world. That at the slightest provocation she could swoon.

"Imagínate!" She'd gasp whenever something offended her fragile sensibilities. More often than not, during such exclamations, a pale hand clutched at the invisible pearls around her neck.

Every morning, Caridad came to work in a starched blouse, freshly powdered, creamed and perfumed as if she was sitting in a breezy veranda. She loved powders and creams and she did without essentials in order to purchase expensive products from Spain. They had all but vanished from Cuba but she could now find them at any Puerto Rican bodega. They were kept behind the counter, inside a locked, glass case, and had to be asked for.

She bought and used them carefully, applying the rose-scented Maja de Myrugia, the delicate lavender of Lavanda Puig and particularly the cream from Heno de Pravia, in tiny dabs to her plump, aristocratic hands. She would never offer any to the others, even in winter when all our hands were red and chapped. Caridad only had one daughter, the unfortunate Celeste, who was born with the wizened, crinkly eyes of an old man. Celeste, I'd noticed, wasn't developing like a normal child, she was slow to reason, had trouble speaking, and she never smelled as sweet as her mother.

A few blocks later, we stopped for Berta, who was in her sixties and came from Formento, a town in Central Cuba that none of us had heard of before. Berta had been in the United States since she was a young girl, long before the Revolution. She came to Union City to work in the lace factories and even though the lace business had long since dried up, she never went back.

"I always meant to return," Berta said, "and now it's too late."

Berta's legs swelled up like hams from standing at the assembly line all day long. As soon as she got in the van, she took off her shoes and massaged her legs — which were blue and knotted with varicose veins. All the way to the factory, she moaned as she squeezed, *"ay, ay, ay."*

The last woman to be picked up, and always the first one we dropped off, was Raquel, who was younger than Berta but often looked much older. And her legs didn't swell up.

Raquel could try anyone's patience, even those, like me, who liked her. All she ever talked about was what she, in Union City, had too much of, and what her husband and the others back in Cuba had to do without. Her husband was serving 15 years in one of Castro's jails. She would never say why, which drove Imperio and Caridad wild with curiosity.

"Chá," Raquel said whenever they brought it up. Not a word, but a sound; hard and final. Her husband was not a character in a *telenovela*. He was not up for discussion.

Raquel arrived in the States with just her three daughters. Most days, she wore her dark hair in a dirty ponytail that sat on top of her head like a little fountain. The only vanity she allowed herself was the orange lipstick that she carelessly ran over her thick lips.

Some mornings it was painfully obvious to me that Raquel had been up all night crying, and I knew that it wasn't because the *telenovela* had taken a tragic turn. I imagined her in her cold little apartment with her little girls huddled around her, all staring at a picture of the missing husband, the missing father. Their sad faces lit by a votive candle — their hearts sick with fear. I imagined her waking up with a pillowcase covered with orange kisses. I knew only too well what it was like to be that lonely.

"They don't even have toilet paper in that country," Raquel said as soon as she took her seat. "They have to use newspapers to wipe."

"Por Dios," Imperio said, "those newspapers are just filled

with pictures of Fidel and his useless promises. Even if there was plenty of toilet paper, I'd still wipe my ass with it."

"Cha," Raquel said.

I could almost feel Raquel's relief when the van pulled into the factory's parking lot. As soon as it had stopped, she jumped out and rushed in ahead of the others, steam trailing from her nostrils.

"She's wasting her time waiting for that man," Imperio said as we hurried across the freezing stretch of concrete. "He's not coming back, I'll bet you any amount of money that he's been executed. *Por Dios*, who knows what he did to those men in the beards."

"You know how it is back there," Leticia said, "all you have to do is look at them wrong and they shoot you."

"Is that true?" Berta asked. "Has it gotten to that point?"

"And worse," Caridad said.

"What could be worse?" Berta asked.

Imperio and Caridad exchanged looks and moved on ahead with Leticia. I fell behind with Berta. It was a very cold November and there were no simple answers.

Raquel could go day after day in silence, but then, when least expected, a lament inevitably popped out of her orange mouth. It was almost like a nervous tick. As unpredictable, uncontrollable, and annoying as that.

"They have *apagónes* every night," she said as we drove home one night. Blackouts. "They live in darkness."

It was a dark blue night in Union City too, the streetlights hadn't gone on yet.

"Raquel," Imperio said, "why don't you get a really long extension cord and run it from your house to Cuba? *Por Dios, mu-*

jer, you could bite it between your teeth and dog paddle back. It's only 90 miles from Key West."

"*Imagínate!*" Caridad said, moving a hand delicately to her neck.

Raquel smiled, too. But embarrassment turned the orange smile crooked. I only half-listened. I kept my eyes on the dark road, waiting for the magic moment when the streetlights would go on.

"*Niiiiñas,* let's talk about something else," Leticia sang out. She always used the word *niñas* to get their attention, extending the first syllable like a telephone ringing. She called us *niñas,* the girls, as if she was the benevolent headmistress of a private school.

"*Niñas,*" she said, "did you watch *Cadenas de Amargura* last night? It's getting good! *La solterona,* the spinster, is not as innocent as you think. I suspect she's been secretly married before and that Jorge Alberto is really her son and that he's the one who paid for her operation."

Leticia wasn't just fanatical about the *telenovelas.* She was obsessed. She talked as if she was a part of them, she delighted in figuring out what was going to happen next, what dramatic new turn and twist the plot would take. She was the first to start watching them. Now we were all addicted. All except Raquel, who daily endured our frivolous chatter.

"How can I enjoy a *telenovela,* when the people back in Cuba are living in despair?"

I felt terrible for poor Raquel. I knew that her husband never wrote to her. I knew that all the information she got was through his family, that their letters painted as bleak a picture of life in Cuba as possible. I knew those letters always included requests for money — but never a word or mention about her husband's situation. Was he dead? Ill? Had he been transferred to another prison? Why didn't he write? Raquel knew nothing. But she held on to the memory of her husband with both hands. She told me that she was sure that one day they would be reunited, and that she didn't care how long she waited or what sacrifices she had to make.

"But why doesn't he write to you?" Imperio asked one day.

"Chá," said Raquel, "do you think they let prisoners anywhere near a pencil? Or a stamp? He's a prisoner and back there that means you don't exist."

Imperio and Caridad liked to pretend that they were concerned for Raquel. I knew they just enjoyed taunting her, getting the kind of pleasure children get out of picking at a scabby knee. But with those two it was better to just ignore them, as I had been trying to do for most of my life. Unlike the other three who rode the van, Imperio, Caridad and I came from the same small town in Cuba: Palamagria. And if you want to know the truth, it was a stinky little town just like Union City, except the weather in New Jersey was worse. It was a place I thought I would never get away from. Then everything changed. Imperio and Caridad left in 1962, three years before I did. I truly believed I would never see them again. Which would have been just fine. After the way Caridad and Imperio had treated me. After the things they said behind my back. After what Imperio's husband, Mario, had done to me. But in 1965, if you were Cuban, you went to Miami or Union City. There were times when I wished I'd stayed in Miami, but I've come to understand why I had to leave.

As the van traveled through the New Jersey gloom, I looked out the window and watched the streetlights turn on, as if a joyful fairy was rushing ahead of me, unfolding the longest diamond necklace in the world. I tried to think of my life that way, as if something beautiful was flying ahead of me, lighting the way, illuminating the darkness. My future was bright. I just had to figure out a way to get there.

. . .

We all lived in the same neighborhood in Union City, just blocks from one another, except Raquel, who lived out toward Newark, where apartments were even cheaper. Imperio and Caridad lived in the same building but on different floors, so they were always together, just like in Cuba. None of us had learned to drive, except for Leticia, who charged us each seven dollars a week, which was how she made the monthly payments on her van.

Riding with Leticia was more expensive than the bus, but to me, it was worth every cent. She picked us up at our front doors every morning and brought us back every night. Although Leticia was a recent exile just like rest of us, she had managed to get some money out of Cuba, and with that money she bought a used, bright-yellow Ford Econoline, tropical yellow, the color of the noontime sun. Imperio and Caridad said Leticia had dollar signs in her eyes, like a cartoon character.

The van had two purposes; Leticia's husband, Chano, used it early in the mornings to deliver pork to butcher shops. He started his rounds at three a.m. and was done by seven. Then he went home and slept all day. Leticia insisted that he clean it up before he handed it over to her. We could always tell when he was running late because the van smelled like a raw pig. Sometimes the floor was still sticky with bloody water from the packing ice. It could be disgusting. But, after a while I didn't even smell it anymore. It's amazing what people can get used to.

"It wasn't money she smuggled out," Imperio often said, "it was jewelry, and who knows where she had it hidden." Caridad always laughed at this, one of her little embarrassed laughs, like a Geisha.

Imperio swallowed her curiosity for as long as she could, and one day she just couldn't hold it any longer. We were all in the van when she finally dared to ask what she had long wanted to know. First, she looked at Caridad with an evil grin. She knew very well that what she was about to ask could put both of them on a bus.

"*Oye,* Leti," Imperio said in her chummiest voice, "is it true that you took jewelry out of Cuba in your *chocha?*"

Leticia didn't bother to answer. She ignored the question the way she ignored the honking drivers that regularly lined up behind her. Leticia's hands, big as a man's, held the steering wheel so tight I feared she would snap it in two. From where I sat I could only see the right side of her face, her thick, square jaw set firm. Leticia had an impressively strong face. Caridad once said it was "mannish." Imperio, behind her back, called her *cara macha,* (man face), and once even suggested that Leticia had hair on her chest.

"*Comemierda!*" Leticia shouted at the traffic. "These Americans drive like they own the road."

She hit the brakes hard to keep from slamming into a passing truck. There was a collective outcry from the back seat as we toppled forward. Even Caridad, who, from the passenger seat, saw it coming, had to place both hands on the dashboard to keep her head from crashing into the windshield.

The van continued on and everyone, a bit shaken but unharmed, settled quietly back into their seats. Dresses were smoothed over knees, hair patted back into place. For the moment, the subject of Leticia's smuggled jewels was dropped. Caridad turned her head back slightly, just enough to exchange a knowing smile with Imperio that said, "It's true, the lack of denial makes it so."

To them it was a big joke, but I wondered what that day had been like for Leticia, squatting in a dirty airport bathroom stall and shoving a handful of rings and necklaces in the most private and sensitive part of her body.

I felt safe with Leticia, even though she sailed through red lights as if they were only decorations and was frequently trailed by a chorus of angry, honking drivers. But her driving record was good, just two minor incidents in the couple of years since I had been riding with her. Imperio said that Leticia drove like a crazy woman on purpose.

"She had those accidents to make driving look difficult, to scare us out of getting our own licenses and our own cars," Imperio said when Leticia was out of earshot.

"Imagínate!" Caridad said, "she put our lives in danger just to keep collecting our money."

Not that any one of us could have dreamed of buying a car. Our little salaries barely covered rent, food, and the monthly payments to Crazy Eddie's for our television sets. We left everything behind in Cuba, arrived with absolutely nothing. No china, no family silver or photos, and definitely no toys for our children. Only Leticia had had the good sense and the courage to shove a handful of valuables into an unmentionable place, and now she alone reaped the rewards. Leticia and Chano, with their three incomes, were the rich ones.

The rest of us were poor, and painfully aware of it. So the fact that for the past three months Raquel and Berta had been stealing from the factory hardly bothered us at all, until Mr. O'Reilly posted a warning sign near the entrance. It was white with big black letters. The word 'crime' was in red! A Spanish translation, roughly scribbled on a piece of cardboard, was tacked just below it:

THEFT IS A SERIOUS CRIME.
THIEVES WILL BE PROSECUTED
TO THE FULL EXTENT OF THE LAW.

THE MANAGEMENT.

The day the sign first appeared, I walked through the narrow door of the factory ahead of the others, found my timecard, and clocked in. I walked right past it. I didn't stop to read it, didn't comment on it.

Jacinto Ramirez, the security guard, stood in front of the door that led into the work area. He was long-necked and long-nosed; every inch of his skin wrinkled and sagged. Jacinto was from Havana and, just because he came from the capital and now wore a uniform, thought himself superior to us.

"*Buenos dias,* Jacinto," I said and tried to get past him.

"*Buenos dias,* Graciela," Jacinto said. I stopped four feet before him, and even from that distance I could smell his dentures. I tried to continue, but he blocked my way, peering into my plastic bag.

Factory policy demanded that all female employees carry our belongings in a clear plastic drawstring bag that dangled from our elbows like a purse. No actual purses were allowed in the factory. My plastic bag contained a wallet, the key to my apartment, a compact, a hairbrush, and a sanitary napkin (for emergencies).

I hated those bags. But they didn't seem to bother the English-speaking employees — *las gringas, las negras, las boricuas.* None of them seemed to give them a second thought.

Us Cubans, we worked alongside black ladies who kept to themselves, Puerto Ricans who refused to speak in Spanish to us, and some white, stringy-haired girls so skinny they looked like they'd blow over if you whistled at them. They knew the rules and accepted them. We didn't.

"The situation is getting serious," Jacinto said pointing at the sign and stepping in front of me as if in a Mambo, "too many people with sticky fingers."

The others had stopped behind me, their arms folded protectively across their chests. I could hear them murmuring. Imperio, not known for her patience, walked right up to him.

"Look, Jacinto," she said, waving her bag in his face, her little body erect and sharp as a switchblade, "if you're insinuating something, just come out and say it."

Caridad took a deep, loud breath, so loud I could hear it. Her hand sprang to her throat. Leticia, Berta, and Raquel stood beside her. Their eyes tracked from Jacinto to Imperio and back again.

"*No señora,*" Jacinto said, flashing his false teeth. "*Adelante,* come in, come in."

Imperio didn't return the smile.

"If they dock us for being late," she said, "you're going to hear from me."

"*Imagínate,*" Caridad said as we entered the main floor, "I can understand inspections on the way out, but does that crazy man think we're smuggling toys *into* the factory?"

"This is getting worse than Cuba," Imperio said.

"*Niiiiñas,* I think he just wanted an excuse to frisk us," Leticia said. We all laughed louder than the comment deserved and continued walking with our plastic bags banging against our hips.

In spite of the laughter, the sign made us nervous. Not that anyone in the van ever thought of Raquel and Berta as thieves or criminals.

For what?

For stealing little plastic doll parts?

No.

Not after all we'd been through. We'd lost our country, had been forced into exile while the *Americanos* had stood by and done precious nothing. They owed us and some free dolls were a small price to pay.

Raquel and Berta innocently believed that by harmlessly stealing a leg here, an arm there, they would have a few complete dolls by Christmas.

"Stealing isn't the problem," Berta said as the van pulled out of the parking lot that night. She dug into her brassiere, pulled out a little rubber leg and handed it to Raquel.

"You're right," Raquel said as she casually took the little flesh-colored limb and dropped it into her clear plastic bag, where another little arm or a torso she had stolen that day was waiting.

"The real problem is that we work on so many different dolls that the arms and legs never match."

We worked on all types of dolls. Dolls that cried, dolls that peed, dolls that pretended to drink from a bottle, cute little baby dolls and frightening baby dolls as big as an actual baby. Dolls that walked, dolls that crawled. Dolls like little fashion models with perfect figures, exotic ball gowns and accessories: necklaces, bracelets, combs, hand mirrors, little purses, even a complete set of matching luggage.

"*Por Dios*, Raquel, it's going to take you forever. And even if you get all the parts, what will you do about its head?" Imperio asked.

"They're never going to let a Cuban work with heads," Caridad said, "not after the problem with Calixto."

Caridad nodded in agreement.

"Calixto was an idiot," Leticia said. "*Se pasó de mano.*" He went too far.

Less than a month ago we had watched as Mr. O'Reilly escorted Calixto Garcia, who worked in shipping, out of the factory.

"What did I do?" Calixto had shouted. "You got no proof. No proof."

Jacinto walked just a few steps behind, acting as if he had nothing to do with the firing of a fellow Cuban. That day, Jacinto became a traitor and Mr. O'Reilly, the enemy. From that moment on, Jacinto was pointedly ignored. "He's dead to me," Imperio said. To the foreman, the Cuban women only offered insincere, lipstick-smudged smiles.

Mr. O'Reilly, whose first name was Barry, didn't seem so awful to me. He did what he had to do. But even before the incident with Calixto, the others in the van had been suspicious of him. Mostly, because he wore his hair in a long, blond ponytail and had a pierced ear with a small, silver crucifix hanging from it.

"There's something wrong with that one," Imperio whispered to Caridad, making circles around her ear with her index finger.

Barry O'Reilly never sat with the other employees in the lunchroom. Instead, he read paperback books by himself. During the little free time I had at lunch, I spied on him.

I was intrigued by the covers of those books of his. I loved the exotic illustrations of dragons, spaceships, and fiery planets; sometimes even alien creatures and robots. I looked forward to new ones he would start.

I was even a little envious that Mr. O'Reilly, for a half-hour each day, could escape to such exotic destinations. My escape, the *telenovelas,* just took me to the same place every night, a mansion or country estate filled with conventional, earthbound romance. Sometimes I wondered if the day would come when I would know English well enough to read the kinds of books Mr. O'Reilly read. I wondered how that would change the way I looked at the world. But to the others at the assembly line, Mr. O'Reilly remained a danger, as if getting too close to him would expose us to a grave and contagious disease.

"Only a drug addict would read those kinds of books," Leticia said as she plugged a little flesh-colored leg into its little flesh-colored socket. She said something similar every time Mr. O'Reilly walked by.

"*Por Dios*," Imperio said, "I'm shocked at the number of people who use drugs in this country. I see it on the news. They're everywhere."

"*Imagínate*," Caridad said, waving a little leg in the air, "we saw them at the park, in groups, young people with long hair, bare feet, and crazy eyes. It gives me *escalofrios*." Shivers.

"And it's not just *los negros*, like in Cuba," Leticia said, tapping the skin of her arm with two fingers.

Mr. O'Reilly displayed every symptom described in the news: the long hair, the weird books, faded denims, his slow and drowsy way of speaking, and his habit of going into the wilderness for entire weekends. Having lost our country to a man who came down from the mountains, Cubans didn't trust anyone who would actually choose to go camping. But Mr. O'Reilly treated us with respect and seemed to enjoy working with Cubans. Oblivious to the contempt around him, he often dropped a word or two of high school Spanish into his greetings.

Every morning he walked past us on his way to his office and said, "*Buenos días*," and we chorused the same back without looking up, sounding as if someone had let the air out of our tires. We didn't take our eyes off the black conveyor belt and the hundreds of little limbs and torsos it constantly delivered to us.

Personally, I thought it was very sweet of Mr. O'Reilly to try to talk to us in our native language. One day I looked up as he approached. I tried to meet his eyes and give him a bit of a smile, just to let him know that, even if the others didn't, I appreciated his effort to communicate with us in Spanish. He sort of smiled back, his face reddened, his feet stumbled a little, and the rubber sole of his shoe made a squeaking sound on the polished cement floor.

After he moved on, I found that I liked thinking about him. He had a nice face, once I got past the long hair and the earring. But the hair could be cut, the earring removed. His eyes were blue and calm, his nose small and straight and sprinkled with just enough light brown freckles that I could almost see the child he'd once been. Yes, a very nice face.

To the others he looked like any other Americano, like the countless others that populated our new town. They were everywhere: walking down the street, driving past in cars, blue eyes staring from billboards holding a glass of Johnny Walker Red, or inviting you to walk a mile for a Camel. They were the enemy and Mr. O'Reilly was too, even though he could have had Calixto arrested but didn't. Never mind that Calixto had been caught smuggling boxes of toy trucks that he planned to sell for profit. Even after witnessing Calixto's downfall, Berta and Raquel continued to steal.

All the dolls we worked on were female, and they all had yellow hair and round, blue eyes. But none of us would ever be allowed to touch one of their heads. The head was the last thing that got attached before the dolls were dressed and packaged. The Cubans, they said, were too new to work with heads. Only the older and more trusted employees, usually American women, pale, trembling, and docile, were allowed to handle complete toys because of all the theft.

"I think it's bad enough that we have to carry our belongings in plastic bags," Caridad said.

"Even if there is good reason," Imperio said with a shaded look to Berta and Raquel, "I think keeping us away from heads is an unforgivable insult. *Por Dios,* we're not all thieves."

"In Cuba, everyone gets to work on everything without discrimination," Raquel said with the voice of a petulant child, her orange lips puckering into a pout.

"Raquel, in Cuba kids use empty rum bottles for dolls," Leticia said.

"Not in my house they didn't," Caridad said, almost a whisper.

"If you think it's better in Cuba," Imperio said to Raquel, glaringly now, "I'm sure Fidel will welcome you back with open arms and a bag full of toys."

Caridad didn't say anything, but she nodded her head in solemn accord.

"Chá," Raquel said, "I'm not talking about Cuba as it is, I'm talking about Cuba as it was."

Imperio and Caridad didn't seem satisfied with her answer; they couldn't stay out of other people's business.

"What good's a rumor if you can't spread it?" Imperio once said.

"Every rumor has a little truth in it," Caridad always added.

That day I took one look at Raquel's face, pinched to the edge of tears, and couldn't stop myself.

"Raquel," I said carefully, "I don't know why you even bother to open your mouth around these two."

Caridad turned until her round eyes met mine with a look of disbelief. Then, her eyebrows lifted almost imperceptibly, her lids opened slightly so that I felt like I was falling into the dark pits of her pupils. Then, just as quickly, Caridad's eyes returned to normal size and she turned back to face the road.

I knew what that look was about.

That look was a warning.

I had secrets.

Chapter 2

CARIDAD

My name is Caridad Rodriguez and, no matter what you've heard, I detest gossip. Sometimes I may share a thought or opinion with my best friend, Imperio. But other than that, I keep my thoughts to myself.

Take Graciela, for example. She is an unfortunate creature living a reckless life, yes. But I wouldn't dream of telling her how to live her life. One would think that after all she went through back in Palmagria, she would have learned her lesson.

But she clearly hasn't, and who am I to say? *Imaginate!*

Looking at her today, sitting quietly in the van, one might think that she is just another decent, hard-working Cuban in exile. But I know better. I know all about Graciela Altamira de la Cruz. I know more than I care to know.

I had known her since we were children, but I always kept my distance. Even as a little girl, she behaved provocatively. There was something off-putting about her. I always got the feeling that she would become annoying if she got too close or stayed too long. She was much too much. For one thing, she insisted on performing in every school assembly, reciting the verses of Jose Martí at every opportunity. Showing herself off. All through school, we were in the same classroom, but we almost never talked to each other. I always sat in the front row; Graciela sat in the back, with the boys.

Los Zapaticos de Rosa, the most famous poem by José Martí, became her specialty. It told the story of a rich girl who owned brand new rose-colored shoes. One day, her mother took her for a walk on the shore and they encountered a woman who had a little girl the same age. The little girl was deathly ill, and they were so poor, there was no hope for her. No hope at all. Overtaken by compassion, the rich girl gave her new shoes to the poor girl. But it was too late. The poor girl had died.

In the beginning, Graciela would just stand on the small stage and recite that long poem, from memory. As she got older, she started to embellish her recitations. In the third grade, she entered the stage carrying a tin pail filled with sand. She spread the sand on the floor so that it looked like she was at a beach and, while she recited, she scooped up handfuls of sand and let it all run through her fingers and back into the pail. She did this as if in a dream, perfectly timed so that when the poem ended all the sand was back in the yellow bucket.

In the fifth grade, she wore pink slippers just like the ones in the poem. *Imagínate!* By the time we were in the tenth grade, much too old for that sort of thing, she was wearing her hair in a big satin bow, the way girls wore them back in the days of *Martí.* It was annoyingly creative, but even I will admit that no one performed *Los Zapaticos de Rosa* like Graciela did; she put her whole heart and soul into it. Year after year, she brought the whole school to tears, and then cheers. She was featured in all the assemblies from the first grade on, getting better and more dramatic as we grew older. Others tried but without anything like the same success. In the Palmagria of my childhood, *Los Zapaticos de Rosa* was everyone's favorite poem. I like to believe it still is.

Of course, at the time, we had no notion what this poem was really about. We innocently believed it was about two little girls, one rich, one poor. We thought it was about how gracious and generous the rich could be to the poor. We were all dying for the chance to give away our new shoes to the less fortunate. Later, when the less fortunate were practically tearing the shoes off my feet as I ran to make the last boats out of the country, it became a different story altogether.

Imaginate! Through that poem, Graciela became something of a local celebrity, but also something of a curiosity, an eccentric you didn't want to get too close to. I really got to know her at Imperio's house. We must have been about thirteen, fourteen years old at the time; just becoming young women. I stopped by Imperio's house one afternoon shortly before summer vacation, and found Graciela teaching her how to cinch her waist with an old nylon stocking. Imperio, in a youthful fit of frustration and despair, had made the silly mistake of turning to Graciela for advice. Poor Imperio was sort of shapeless. She was not developing the wide hips and narrow waist every Cubanita desired. She was skinny, flat-chested, and lacked a single womanly curve. Her stomach bloated out forward and sideways. She had a pretty face and interesting, curly hair, but from the neck down she was a bit of a disaster.

In those days, the style was bright-colored blouses, starched and off-the-shoulder, narrow skirts with ruffles at the knee and wide belts with matching purse and shoes. The belt was worn as tightly as we could stand it to give us a desirable silhouette, because a girdle could only do so much. The hips were just as important as the breasts. Graciela could cock a hip like opening a drawer, and just by walking down the street she could make men spin like tops.

I sat on Imperio's bed and watched as Graciela studied her carefully. Graciela was undoubtedly flattered, and yes, honored, to be invited into our world. *Imaginate!* We played records and Imperio's mother brought in pastries and lemonade, which Imperio and I consumed with glee. Graciela hardly ate, which I found rather insulting. That afternoon, in front of my very own eyes, Graciela convinced Imperio to wear the nylon stocking 24 hours a day for as long as it took to train her waist.

The first time Imperio fainted was in the middle of English class. It was a particularly hot afternoon, the kind of afternoon that makes you feel like a lizard, drowsy and changing colors. Well, one moment Imperio's sitting in front of me, the next she has melted to the floor.

"It's the heat," Graciela said, and rushed to help her up. Imperio looked green, then blue, then white. I walked her outside until she could catch her breath. The same thing happened several times until the teacher discovered the source of the problem and cut the stocking off. Not long after that, Imperio found a boyfriend, a young man named Mario Santocristo, who noticed her because she kept fainting. Until then, Imperio had been just another girl among the others at school. But the fainting spells made her quite popular. As it happened, Mario liked her just as she was, short, skinny, and ill-tempered, and she happily gave up trying to be a curvaceous beauty.

Much to Graciela's frustration.

Imagínate! She actually believed that if Imperio kept that thing tied around her waist, it would give her a nicer figure. If it had been up to her, she would have kept poor Imperio in a constant state of suffocation.

Graciela had no such worries. She wasn't necessarily prettier than the other girls, but there was an exaggeration about her, partly God-given, partly created by her for her own personal reasons. No reasons I could even begin to imagine. Why would somebody want to stand out like that? I believed in a subtle, elegant beauty. But not Graciela.

Immediately after her fifteenth birthday, she transformed herself. Her belt was always wider than everyone else's, and instead of the pleated skirts we all wore, with two or three crinoline half-slips underneath, she wore very tight ones, as tight as she could, to better display her curvaceous figure. Of course, Graciela did have the advantage of height. She was much taller than girls usually grow in Cuba. Not to mention that her heels were higher and narrower than anyone else's in Palmagria. And her makeup! Well, let me just say she had a tendency to do everything bigger and brighter and leave it at that. She didn't even wait until she was fifteen, the way decent girls from good families did, to start wearing makeup. Long before her *quince años,* fifteen years, she was painted up and getting more attention than she deserved. To this day, she can draw on her eyebrows to perfection, even while the van is moving.

I suppose you think I am being *criticona,* but I deny that. It's not my character. If anything, I am very accepting. I simply know her too well. Not that there was ever much of a mystery to Graciela Altamira. Not for me, anyway. She lived in the nicest house in the worst part of town. Right next to her front door there was a narrow alley that led to what we call a *solar*, which is a cluster of one-room huts where the poorest of the poor live, where they still cook with wood, where everybody sleeps in the same bed, and there are so many skinny, bloated-bellied babies running around that it looks like some kind of refugee camp. Only the people who lived there dared go inside. If I slowed down a little while I walked by, out of the corner of my eye I could see how they lived in there. It was rather disgusting.

There were always two or three old women sitting outside with the sun cooking their skin, their big, flowered skirts hiked up above their knees, *chismeando*, while they ate a mango or a slice of watermelon. They looked at me in exactly the same way I looked at them, *con sospecha*, but I always said, *"Buenas."*

A lot of the women from the *solar* made their living as domestics. They came to our houses to cook, clean, and wash our clothes. They were rough women who never thought twice before getting into hair-pulling fights with each other. But in our houses, they were more civilized. Everything was, *"Si señora,"* no matter the request.

Their men were another story. They were fishing or they were drunk. Mostly they drank. And they drank so much they slept on the sidewalks, sometimes even in the middle of the street, or wherever they fell down, or passed out, or whatever it was those people did. So it was up to their women to provide for all those dirty, bloated children.

Imagínate! Graciela lived among those people all her life. Until she married. Not that she married right away.

The rest of us had been married about two years when Graciela and Ernesto de la Cruz got together. Three of us who attended the same schools, Azucena Martines, Cuca Soto, and me, were already pregnant with our first children. Actually, Cuca

Soto was on her second or third. I lose count with her. You could say she was making up for Imperio, who for some mysterious reason refused to conceive. The decent women of Palmagria limited themselves to one or two children. It was only the very poor who insanely had as many babies as God would send them. But even I have to admit that Imperio took it too far, and her husband didn't seem to care.

I married the perfect man, Salud Gutierrez. Salud was a chiropodist, which is practically a doctor. Sure, there were times when I looked at his hands and thought, "All day long he touches people's feet, digs out rotted toenails, cuts out infected calluses." But then I forced myself to think about all the money he made. In a town like Palmagria, where most everybody walked miles every day, his services were in great demand. There was always somebody limping painfully into his office.

And Salud, in spite of his limited education, had a talent, an instinct that no amount of schooling could provide. He had no close friends, but people respected him, and he was the only chiropodist around. Everyone called him "El Medico."

Ernesto de la Cruz was the last person I ever expected would get involved with Graciela Altamira, and he would live to regret it. He was our former teacher; a teacher so loved and respected, they even made him principal. The youngest principal the school had ever had. He was not one of those dreamy teachers that make girls swoon during class. Handsome he was not, not even a little, but he was attractive in his own way. And solid. People always said that Ernesto de la Cruz was solid.

"*Un verdadero caballero,*" they said. A true gentleman.

He was always punctual, prepared, and ready to teach. He did not have a sparkling personality, but his lectures were always interesting, so students rarely fell asleep during his classes. Unlike other teachers we had, who could just as easily have been driving a bus for a living, Ernesto de la Cruz loved his work, you could tell. It was this passion that made us pay attention. When they promoted him no one was surprised.

"*Se lo merece,*" they said. He deserves it. They honored him with bottles of red Spanish wine and boxes of cigars, which he accepted graciously, humbly. Everything in his life seemed to be going well, perfection. Until the day when tragedy struck. After that, nothing was ever good again.

His wife, Josefa, may she rest in peace, died unexpectedly of a heart attack. No one could figure out how someone that young could die so suddenly of a heart attack, but that was exactly what happened. They had been married about ten years and one afternoon when Ernesto went home for lunch, which he did every day, he found her fully dressed and peacefully asleep in their bed. She never woke up.

Imagine what that must have been like! *Imagínate!* The news spread quickly and everyone felt terribly sad — unusual in a town that celebrates the misfortunes of everyone else. But Ernesto de la Cruz was special to us. He had touched all of our lives. I remembered him standing in front of the chalkboard, year after year, his fingertips white with chalk dust. He was a man of letters, a cultured man who read thick, leather-bound books and listened to classical music. Bach, Beethoven, and Mozart could be heard floating out from the windows of his house on Sunday mornings. And even though that was not the kind of music we associated with happiness (Palmagria being the sort of place where radios went on at breakfast and stayed on all day long, shaking our houses with the rumba, the samba, and the cha-cha-cha), somehow we knew that, in their own quiet way, Ernesto and Josefa had a happy home.

I often saw Ernesto and Josefa at the movies. They seemed to enjoy all sorts of films, from adventures to love stories. Whenever the program changed, they were first in line, holding hands like newlyweds. Or sometimes I'd see them sitting side-by-side on a park bench, watching people walk by. Everyone said 'hello' to the professor, and he always said 'hello' back and included your name.

"Hola, Caridad," he always said to me. He remembered the name of each and every student he ever taught. He had an impressive memory. Josefa would just smile slightly and nod a greeting. She was not the kind of woman to make a big show of herself. In fact, I think she would have been embarrassed by the spectacle of her own funeral.

Imagínate! The funeral was held at Señora Santa church, of course, and attracted such a crowd that people were mobbed around the block. Many of them were Ernesto's former students come to pay their respects, along with their children, their parents, and even the most distant of relatives.

"Hurry," one woman said as she scampered up the steps with three small children in tow. She was wearing white high heels and a tight black dress, much too tight for the occasion.

Everybody wanted to be inside that church.

Shouts swarmed around me: "Save me a seat!" "Meet me inside!" "I can only stay for the beginning!"

It was as if they were going to the first night of the most popular movie in the world.

But let me tell you, those who weren't able to get into the church were the lucky ones. Inside it was so hot, I could barely catch a breath. *Por suerte,* I had my cardboard fan, as did many others. Those who had not thought ahead fanned themselves with whatever was available: a hymnal, a folded newspaper, a magazine, or a hat.

Meanwhile, at the altar, Padre Anselmo struggled to say something of significance about Josefa. Sweat poured out of him as he tried to come up with something other than the usual. I couldn't really blame him. Who really knew Josefa and what had she done? Nothing to speak of. She was not a member of a charity, she didn't leave children or pets behind, had no close friends, kept to herself. All she really did was take care of Ernesto, which we all appreciated. Ernesto had been her life. And so it was that the sermon and eulogy were all about her husband's achievements, accomplishments, and his unimaginable pain "at this dark moment," rather than anything to do with Josefa.

"Stay close to him," Padre Anselmo said, pointing at Ernesto's bowed head. "Today is almost like a feast day for him compared with what's to come. The funerals, the masses, the burials, all keep us so busy we almost don't know what has happened. The dearly departed is still above ground, still with us," he said pointing at the coffin in front of him. "His most trying days are yet to come. After she's buried, after she's gone."

Here, Padre Anselmo paused. And I could see, because I had one of the best seats in the church, that a little light had gone on inside his bald and shiny head. It was his job to make us cry and he was not going to let us out of that sweltering church until he had done it.

"Tomorrow our beloved friend and teacher will wake up alone," Padre Anselmo said, pausing to make sure we were all listening. Fans, missals, magazines, and hats all stopped in midair. Only an occasional tickling cough could be heard.

"He will walk around his lovely home expecting to hear the cheerful voice of his beloved wife and it will not be there. He will smell her scent, still lingering, but he will not hear her footsteps, nor receive the gentle kiss which always greeted him upon awakening."

He stopped to take a well-rehearsed breath. I heard sighs all around.

"He will walk through his days," the priest went on, "with a broken heart. He will attend his classes and impart knowledge as he always has but he will not be the same man. His eyes will be like shattered glass and his heart a field of pain."

I watched as Ernesto dropped his face into his hands as his shoulders began convulsing with sobs. I heard all the women start to let go, as they always, inevitably, did. The wailing began. The fanning started up again. Padre Anselmo continued to talk though he could hardly be heard above all the noise, but that was not his concern. His job was done.

I felt my own warm tears.

To make bad matters worse, someone had the well-intentioned but terrible idea of hiring a violin player to accompany the long, slow exit from the church. As soon as the pallbearers picked up the coffin, the violin music began. The strings cut through our hearts, uniting us in our grief. Most of all, we grieved for our beloved teacher. His pain was our pain. His loss was our loss.

Outside the church in the scorching sun, we could barely move. It took what seemed like hours to get everyone out and on their way to the cemetery. I watched patiently as eyes were dabbed, handkerchiefs passed hands, noses were blown. Imperio came and stood next to me.

"It's like a disgusting competition," she said, "to see who can suffer the most, who can squeeze the most fluids out of their useless heads. *Por Dios*, they hardly knew the woman!"

I knew she was only saying those words to keep from showing her own emotions so I just nodded, the way I often do with Imperio. She is a good person, she just seems a little cold-hearted sometimes.

"And did you see who slithered over to Ernesto, like butter on bread?" She said as we started walking.

"No," I said.

"Graciela, who else?"

I looked around but finding her in the crowd was almost impossible.

Most everyone who had been at the funeral went to the cemetery. It was an exhausting procession; the hearse creaked slowly, first over cobblestone and then on the bumpy dirt road. It was a rough, hot, dusty walk, but we couldn't let our professor bury his dear wife all alone.

Most of us had rushed to his house the moment we heard that Josefa had passed on. Those of us who were most familiar with him went inside where we drank café, ate white cheese on crackers and told stories until sunrise.

Graciela was there that night making trips to and from the kitchen, passing out *galletas* like she was one of the family.

And now I saw her.

Oh, she was much too much.

I tapped Imperio on the shoulder. "There she is."

"*Que te parece?* What do you think?"

Imperio smiled, a tight-lipped grimace, no teeth. Together we kept an eye on her.

Graciela had somehow managed to be right next to Ernesto, where she remained all the way to the cemetery. Imperio and I saw when she pretended to trip on a rock and he took her by the elbow. We were there when they were lowering the coffin and tears brimmed her eyes, tears that flowed as clean and clear as if from a mountain spring, (Graciela, out of respect, had not worn a speck of makeup that day).

I watched as Ernesto reached into his breast pocket and offered her a handkerchief, which she used to daintily dab her cheeks.

"A handkerchief that Josefa washed, ironed, and perfumed, just before she died." Imperio said out of the side of her mouth.

I barely heard what else she said because I had noticed that the stubborn and thoughtless violinist had followed us to the cemetery and had started to play again. Couldn't he hear the wails and sobs already crowding the graveyard? Did he have to make it worse with his mournful music?

It was clearly having the same effect on Imperio.

"I can't stand it any longer," she said and walked right up to him. He saw her coming and a defiant smile spread across his face.

"You have to stop," she said, very respectfully, or so I thought. (Although from the furor that it caused later, one would think she had attacked the man with a hammer). He refused. He continued to wring those depressing sounds out of his instrument. Personally, I was shocked at his insensitivity. But scrawny, old, and hunched over with arthritis, he was no match for Imperio.

So she grabbed, I mean, took — the violin from him and stuffed it — placed it — very carefully in its case. She held onto it for him until the body was safely in the ground. Then, and only then did she return it to him. That was all she did. Don't think for a minute that I didn't hear about it from everyone I ran into for the next few weeks. I thought most everyone had been relieved when that dreadful music stopped, and everyone was, except those who always had their tongues wagging, those who were always ready to start problems. In Palmagria, there was never a shortage of those.

Imagínate. Poor Josefa was barely cold in her grave when Ernesto started to visit Graciela at her parents' house. The first time we thought nothing of it. But then we saw him go there again and again — sometimes with flowers, sometimes with a greasy bag of *churros.*

"That can only mean one thing," Imperio said.

I simply nodded. That first time, we just happened to be passing by when we saw him at her door. In short sleeves, like he was visiting relatives. After that we made it a point to walk by after dinner, just to satisfy ourselves that what we thought was happening really was.

"*Por Dios,* by the time a man comes to your house with *churros,*" Imperio said, "he's already had plenty of time and encouragement to take that step, if you know what I mean."

Oh, I knew exactly what she meant. I did not need to be there to know exactly what was going on in the living room. I knew that Graciela and Ernesto would be on the sofa, holding hands. That Graciela had forced her poor mother into the kitchen to brew *café* and arrange the deep-fried pastries on a fancy plate, and that her father was sitting on an armchair opposite the couple, talking business and politics — man to man — with Ernesto. Making a connection, under Graciela's watchful eye, adopting him as his own son against his better judgment. She was controlling everything. Of course she was!

Ernesto de la Cruz was a catch. Even if he was a widower, which usually put a black mark on a man. In other parts of the country, it may have been different, but in Palmagria and the rest of our province, a widower was expected to remain that way for the rest of his life, because no self-respecting woman, no matter how desperate, was going to get close to a man with the stench of death still clinging to him. *Imaginate!* Everyone knew that in his house still hung the picture of the dearly departed wife. That white flowers had to be placed under it. And that at Christmas, Easter, on her birthday, on her Saint's Day, and on the anniversary of their wedding, and of her death, they would have to make the trip back to the cemetery, back to her grave, to offer flowers and beg forgiveness. Everyone knew that if the spirit of the deceased didn't approve of the new wife, there would be trouble — sometimes manifested by apparitions, warnings, or plain bad luck.

Graciela's parents were superstitious and terrified. But Graciela ruled over them. It was obvious to me that they had received a good talking to. Clearly, Graciela convinced them that Ernesto was an exception, that he may very well be her last chance at a good marriage. So her poor parents had to go through the motions, reluctantly followed the rules of courtship.

"It's sort of like a shotgun wedding," Imperio said, "except in this case, it's the bride who is holding the shotgun."

"It is much too much," I said. "The situation verges on blasphemy."

"Por Dios," Imperio said, "Josefa's mother is still in full mourning. Graciela's parents can't look their neighbors in the eye."

But we knew there was nothing anyone could do. Graciela had always intimidated her parents. Unheard of in Palmagria, where parents held the right to govern their grown children, and their children's children, until death and often beyond.

How Ernesto went from quiet, sedate Josefa to crazy Graciela is one of the great mysteries of Palmagria. There are many stories about how Graciela managed to snag Ernesto. Some said she sat in his class day after day without bloomers. *Imagínate!* Some people will say anything. Once I got over the shock, it was not hard for me to figure it out. Graciela was no mystery to me. She was so transparent it was almost indecent. The answer was simple. She wasn't getting any younger. Most of the men in our age group were spoken for, and Graciela's desperation was starting to show. It got so we were uncomfortable when our husbands were around her. So, even though the union of Ernesto and Graciela was not one we approved of, not even a little, we were almost relieved.

From the start, there was trouble.

I remember that wedding very well. Not because of the wedding itself, but because of the horrible event that took place on the very same day.

Imagínate! The wedding was held at the exact same church where Josefa's funeral had taken place just a few short months before. There was a smaller, less ornamental chapel in Palmagria, and certainly the wedding of a widower did not call for such a big to-do, but Graciela insisted on the big church and Graciela got it. Fortunately, she had the good sense to settle for just the wedding ceremony and not the endless Latin mass, so the whole ordeal was relatively brief.

Immediately after the chaste kiss that I truly hoped would unite them for life, with a sigh of resignation, we stood up to leave.

"*Gracias a Dios,*" Imperio said with a roll of her eyes as we filed out of the church, "it's finally over."

Arroz Blanco, a local lunatic believed to bring good luck to brides, was standing just outside of the church, and Graciela, in one of her typically false and exaggerated gestures, walked out of the church (to a half-hearted showering of good wishes) and handed her wedding bouquet to Arroz Blanco.

Arroz Blanco took the flowers greedily, her demented eyes like two spinning marbles. Graciela continued on, walking proudly, smiling and waving as if she had just set a great example for us all. As if to say, 'Look at me! Look at how lovely and generous I am to the less fortunate. Why, I've grown up to be just like Pilar in the poem. I would give her my pink shoes too, if I had them.'

Graciela did not see what Imperio and I saw. As soon as Graciela had moved on, Arroz Blanco promptly started to eat the bouquet, as if she were a goat.

We looked at each other with tears in our eyes. Imperio was the first to go, and I'm afraid I didn't hold back much longer. I felt terrible, but how could we not laugh? The sight of that poor, demented creature eating Graciela's wedding bouquet like it was a salad was much too much. That was bad enough, but the last thing Graciela needed was the sad spectacle that was taking place in the tenement next to her house.

"It's a bad omen when your own parents won't attend your wedding," Imperio was saying as we walked from the church to Graciela's house after the wedding. We were strolling leisurely, taking our time. The afternoon sun was mild, the sky was a beautiful, brilliant blue. The only thing that would have made it a more perfect day for a wedding would have been a quick, thick, rain shower. It means good luck. But the only black cloud that day was Graciela's parents refusal to attend the wedding.

"Graciela said they were not feeling well."

"Both of them?" Imperio asked. "I don't believe it. Do you?

Cuca Soto told me that this morning she heard shouts coming from their house."

"They have to know what a slap in the face this is," I said. "Their only daughter."

"*Por Dios,* she's their only *anything,*" Imperio said, picking up the pace. "The father of Azucena Martinez got out of his deathbed just so he could walk her down the aisle, then he went home and died. Remember?"

Imperio was getting so worked up that I could hardly keep up with her. The shoes I had bought just for the wedding were killing me. I knew Salud would not approve, so I didn't complain. How would that look? After all, I am the chiropodist's wife.

As we turned the corner, I was shocked by the staggering amount of people standing outside Graciela's house. For a split second I felt the stirrings of jealousy, like a subtle altering of my pulse that so many people had come to wish her well on her wedding day. Surprising, because when a girl marries late in life — Graciela was already 22 — or marries a widower, the celebration is played down. Rather than a big party, there is more of a wake, a polite little *brindis,* a toast, just the immediate members of the family, and one or two of the bride's and the groom's closer friends. Cake is served, champagne is poured, someone says a few words and everyone goes home. No music, no dancing.

So the excitement was completely unexpected.

"It's that type of neighborhood," Imperio said, and stopped to survey the pushing, sweating, crowd. "Poor people are all very close and in each other's business all the time."

But we soon discovered, the cause of the commotion was not Graciela's wedding. It was something even more horrendous.

First I noticed the ambulance and I said, "Oh, something horrible has happened to Graciela's father."

"Maybe he really *was* too sick to attend," Imperio said as she slowed down to a stop.

Then we saw both her parents looking through the window, their faces so pale they looked like two wax figures, but both very much alive.

And then the ugly story emerged from the depth of the *solar.*

"Drowned . . ." was all I heard at first; like a whisper out of a nightmare.

". . . kill their own children . . ." someone else was saying as I passed by. I wanted to get closer to where Graciela was.

". . . the mother, I'll stake my money on it . . ." another finished, callously. How could he know? I wondered. Why is it always the mother?

Buzz, buzz, buzz. Everyone whispered at once. It was like walking through a beehive. Imperio, who's smaller and faster, disappeared from my side and returned a moment later with the news.

"Dios mío," she said, both hands on her cheeks, "someone in the *solar* drowned a newborn baby in one of the outhouse latrines. And the military police are going from hut to hut, inspecting all the women to see who looks like she might have just delivered."

I shuddered to think of the humiliation those women must be suffering, to have to get so intimate with a sweaty, insensitive policeman. It was much too much.

The crowd was getting thicker, louder and smellier by the minute as word spread through to other neighborhoods. People rushed in as if someone was handing out free money. I had to dig the heels of my new shoes into the ground to keep from being swept into the alley by the gawking, curious mob.

I managed my way closer, to get a sidelong glance. Suddenly, I caught a glimpse of Graciela, in her white dress and veil. She zigzagged through the crowd, pushing people aside trying to make it to her front door. It was at that moment that I heard a collective groan, as if the crowd had gotten a whiff of something vile. It erupted like a wave, starting at the front and working its way to the rear (by now there were people all the way round the block). At that moment, Graciela stopped and turned quickly, looking like a trapped, frightened animal as she came face to face with Pepe Medina Ynclan, a young man we had known all of our lives. He'd been in our class at school. One of the best looking men in Palmagria. But we didn't have much to do with him since he'd joined Batista's secret police, which was no secret at all. People like that, no matter how attractive, it was better to keep at a distance.

Now, Pepe's handsome face was pale, his eyes red with tears, his nose running. The fluids met at his chin and dripped onto a small bundle wrapped in the dirty pink blanket he was holding close to his chest. The people around me could not stop commenting and speculating.

"He rescued the baby . . ." someone said.

"He didn't rescue it, he pulled it out of the latrine," someone else countered.

"What a nasty job . . ."

"That baby is dead."

"What sort of mother . . . ?"

I kept my eye on Graciela. Her white dress, in the midst of the dirty crowd, seemed to absorb all the sunlight and reflect it back. Those closer to her moved back, as if scorched by its glow. Her first reaction was to send a hand to her mouth, as if to cover a gasp. Instead, she made the sign of the cross slowly, her eyes locked with Pepe's. Then she stepped aside, allowing him to continue on to the waiting ambulance. Graciela gathered her white skirt and ran up the three steps to her house. Before she entered she took a final look back, as if searching down from a great height for someone in the crowd. Ernesto? Then, her white veil swung back around and slowly, without a sound, the door closed behind her.

Seconds later, Ernesto, in his shiny brown suit, knocked lightly at her door. It opened just wide enough to let him in. It was like a moment slowed down in time as the crack of darkness inside the house opened wider, just wide enough to swallow him. Then, quickly, it closed again. Can you imagine a more horrendous wedding reception? It was talked about for weeks. For weeks!

Imaginate. But that was not to be the most dramatic episode in Graciela's life. Oh, no. The woman we see every day in Leticia's yellow van, the one who rides with the rest of us decent ladies, her knees demurely pressed together, the one who consoles Berta when she is in too much pain to walk, the one who immediately forgives Raquel whenever she babbles on about her husband and, with little regard for our feelings, insists on reminding us of how horrible everything is back in Cuba — she may seem like one of the girls now but it wasn't always like that.

Chapter 3

IMPERIO

Some of the girls in the factory say that I have ice water in my veins. That I don't have feelings. That there's a calculator where my heart ought to be. A calculator! I shit on them. *Por Dios!* I consider myself practical, sensible, and realistic. That's the way I am and if you don't like it, don't come around. Don't come crying to me.

"Stop rubbing your damn legs and whimpering," I said to Berta one morning after she kept us waiting fifteen minutes. "If you're as sick as you say you are, go see a doctor." Graciela looked at me like I just slapped the old woman across the face. But how much is a person expected to take? How much? Maybe I see things much more clearly than others. If you ask me a question, if you say to me, "Imperio, what do you think of such and such?" I'll tell you the truth. My truth. If Berta's looking for someone to put an umbrella into the bitter cocktail that is her life, she can go to someone else. I don't make ugly things pretty.

I don't put sugar in my coffee, I don't beat around the bush, but I do expect her to be ready when the van arrives and to not take forever getting in and out. For me a situation is either black or white. And that's the way I like it. But Graciela defends her. Defends her! *Por Dios!* Graciela has never been reasonable. Not now in Union City, and not back in Palmagria. She had always let her heart and not her brain make all the decisions. She sees herself as romantic, soft, and caring. An innocent. Innocent my ass. I think she's an idiot. Listen, if you're stupid enough to let your heart rule your life, then heartache is sure to follow. Graciela should have known better, particularly in Palmagria.

There's no point describing the beaches and the palm trees and the sunsets. You go to any tropical island and you're going to find just that. So what?

Palmagria was a very small town that followed very specific rules. If you grew up there, as Graciela did, you knew that from the cradle. If you came to visit, you learned soon enough. Usually the hard way. There was no gray in Palmagria and the rules were tougher on women. I'm not saying that was good or bad, it was the way it was. Girls who couldn't live by those rules moved to La Habana. It was only a few hours away by bus, but as far as the people of Palmagria were concerned, on another continent.

In La Habana there were no rules. People did what they wished without worrying about what others thought. In La Habana, women could wear two-piece bathing suits at the beach, live in their own apartments, dye their hair different colors, have love affairs with married men, or black men, even other women if they wished. But they couldn't do such things in Palmagria.

Por Dios! If a woman moved to La Habana for some other reasons, to further her education or just to enjoy a different way of life, people back in Palmagria still whispered that she went away to be a *lesbiana* or a *prostituta*. That's why the very few who left, and I can count them on one hand, never returned, not even for visits.

Graciela should have left as soon as she could and never come back. She never fit in. She had different ideas, and the more she tried to live like the rest of us, the crazier she got.

At first, after that ridiculous wedding to that unfortunate man, everything seemed to be going reasonably well. Much better than anyone expected. Certainly much better than I ever thought possible. Ernesto, the poor fool she married, was a popular teacher, but not with me. I always found him to be irritatingly high-minded, with his thick books and classical music, and that wife of his, Josefa, who was boring as dust. As dust! May she rest in peace.

Caridad suggested that maybe it had done Graciela good to finally get out of her parents' house, which was more like a battlefield. Her father, Guillermo, was a weak man, so weak that Graciela's mother, Irma, had been disgraced by countless miscarriages. From what I've heard, time and again she got pregnant and then lost the baby. People said that, "Guillermo's glue didn't stick," that "his eggs were runny." So when Graciela was finally born, it had been something of a miracle. Well aware that Graciela had tried to rule in that house from the start. But as weak-willed and puny-spermed as her father was, her mother was strong. *Por Dios,* a woman who would have that many bloody incidents and still try again and again had to be strong. But Graciela was even stronger. Irma's struggles to make something decent out of her only daughter were legend in Palmagria. Legend! And Graciela had disappointed her to the very end. She married a widower. Even if it was the distinguished Profesor de la Cruz, who could blame her parents for not attending the wedding? Not me. It must have been clear to Irma that Ernesto was just a slightly more successful and respected version of her gutless husband. Guillermo worked his entire life at *la papelería*, the stationery store, for practically no money simply because he didn't like to get his hands dirty. Who would want that for their daughter? Not me.

If you ask me, that wedding never should have happened. But regardless of what I thought, marry they did. The newlyweds moved into Ernesto's house near the school, definitely a much nicer neighborhood than where Graciela had lived before.

In her new home, Graciela had to make do with whatever had been left there by Josefa, because at that time, the stores were completely empty. The United States had imposed some sort of an embargo on us, which we didn't take very seriously at first. *Dios Mío!* Most of us didn't even know what an embargo was. But we learned fast when we started to feel the lack of everything. People called it El Bloqueo, the blockade, because 'embargo' was just too pretty a word for what was really going on. It made me furious to walk by stores that used to bulge with window displays and see them totally empty, nothing but cobwebs and dust. And on those rare occasions when eggs, bread, or milk came in, lines formed around the block and fistfights broke out. Stupid, desperate people fought each other in the streets just to get a better place in line. They bloodied each other over a can of beans.

Graciela was like a rock through all this. She developed a quiet determination I had never seen before. She was like another person, this married version of Graciela. Gone were the flirting eyes, the annoying and embarrassing desperation she displayed whenever men were around. I watched her carefully. I had a hard time believing that a woman could change just like that.

We stopped to chat with her and Ernesto after a late showing of "La Dolce Vita" de Fellini at the Cine Carreta. It was a very warm night, and it had been even warmer inside the theater, where the idiots in the balcony insisted on treating the movie like pornography. They shouted dirty words whenever something even remotely sexy appeared on the screen.

Caridad and Salud were with us that night, and after the movie the six of us lingered at the corner just for a moment. I had seen Ernesto and Josefa under similar circumstances so many times over the years that it felt a bit odd to see Graciela standing in her place. Ernesto had his arm around her, and they looked like any other couple. Don't ask me why, but I got the feeling that not all was as it seemed. The movie, which had been seen all over the world but had just reached Palmagria, was all anyone could talk about for weeks.

"I liked hearing Perez Prado during the striptease," Graciela said.

"Yes," Ernesto said, "of all the popular songs of recent years, 'Patricia' is one of my favorites." Graciela nodded her head as he spoke, completely agreeing with every syllable.

"You could hear the music over all the shouting?" I asked and Graciela laughed. But she laughed like she was doing me a favor, which was interesting because I didn't mean for my comment to be funny.

And then Mario said, "I liked the Swedish blonde with the big tits." I could have killed him.

"Mario," Graciela said, "you belong up in the balcony with the bad boys."

And then she looked at Ernesto and wrinkled her nose at him and he kissed her right on the tip of her nose.

"Where do you think I found him?" I said, but no one was listening, they were so impressed by the newlyweds affection. I was thinking, this old fool doesn't know what he's gotten himself into. I mean, just one look said it all. He was short, balding, thick glasses, and bland in every way. And say what you will, at that time Graciela was luscious. That's the only word for it.

We said good night and watched for a moment as Ernesto and Graciela walked away, arms around each other.

Caridad and Salud walked with us in silence for a while.

"Graciela seems different," Salud said. "More calm."

Mario started to whistle the music from the movie.

"Marriage changes a girl," Caridad said.

"Marriage should," I said. But I wasn't convinced.

The next afternoon I paid Graciela a little visit. She didn't seem surprised to see me and welcomed me with open arms. And it was then that I saw what a ridiculous effort she was making to be a good wife. But it almost seemed like an impersonation of a good wife. I knew she was making a grave mistake when I noticed that she had taken down all photos of Josefa and put them away. She had taken them right off the wall. All that remained were the nails sticking out. There would be no flowers for the former mistress of the house either, and no visits to the cemetery. Not at Christmas, Easter, or any of the anniversaries. Josefa was dead and buried, and that's the way Graciela wanted her.

Graciela had given Josefa's old pots and pans a good washing and traded bedsheets with her mother. I couldn't exactly fault her for refusing to conceive her children on a dead woman's bedding.

She seemed to have at last settled into a comfortable life. She had finally become one of us, or so I thought. I continued to have my doubts.

She gave birth to two boys in short order. The first she named Ernestico, after his father, the second, Manolito after a famous bullfighter. She seemed determined to make her marriage work, which is what baffled and enraged all of us later on, after the truth was revealed, after the scandal started, after doors began to slam in her face. In her face!

Ernesto didn't make a lot of money, and Graciela wanted things. But things were scarce and the black market was expensive. So, she set herself up as a manicurist and was very successful at it, because she rendered the best "Cuban" half-moons in town. The Cuban half-moon was a pearly-colored crescent painted with precision exactly where the nail met the cuticle. Graciela was masterful at it, an artist. When she did our nails it looked as if all our fingers were smiling. The women who had been doing our nails for years (sloppy, uneven edges, smudges) were left without their best clients. Graciela dealt with their resentment by ignoring them. She opened her door wide for business, and what could we do? We had to support her and besides she was absolutely best.

It soon became very fashionable to have Graciela Altamira de la Cruz do your nails once a week. Word spread and women came from as far as Niquero and Bayamo. And Graciela, who had always wanted to direct fashion and set trends, at last had all the snooty, upper-class girls of Palmagria literally at her fingertips.

Every Wednesday afternoon, while our husbands and children slept the siesta, you could find a group of us younger wives reading Graciela's fashion magazines and blowing on our newly lacquered nails; telling stories, sharing gossip, and dreaming out loud. This was our time. We sat around Graciela's dining room table in the cool darkness of her house while, outside, the sunshine raged or rain poured down. Caridad and I had started smoking mentholated cigarettes, which Caridad made by putting a handful of regular cigarettes into a glass jar with a dab of Vick's Vapor Rub Ointment on the lid, and sealing it tight for a week. We smoked without our husband's consent, and listened to the latest records. We were crazy for the heartbreakingly romantic *boleros* by Los Zafiros and Luisa Maria Guell. It was at that dining room table that new fads were discussed, hemlines were lifted or dropped, colors and patterns adopted or discarded.

Everything in Graciela's life seemed ideal from the outside. *Por Dios,* how was it that none of us took even a moment to notice that Graciela, hunched over finger after finger, quietly trimming cuticles and outlining those perfect half-moons with the precision of a surgeon, for nothing but a few precious coins, was slowly losing her mind?

Yes, it must have been insanity. Insanity! Complete and absolute madness. What else would drive a woman in her position, in a town like Palmagria, to do what she did?

People blame the Revolution for every crazy thing that happened back then because people always need to find something to blame. After the Revolution, our town changed. As if everyone had just lost their minds. And who wouldn't have? *Por Dios,* who suffered a bigger blow than Palmagria?

The entire town, except for a few and we all know who they were, had been against Batista and had blindly, *blindly,* done everything imaginable to put Castro in power.

Palmagria, as insignificant a town as it was, had a very lucky geography. Its southern end ran into a natural bay in the Caribbean, and its northern end was located at the foot of the

Sierra Maestra; the mountains where Fidel Castro trained his hairy men. Almost everyone in Palmagria was involved with the Revolution in one way or another. Foolishly, people smuggled arms, food, and cash to the bearded rebels in the mountains, risking their lives. Idiotic young men went up there with nothing but a desire for freedom, counting only on the protection of the Saints and the useless prayers of their mothers. Even Mario got swept up in it and came home one day with his eyes full of fire.

"Mario," I told him, "you're no revolutionary. What are you going to do, sleep in a trench?" As soon as he sobered up, he admitted I was right.

But most women were not as smart as me, and they willingly sent their husbands up to be killed. When Castro finally took power, they congratulated each other on the streets for a job well done. Never mind that now they were widows with mouths to feed and no way to do it.

"*Ganamos,*" they shouted from street corners. We won.

The people of Palmagria knew they were not completely responsible for Castro's victory, but they were certain that the town had played an important part. Everyone looked forward to a country free from foreign oppression, the Cuba *libre* everyone talks about now.

Everyone but Graciela, I suppose. One breezy July afternoon in Graciela's dining room, I first noticed that something wasn't quite right with her. The radio was transmitting one of Fidel Castro's interminable speeches direct from La Habana.

Graciela had already finished Caridad's nails and was now working on mine. Caridad sat on the sofa near the window, her nails still wet, her fingers stiffly extended, a mentholated cigarette held carefully between an index and middle finger. Her eyes were fixed on the radio, as if she expected to see the now familiar bearded face, the waving flags, the reaching hands, or the sea of faces that filled the Plaza de la Revolución.

I sat across from Graciela, my hand in hers, and watched as the little brush made graceful strokes across my nails. Suddenly, and for no apparent reason, Graciela let go of my hand, walked to the radio, and without so much as an 'excuse me,' turned it off. She responded to our glaring stares with a shrug. With a shrug!

"I can't stand all that noise," she said and went back to my nails.

But it was no use. Fidel Castro's voice resounded and echoed from all the other houses so that everything he said seemed to repeat itself.

"It does great honor to all of us that the Soviet Union," Fidel said, *"has sent the man who has just made the first flight in space to be with us this afternoon."*

The astronaut must have stood up because about ten minutes of shouts and applause followed.

"So it's true," I said. *"Por Dios,* we're in bed with the Russians."

"Imagínate," Caridad said, her eyes big and wide as she considered what this would mean to us.

"I've had just about enough of this *revolución.*" Graciela said. "We've had governments change many times before without so much commotion and backslapping. Who cares?"

She had finished my last nail, and I noticed that they were perfect. She calmly collected her tools: the roll of cotton, the bottle of acetone, her emery boards. When she was done packing everything into her pink plastic box, she stood and gave us a look that could only mean goodbye.

All the way home, I couldn't stop thinking about the Russian astronaut. Lately, the word 'communist' had been on everyone's lips. But what did it actually mean?

It was not a new word. Certainly I was aware that communist countries existed. But that was worlds away, in Russia and China. I could not imagine what it would mean to us. I had seen photographs of uniformed Chinese soldiers standing at attention and looking more like dolls than men. And of Russian soldiers marching the strangest little ceremonial steps in front of buildings that looked like they were topped with onions. But that was always in countries so distant that they didn't even share our alphabet. To me, it always seemed to be taking place in a different time as well, either in the distant past or far into the future.

There had been mention of communism as far back as I could remember, but not any more than we talked about the Nazis in Germany or the Fascists in Italy. There had long been a communist party in Cuba, but it was so small and inconsequential that it could be easily ignored. They were no more a threat than Jehovah's Witnesses were to Catholics. *Por Dios,* there were no real communists in Palamagria.

But then, unexpectedly, sympathizers started to emerge. People we had known all of our lives turned suspect. A book by Karl Marx was discovered in the public library, and it had been read so often and so feverishly that its spine was broken. I looked into the eyes of my neighbors and began to wonder if they might be the ones. What if they were the communists?

There was a Chinese family that had always lived in the center of town. No one but their next-door neighbors really talked to them, and that was at arm's length. The Chinese family did what Chinese families always do in small Cuban towns. They raised vegetables for market and took in laundry.

But now everyone wondered, were they the communists in Palmagria who were pushing this new movement on us? Or worse, communist spies?

"I don't trust *los chinos*," Caridad said, and stopped taking her sheets to them.

I continued to take my laundry to the Chinese, but kept my visits short. I dropped off and picked up, and made sure no one saw me going in or out. While I was there I took a quick peek behind the counter to see if there was anything subversive lying around: a pamphlet, a leaflet, a flag. It seemed as if from one day to the next, the people of our town were divided. Suspicions were aroused.

There were those who were desperate to leave the country, those *who hated* the people who were leaving the country, and the rest of us who were caught in the middle.

People like me were frozen with fear and indecision. We were not the sort of people who dreamed of a life in other parts of the country, let alone the world. We were born in Palmagria and, in spite of its problems and defects, we expected to die there, be buried there, and spend the rest of eternity there. That's the way it had always been. Occasionally, someone ventured out, driven by some strange desire that no one could understand. But for the most part, we stayed.

It was easier for the wealthy to get out, they had always kept one foot in Cuba and another abroad. It was not unusual for them to have a big house in Cuba and another in Miami Beach. They sent their children to universities in Spain or the United States. They were used to entertaining foreigners who came to visit in yachts and private airplanes.

For the very poor, there was no decision to be made at all. Very few had the education or even the mentality to consider going to another country and learning another language. They could barely get along where they were born. Besides, the new administration was all about them. There were slogans on walls now offering them a brighter future. There were organizations dedicated to their care. Politicos of humble backgrounds, who had risen to prominence only after the Revolution, made fervent speeches, telling the poor that it was time to rise up out of their pitiful lives and take their rightful place in society. Every day, these new saints of the people served themselves up as examples of the new success.

You couldn't leave the house without running into some sort of demonstration. Banners and flags appeared everywhere. Uniformed men and women became so common that, after a while, we hardly took notice of them. They walked around rigidly, their faces set hard with responsibility. They always saluted us as we walked by. They demanded respect. They were not friendly people, these rebel soldiers. They didn't smile, they didn't dance; it was as if, suddenly, they had stopped being Cubans. As if something hard and harsh had invaded their souls.

"*Imagínate*," Caridad said as we crossed the street, "even a couple of ladies like us simply walking to the store get the military treatment."

We didn't know what to do.

"Do we salute back?" she asked me.

"Just wave," I said, "see what the hell they do."

So she just waved, "*Que tal?*" And smiled the way she always did. In Palmagria, you greeted your neighbors no matter how you felt about them. It was considered good manners. I didn't, if I didn't like you, you knew it. But with these new people, I was always a little concerned that waving or not waving, smiling or not smiling, was somehow wrong or disrespectful. That they might take offense. If forced to, I waved, but I never smiled. Never! And I certainly was not about to salute them.

That summer, everything took on a military tone, as if the

entire town had been enlisted. As if the Revolution wasn't really over, as if we were now in a new and confusing war and the enemy could be just anyone.

"Take back your country!" People shouted on the radio and from street corners.

There were marches and speeches almost every day.

Too many took the slogans too seriously, and a rash of crime erupted almost overnight in a town where, before the Revolution, people had rarely locked their doors. *Por Dios*, our windows were always wide open, and everyone knew everyone else.

Guajiros were being told that everything belonged to everyone, and that it was theirs for the taking. Those with nothing, who just needed an excuse, started to help themselves.

Those of us who had even the tiniest bit more than others became their targets. Poor families trained their children to sneak into our homes during the day and hide. Then, at night, they quietly unlocked the front door while we slept, and the adults then tiptoed in and cleaned us out. Many families woke up to empty houses; everything that could be taken, had been. Fear took hold. I'd see people sitting on the front steps of their house waiting for the authorities, their heads in their hands, and I knew without asking that they'd been hit. There were serious reports and investigations, but *olvídate*, forget it, once you were ransacked, you stayed that way. And it wasn't as if you could just go to the store and replace what had been stolen.

Caridad, who had the courage of a goldfish, stopped sleeping.

"*Imagínate*," she said, "people are afraid to go outside. They're getting guard dogs, the most vicious ones they can find."

She was right. Our town was now overrun with *guajiros* who came down from the mountains like a swarm of locusts to seek their fortune. You could see the hunger in their eyes, their desire for more. This was their moment after a lifetime of poverty, and they were going to take full advantage of it. They were dark and weathered and ill-mannered, these people. Their children, used to life in the fields, would shit on our sidewalks. Not that Palmagria was the most elegant place on earth. But there were certain things we did not do. *Dios Mío!* Shitting on the sidewalk was definitely one of those things. Definitely!

"Isn't it enough?" Mario said, "that the Land Reform Act has given them all the land the Americans left behind? Free land just for the taking. Isn't it enough that schools are being set up for them, that they're being taught to read and write? Isn't it enough that they're all being vaccinated? Why do they have to come here? What's here for them?"

I told Mario again and again to keep his opinions to himself. But, after a few drinks, he always forgot. Always.

The only other time that Palmagria had been invaded by these primitives was during hurricanes, when the rivers overflowed and flooded their houses. *Guajiro* families came into town cold, wet, frightened, and useless; not with that air of entitlement they had now. We gladly took care of them, gave them shelter, food, dry clothing and blankets, because we knew it would all be temporary. Once the water drained out of their fields, they always returned, in slow-moving caravans: wooden *carretas* filled with donated supplies, pulled by oxen and mules. Back they always went, if reluctantly, to rebuild their lives as best they could. Sometimes, one or two families remained in town. Even if they weren't immediately welcome, with time they were absorbed and eventually forgotten.

Por Dios, now they were everywhere and they were not going back. Now they had it better than at any other time of their lives. The homes of the wealthy, houses that had been in the same family for centuries, were being vacated and handed over to these so-called 'Heroes of the Revolution.' Families that had been living in shacks with dirt floors found themselves in ornate mansions with swimming pools and servant's quarters. Venerated buildings now housed reinvented organizations. Instead of Boy Scouts, we now had The Young Pioneers, which everyone said was dedicated to brainwashing the young into the communist way of life. All children were forced to join, regardless of what their parents felt. The new government was focusing as much on the young as on the poor. It was, they trumpeted, their 'investment in the future.'

I had never cared too much about politics. I always figured things would take care of themselves. That day when Graciela turned off the radio, I knew that what she'd said was true. There had been revolutions before, assassinations, and crazy elections when even the dead could cast a vote. But I could tell that this was different, this time there was a solid plan. *Por Dios,* they were going after the most ignorant and impressionable segment of the population. There was a plan, a design, and it seemed to me that the aim was to destroy what we had managed to create for ourselves through hard work and determination. To take away what little we had.

People like me were putting up a fight. Not a loud one, because we knew that would immediately land us in prison. But small things. We started withdrawing into our own little ways. Many parents kept their children from attending the mandatory Young Pioneer meetings. It was the revolt of the middle class, which was curious because up to that point the world didn't think Cuba had a middle class. *Por Dios,* according to the Revolution, the country consisted of those who lacked nothing and those who had nothing, but that was not entirely true.

Yes, there were very rich people who owned just about everything, and they were foreigners; mostly Americans. Yes, there was a tremendous number of peasants who owned nothing, not even the tiny square of land they slept on. But there have always been people like that in every country in the world. Who ever said life was fair? In Cuba, there were also plenty of families who owned their own homes and their own businesses, even if it was just a greasy mechanic's shop or a seamstress' workshop. People had a very definite way that they wanted to raise and educate their own children.

When the private and religious schools started to close down because they refused to change to Marxist textbooks, many decided to keep their children home instead of sending them to public schools, where communist indoctrination had already begun. When the officials started to notice that there were many children who were not completely taken in by their propaganda, that parents were keeping their children out of school, a terrifying rumor began to circulate, sending everyone into a frenzy. A frenzy!

It all started when someone said that Fidel was going to send his twelve-year-old son, Fidelito, to the Soviet Union to be educated by Russians. On the day we were all whispering this rumor, my younger sister Clarita ran into my house in tears.

"They say they're going to send all children from twelve to fifteen years old to the Soviet Union," she said through a runny nose and slurpy sobs.

"It makes perfect sense to me," I told her. "From twelve to fifteen, they go to the Soviet Union to become perfect little communists. Then they return, and from ages fifteen to eighteen, they are thrown into the military. After that, they'll be pissing Red."

Maybe I am too practical, too sensible, and too realistic. Maybe what they say about ice water in my veins is true. *Por Dios,* I see things for what they are. Of course, this wasn't what Clarita wanted to hear, but I can only tell the truth. I felt that if she was going to make the right decision, she needed to have all the information. To just console her with lies would have been criminal.

In a panic, parents started to send their children to the United States to stay with relatives or with church groups, just temporarily, to keep them safe. We could not imagine what would happen to a child in the hands of the Russians or how they would endure those harsh winters without the comfort of their family. Twelve-year olds are still very young. My friends tended to pity me because I never had any children. Never to my face, of course, but I could see it in their eyes. Well I pitied them! And now I felt, not quite superior, but, certainly blessed.

When it came to children, my sister Clarita won the *lóteria;* vulgarly delivering five kids in about as many years, each more annoying than the next. Unlike me, Clarita was voluptuously endowed with wide hips and large, soft breasts. And our natures were at opposites, too. Clarita did not posses one ounce of suspicion and could never hold a grudge. Whenever there was something about a neighbor or a friend that I wanted to discuss, she always pushed me away and told me that she was too busy taking care of her family to think about such things. She's too kind, too soft-hearted, my sister. Her kids ran circles around her and her house always looked like a tornado hit it. Sometimes I thought it would serve her right if they took away some of her damn kids and sent them to Siberia. Maybe an experience like that would pull her head out of the sand. She was trapped. She couldn't suddenly pick up everything and move with five kids to the United States.

Although, at the time, most of us were sure Castro couldn't last, and we were determined to continue our lives just as we always had. A lot of people had already left everything behind, thinking that when they returned a few months later, it would be there waiting for them. But I knew that was not true.

I knew that once one of those *guajiros* got into your house, you'd have to set fire to it to get them out.

It was in this time of rancor, suspicion, and regret that Graciela made her biggest mistake. *Por Dios,* whatever she got, she had coming. If you tie a rope around your neck, there's plenty of people in Palmagria who were more than happy to lead you towards the gallows.

Chapter 4

GRACIELA

Most days I didn't miss Palmagria at all. Palmagria was in the past. It had been raining cold and hard in Union City and I was almost glad to be inside the factory. Grateful for the dolls that came to me naked, cold, and incomplete. The dolls had perfectly round holes where their legs, arms, and heads should be. They glided by endlessly, reflecting the fluorescent lights that hung above. We assembled them limb by limb until they started to take human form. They came fast and were handled roughly, quickly by our frantic, minimum wage hands.

Later, they passed through a clear plastic curtain and into a dustless room, where their heads would be added. They moved on down the conveyor belt, to the place where the journey became slower, where gloved hands handled them more delicately. They would be as lovingly dressed and combed as an infant's corpse. Tiny bunches of plastic flowers were added to their curled and lustrous hair, and then they were carefully placed in boxes without a ruffle out of place. Eventually, they would find their way to little girls all over the world. They were given special names and treasured. They listened to sweet confessions and plans for the future, they heard of boys and dates, graduations and wedding plans. They were wept on and held tenderly during dark and frightening nights. They sat on canopied beds fragrant with the carefree smell of little girls. Their unblinking eyes observed the delicate passage from girl to woman. And they lived on, long after they had been discarded, with the complete certainty that they would never be forgotten.

At the assembly line, day after day, I stood across from Caridad, the ever-moving conveyor belt between us. Imperio stood to her left, Leticia to the left of her, Raquel on my right. Berta always stood next to me, on my left.

Beyond was the department that attached the heads. We could see them in there moving slowly, luxuriously. It was like an exclusive neighborhood that we could walk through but couldn't afford to live in.

The women in "heads" made more money and dressed better than us, and every Friday they all went to the automat down the block for lunch. They always returned chatting and happy as if they'd just been on a Caribbean cruise.

Berta and Raquel eyed the women from "heads" with scorn while they waited for the day when they could work in that department. Waited for the day when they could start to steal the precious plastic heads that would complete their stolen dolls. Berta and Raquel lived in envy and fear. They were jealous of the white women who not only get to work with heads, but could most likely afford to buy one.

They also lived in fear of Mr. O'Reilly. What if he exposed Berta one day, like he did Calixto? What if a little leg or arm accidentally fell out of Raquel's skirt as she walked past Jacinto? Berta always stopped and crossed herself as she walked past the warning sign.

But in spite of the sign, the plastic bags, the overall feeling of mistrust, and the growing disapproval of the others in the van, Raquel and Berta continued to steal doll parts. Fridays were their big days, sometimes they were so excited that they traded doll parts while the van was still in the factory's parking lot.

"You can at least wait until we're on the road," Leticia said, "I don't want to be caught with contraband."

As the van made its awkward way down the boulevard, Caridad pointed at Raquel and Berta with her lips. It was a quick, almost imperceptible puckering and unpuckering.

"*Por Dios,*" Imperio said, "look how jumpy you two are. You live as if you were still back in Cuba under the eyes of the Committee for the Defense of the Revolution."

"I don't dare steal a thing," Caridad said, "not an arm or a leg," and turned up her nose as if the thought was too unpleasant to consider.

"Even if I did have a child," Imperio said, "I'm not stupid enough to risk my job for a plastic doll."

"You don't know what it's like, Imperio," Raquel said, "the girls want things that I can't buy for them."

"Personally, I don't see the harm in it," Berta said between her 'ay-ay-ay' and the rubbing of her legs. "The factory owners will never miss it. They're richer than God."

"The poor houses and the jails are full of honest people," Raquel added.

"I don't know why you put up with it, Leticia," Imperio said, "these two could get all of us fired. Fired!"

"Or imprisoned," Caridad added with a tremor. "*Imaginate!*

Then where do we go? Our reputations will be ruined. No one will hire us ever again."

"*Niiiiñas,* calm down," Leticia said as she took a turn so close to the curb that two wheels of the van bumped over its edge and onto the sidewalk. "No one's getting fired; no one's going to prison." As she maneuvered the van back into traffic.

Raquel wanted dolls for her daughters. And Berta had seven grandchildren from her grown son who lived in Venezuela and barely kept in contact with her.

"In Cuba, it would be different," Raquel said, "In Cuba, families stay together."

Sometimes we drove past the department stores where our dolls were sold, and there they were, blond and shiny, smiling through the clear plastic windows of their pink-and-yellow boxes. We knew how much they cost. We knew we couldn't afford them.

"That's money we can send back to Cuba," Raquel said.

"You're sending money again?" Caridad asked. "Then what's the point of the embargo?"

"Raquel," Imperio said, "how are we going to get Fidel out if you continue to send him money?"

"It's just twenty dollars a month," Raquel said, "They can do a lot with twenty dollars back there. They send me letters. Those letters will break your heart."

"Don't read them," Imperio told her.

"Don't you understand, Raquel?" Caridad asked gently, as if talking to a child. "It defeats the purpose."

"*Por Dios,* Raquel, do you want to stay in this country forever?" Imperio almost shouted, her face starting to flush with frustration. "Do you want to work in a factory all your life and freeze every winter? Do you want to end up old and crazy and eating cat food in a shelter? Think about your girls. Your husband did whatever it was he did without thinking of the consequences."

"He did what he did." Caridad echoed, the words just hung there. Raquel said nothing.

"Whatever it was." Imperio added.

Then everyone fell silent for the rest of the way home.

Raquel didn't care. She continued sending money home, and she and Berta continued stealing doll parts.

It was just a little leg here, a little arm there. Mostly on Fridays, sometimes on Wednesdays. Or Mondays, depending on how things went that day. Sometimes they felt particularly lucky, or safe. They played a careful game. But not everyone was as careful. Some people always went too far. Calixto Guiñon's sad example haunted us.

On Christmas Eve, what we call *Noche Buena*, the good night, we gathered in Leticia's apartment because it was the biggest. She had two bedrooms. Chano gets pork at a discount, so that's what was in the oven, a big, fat hunk of pork. I sat in the kitchen with Imperio and Caridad, sipping from a glass of red wine while Leticia cooked. She was making *congri* and *yucca* and the whole apartment smelled of olive oil, garlic, and laurel leaves.

The men stayed in the living room. From the kitchen, I could hear Mario going on and on but not a word from Caridad's husband, Salud, or from Leticia's husband, Chano.

"Where are the Americans?" Mario said, his voice getting louder. Salud didn't answer. His best defense against Mario's rants was to let him go on and on until he ran out of steam.

"All I see are *judios, negros*, and *italianos, viejos.*" Mario said.

"*Fíjate,* the Jews own all the businesses, the blacks are enslaved in factories or getting drunk at the corner, and the Italians won't have anything to do with us. Their skin is the same color as ours but they treat us like negros."

From where I sat, I could see him. At first glance, you'd think Mario was as white as the Americans he railed against. His hair was the color of copper wire, his eyes a very light brown. But if you looked carefully, you could see his mulatto features, the sinewy body of an African and the taut, yellow skin of a Chinaman.

The room was too small for him, most rooms in America were, so he just took one step forward and another back, one hand in the loose pockets of his pants jiggling the coins and keys he kept in there. In the other hand, he held a beer. Not his first or his second. Salud and Chano had sunk down on the couch; their stomachs looked like someone had stuck beach balls under their plaid shirts.

"And forget about Miami," Mario went on, his annoying voice getting louder and blurrier, "all the gangsters from Havana control Miami. You can't open even a tiny business there without greasing somebody's hand. The only way to make any money is with *la bolita.*"

My boys were out in the hallway playing with Celeste, Caridad's daughter. I could hear them running the length of the narrow corridor and up and down the stairs, laughing and shouting at each other. Twice, Leticia's neighbors, Americans in red-and-green sweaters who were still getting used to having Cubans in their midst, had come to complain about the noise.

"Graciela," Mario shouted from the living room, "do something about your monsters."

"What am I supposed to do? Tie them to the couch?" I shouted back.

I wasn't going to let Mario ruin Christmas for me. Even with a gut full of beer, he knew better than to push me too far. He was lucky I didn't march into the living room and slap his drunken face — after what he put me through.

I had already talked to the boys about being too loud; there was nothing else I could do. After all, it was Christmas, and Christmas was for the children.

"*Por Dios,* Graciela," Imperio said, "you let those boys run wild."

"Celeste is out there too," I said. "Why don't you say anything to Caridad?"

"I doubt that it's Celeste that's bringing the neighbors to the door," Imperio said with a quick look to Caridad.

"*Niiiiñas,*" Leticia said to no one in particular, "don't start." Then she dumped the *boniatos* out of the pressure cooker and a cloud of steam filled the small kitchen.

I let the subject drop. Celeste ran in and her father jumped up off the couch as if he'd been hit by an electric current.

"There's my *tesorito,*" he said. My little treasure. Celeste was red-faced and sweating. She sat on her father's lap, even though she was getting much too big for that. Her ruffled skirt hiked up over her thick, hairy thighs. I watched Caridad as she took a sideways look at them.

"*Celestica,*" Caridad said, "no more running for today. *Me escuchas?*" You hear me?

In response, Celeste jumped off her father's lap and ran back outside, slamming the door. Caridad shrugged as if she didn't care, but she gave her husband a look that would kill a goat. Reluctantly, he got up and followed Celeste.

The front door opened again, and I was relieved to see Raquel and Berta. Raquel's little girls looked adorable in matching corduroy dresses, but Raquel looked like she's just fallen out of bed. Even her orange lipstick seemed pale and lifeless; her complexion was greenish. Still, she came into the kitchen with hugs and kisses and a *"Feliz Navidad"* for everyone.

Berta also squeezed into the small kitchen, and for a few minutes, it was just like being in the van, except we weren't being tossed from side to side, no one was honking at us and it smelled like delicious roast pork, not raw.

"What are we going to do about presents?" Raquel asked. "I can't give the girls headless dolls."

"I can lend you a few *dolares*," Leticia said, but she kept her back to us, which meant she didn't really want to. "Go buy them a little something."

"I can't do that," Raquel said in a whisper that only Leticia was supposed to hear. "You've already done enough for us, I can't go deeper into debt right now."

I had suspected that for the past few months, Raquel had been riding in the van on credit. Leticia didn't want anyone to know about it because she was afraid all of us would ask for a free ride, or credit, or a discount.

"Por Dios, Raquel, don't be a martyr," Imperio said. "Take the money. You can pay her back."

But Raquel wouldn't hear of it. She just shook her head, her ponytail bobbing like she was something you'd hang from the rear-view mirror of a car.

"I can't afford postage and gifts," Berta said, rolling down her knee-high, orthopedic stockings. "It's one or the other. Do you have any idea what it costs to ship a package to Venezuela? I sent them a nice card, the kind with the fake, glittery snow pasted on it."

"That sounds nice, Berta," I say. I glance down at her exposed legs; the blue veins were swollen and knotted.

"Why are you all driving yourselves crazy?" Imperio said. "Just move Christmas to January."

In Cuba, January 6th was when the Three Kings deliver the gifts to the children. We didn't have Santa Claus like they do here. Our presents came by camel, brought by the Three Kings, the same way frankincense, gold, and myrrh were brought to baby Jesus. So Imperio, who has always been practical to the extreme, changed the tradition back to what we had always known.

Over the screaming protests of the children — and I hate to admit it, but my boys complained the loudest — we postponed the gift exchange until January 6th. Which was fine with me because all I had purchased for the boys were two drawing pads and two boxes of coloring pencils, far from what they wanted. Their letter to Santa Claus was long; the toys they asked for were expensive. They wanted a TruAction Football Game, a Dick Tracy Copmobile, a Tasco Deluxe Microscope, a View Master Projector. I was more than willing to put off their disappointment for a couple of weeks, hoping their father would remember to mail them a few extra dollars for the holidays. Yes, January 6th was just fine with me.

The sky over Union City turned even darker, and the winds grew colder. Christmas came and went and still no heads for the dolls.

It seemed to me like we'd just celebrated New Year's Eve the way we always did — eating a dozen grapes, one for each month of the year, and singing Cuba's national anthem, *"que morir por la patria es vivir,"* and weeping from homesickness into a glass of Spanish cider — and when we came to, it was already the 6th. The day came with icy winds and freezing rain, followed by a snowstorm that we thought would last forever.

Once again we gathered at Leticia's. Berta's grandchildren only received a card and Raquel's little girls got headless dolls.

"What good is a doll that doesn't smile?" Berta asked. She had her swollen legs propped up on a dining room chair, and I noticed that some of the varicose veins had popped open and where there were once blue ropes and knots there were now bandaged sores.

"Listen, Berta," Imperio said, "I think you need to worry less about toys for those grandchildren of yours and pay more attention to what's happening to your legs. You want to end up in a wheelchair?"

Raquel's girls didn't seem to mind the headless dolls, but it was a sad day for us all, watching them play with what looked like plastic victims of unspeakable crimes. The only one who had a normal reaction was Caridad's daughter Celeste, who took one look at the dolls and ran screaming like the devil.

"In Cuba, children get no presents at all now," Raquel said, her voice coming from a great distance. "In Cuba, Christmas has been canceled."

For the rest of the winter, we offered each other solemn faces as we sat in the overheated van day in and day out.

I mostly stayed huddled inside my tiny apartment and never opened a window. I disappeared into a thick, dark overcoat and layers of wool, scarves, gloves, hats. My face turned dry and ashen, my hands red and raw. My lips became so chapped and cracked that I was reluctant to smile. The air inside my apartment was oily, dust stuck to every surface. Fortunately, the outdoor furniture was easy to keep clean. It was so different from winters in Palmagria where the windows stayed open to the cool breeze and the scent of gardenias perfumed the houses, even in January.

I was beginning to think spring would never come. Everything green had vanished. Then, early one morning, I stepped out onto the sidewalk. The freezing weather had subsided a little, and while waiting for the van to arrive, I heard a strange sound. It was a tiny sparrow, all alone, perched on a tree branch and chirping feebly. It was the first sign of spring and a pathetic one at that — just a speck of life on a bare branch. I looked up at that tiny, gray creature singing its little heart out, trying to convince me with all its might that things were going to get better, and suddenly I appreciated our big, annoying, loud Cuban wildlife so much more.

Our house in Palmagria had always been surrounded with sounds that I had taken for granted. Every day, I turned a deaf ear to the early morning call of the roosters, the gruntings of the pigs, the lewd calls of the talking parrots, the mangy dogs that barked at everyone who walked by.

In Union City, those sounds had been replaced by the constant, monotonous humming of traffic, interrupted only by an occasional car horn or the razor sharp sound of a speeding train as it cut through the winter gloom.

Leticia kept the heat in the van turned up so high that someone was always either rolling down the windows or complaining about the wind. The front windshield fogged up. Whoever was riding in the front seat had to constantly wipe it with a rag. It was a task we performed gingerly, apprehensively, as if at any moment the rag was going to burst into flames in our hands. There were times when we couldn't wipe fast enough and the van ended up on the sidewalk. Everything was so thick with snow that it was impossible for Leticia to see where the road ended and the walkways began.

"Slow down, Leti," Berta said, "are you trying to get us killed?"

"You don't like it, take the bus," Leticia said with arrogant confidence because she knew that with all the Cubans suddenly crowding every corner of Union City, any one of us could be easily replaced.

"*Imagínate*," Caridad said, a hand to her throat as if a big, flesh-colored butterfly had landed there.

"*Por Dios*, stop complaining," Imperio said. "Did you leave your country to ride a stinking bus."

It wasn't so much the buses as the waiting that we feared. Waiting alone for a bus in Union City in all sorts of weather, or in the dark, terrified us all. As much as we grumbled, we were grateful to have Leticia and her ugly yellow van.

Many things divided the passengers of that van. Bickering was almost constant. It was the *telenovelas* that united us. No matter how bleak the weather, how dangerous the driving, or how annoying we found each other, when the topic turned to the current *telenovela*, everyone cheered up.

I liked the *telenovelas* for their predictability. It was comforting to know something was going to work out, that the dark-haired girl was always going to be good, the blond was always going to be bad. That if you were born poor, you would end up rich; if you were illegitimate, it would be discovered that you had been switched at birth. But most importantly, if the love of your life was engaged to marry someone else, he would be yours in the end.

There was only one thing none of us in the van could ever be sure of, and that was when the first kiss between our favorite new couple would take place.

Night after night, I watched the destined lovers get closer and closer, until the maid interrupted them, or the hateful blonde fiancée made one of her numerous untimely entrances.

The man's eyes, big and dreamy, held the woman's gaze. At first, she was shy in his presence. But over time, she started to return his looks.

Whenever he walked into the room, her lips parted slightly and quivered with the anticipation of that first kiss. Her lips were perfectly painted, meticulously outlined in dark, filled in with light. Because in our *telenovelas,* everybody wore a lot of makeup, even the maid.

The show also tortured us with romantic music. As the music swelled, there were long, simmering silences between the two future lovers. They got closer and closer and closer. And then that spoiled, rich blonde always walked in, big, sculpted curls crowning her arrogant head.

"Isn't it highly irregular that you would be in this wing of the house?" she asked bluntly, her eyes narrowing to slits. "I thought it was forbidden . . . to servants."

The romantic music stopped. Cymbals crashed. A window blew open.

I felt the word "servant" like a sharp slap in my face, because I knew that the dark-haired girl was actually the rightful owner of the *finca.* That she had been switched at birth. It was just a matter of time before the only person who knew the secret — usually an old lady — took to her deathbed and whispered the truth to the local priest during Last Rites. But that could take days and days, weeks even! The old lady's agony lasting forever, the moment of that first kiss promised and then withdrawn or interrupted again and again.

I sat on the edge of one of my folding patio chairs in my little American apartment; the once-white walls closing in on me. While the boys slept peacefully in the next room, I clutched a pillow to my chest. I leaned in closer as the old woman started to say what I'd been waiting for months to hear.

"There's something I must confess," she said, struggling to speak, extending a claw-like hand, pointing at nothing with a crooked finger. (The old woman was almost always played by a fat actress who looked healthier than anyone else on the screen).

But as I watched, I truly believed she was dying, I believed it with all my heart.

The old lady struggled and struggled to confess, day after day, episode after episode, she fought between death and the truth. And every time she was about to tell all, the blonde one stopped her.

"Don't try to speak," she told her with feigned concern, leaning closer to the bed, making everyone in the room believe that she was good, not evil, like I knew she was. "You must conserve your strength, don't you agree, Doctor?"

The doctor looked at the dying woman with wise, scientific eyes and caressed his chin whiskers.

"Yes, you must conserve your strength," he agreed, mesmerized by the vile, blonde beauty.

The old woman leaned back into her pillow her expression pained from having to swallow the truth so many times.

The dark-haired girl cast her eyes up to heaven while the blonde let out a sigh of relief. The music always chose that moment to start again; light piano tinkled like raindrops on a lake. The dying woman glanced feebly at the people surrounding her — from the scheming blonde to the dark-haired girl, over to the handsome landowner, to the priest, the doctor, and back to the blonde, who stared daggers. The music became harder, more dramatic, and voices start to emerge from closed mouths.

That was the part I like the best in any *telenovela*, because they let you hear what everyone was thinking.

"Please don't die and leave me all alone in this horrible house," the dark haired girl implored with her eyes, her overlaid voice echoing a little.

"What could she possibly know?" the landowner's deep, masculine thoughts wondered, "This sweet old woman who has been a servant in our house since long before I was born?"

And then, so clearly that it felt as if everyone in the room could hear it, the thoughts of the blonde are revealed!

"Die now, you old witch. You will not ruin my plans. I will marry Francisco, and none of you will ever set foot in this mansion again."

After a really good episode, I couldn't wait to get in the van and talk about it with the others. Week after week, month after month, the *telenovelas* gave us new topics to discuss. They had titles that stayed with me forever: *Dear Enemy*, which was about twin sisters; or *The Privilege to Love*, about a half-caste slave. My favorite will always be *Cadenas de Amargura* — *Chains of Bitterness* — about an evil spinster with a dark secret.

It wasn't always fun and giggles in the van. Some nights, it filled up with the kind of sadness only a group of very unhappy women can generate. None of us ever dreamed we'd come to Union City to work in a toy factory, or any other kind of factory for that matter. After a long day of plugging tiny plastic arms into tiny plastic sockets, we were all too tired to talk, lost in our own thoughts, our own worries. Like on the day when Berta first fell down. One minute she was standing at the line, the next, she was on the floor. I was the one closest to her, so I bent down to help her up. But she was out cold. I could hear the others shouting, "Emergency!" And then Mr. O'Reilly was there. Together we helped her up and practically carried her to his office. He guided us to his desk chair, which had wheels on it. We tried to get Berta into it, but the chair kept rolling away. By the time we got her in it she was already coming to.

Mr. O'Reilly was very nice to her. He even got a paper cup of water for her to drink.

"*Estas buena?*" he kept asking her in his bad Spanish. What he was asking her over and over was 'are you sexually aroused?' I didn't have the heart to correct his Spanish. And if I hadn't been so worried about Berta I would have found it falling-down funny.

That night, on the way home, I looked from face to miserable face: Berta, Raquel, Leticia, Imperio, and Caridad. I wanted to hear their true thoughts like I could in the *telenovelas*.

The van traveled carefully along the now familiar streets. We had nothing better to do than to look out at the squares of green lawns in summer, or white in winter. At rows of little houses separated by rusting chain-link fences, the air-conditioning units that stuck out of windows like leaking tumors. Just when I thought the van would explode from the unrelenting misery it was transporting, Leticia said the magic words.

"*Niiiiñas*, I'm sure of it! *Esta noche se besan.* Tonight they will kiss."

"Not tonight," Berta said, in a voice that belonged to a sleep-walker, "Tomorrow."

"Berta's right," I said, "tonight the old lady dies, and tomorrow they will kiss."

"You will not ruin my plans," Imperio said, imitating the

blonde to perfection, "I will marry my Francisco and none of you will set foot in this big mansion again."

"*Imagínate,*" Caridad said.

After that, we couldn't stop laughing. And every time we did, Imperio repeated the line and got us going again until one by one we were dropped off.

My relationship with the ladies in the van was a strange one. They weren't exactly my friends, and I wouldn't trust them, particularly Imperio and Caridad, to take a dog out for a pee. But, in a world full of foreigners, all we had was each other.

Imperio had been a classmate from the first grade. Caridad had attended that same school, but back then, we never talked. Caridad was like a little pampered Pekingese. Her mother brought her to school every morning in little starched dresses and perfect patent-leather shoes, and dashed her home as soon as the first bell rang. Off she went to ballet or piano lessons.

I met her when I was fourteen or so, through Imperio, and the three of us became friends, sort of. There was always something about Caridad that kept me at arm's length. She was warm, kind, and well-mannered, but it was as if she'd gone to the Catalogue of Decency and chosen how she wanted to represent herself. Even as a young girl she was like a crowned nun, very pious and serene, until you noticed how she carried her head. It was somewhat easier to be friends with Imperio, as irritating as she could be, and in spite of that horrible man she married, at least you always knew what you were getting.

After they both left Palmagria for this enormous country, I thought I would never see either one of them again. And that would have been just fine with me. But life had other plans.

Chapter 5

CARIDAD

Imaginate!

It all started when poor Berta fell. One moment she's standing across from me working, and the next she's sprawled out on the concrete floor of the factory. She fell slowly, as if she was trying to lie down on a bed and someone had pushed the bed away. I was so embarrassed. If poor Berta wasn't feeling well, why didn't she just excuse herself. Naturally, Graciela, who was working next to Berta, went into hysterics.

"Berta! Berta!" she screamed in that overly dramatic manner that makes me shudder. I could feel the Americans watching us.

Graciela was kneeling over her, and the conveyor belt was still going. Berta's and Graciela's pieces were still coming.

"Emergéncia!" Leticia shouted. But no one came to slow down the belt, doll parts were piling up. So the rest of us had to move faster to pick up the slack, not just for Berta but for Graciela as well.

A few moments later, Mr. O'Reilly came running out of his office and between him and Graciela they half-carried, half-walked Berta to his office. He didn't slow down the belt.

The doll parts were coming fast. Imperio just started picking them up and setting them aside.

"They can deal with these when they return," Imperio said. "Maybe Leticia considers this an emergency, but I think of it as an unscheduled coffee break."

I was working so fast I barely heard what Imperio was saying, but not so fast that I didn't see what was going on because from where I stood I could see into Mr. O'Reilly's office, which was almost all glass. I saw it all as clearly as if I'd been using binoculars.

He pulled out his desk chair and they got Berta into it. Poor Berta's face was pale and slack, her tongue was practically hanging out. Mr. O'Reilly was kneeling in front of her, fanning her with a paperback book and saying something.

Graciela was standing between the two of them but then leaned forward so that her breasts were practically in his face.

I could see Berta's mouth moving, so she was saying something, which meant she was alright. I sighed with relief and tried to set my sights back to my work. But, then I saw Mr. O'Reilly get up and walk to the water fountain. He returned with not one but two paper cups of water.

Berta sipped at her water and started to sit up. Graciela accepted her cup of water and held it, her eyes locked with Mr. O'Reilly's like she was at a cocktail party. She took a sip and smiled and I think they forgot poor Berta was even in the room.

I'm not one to judge, but it seemed to me that after that little incident, Mr. O'Reilly came around much more often. Instead of just walking by and saying *"Buenos dias,"* he now stopped for a moment, stood right between Berta and Graciela. And she just continued working as if she wasn't aware that he was standing there. But that's her strategy. Graciela has always played a good game.

Even during those awful days back in Palmagria when the rumor had almost become a shout, her hand was warm, her grip was firm, and her brush strokes as precise as ever. I sat across from her, my hand in hers and searched her eyes while she lacquered my nails, but her eyes gave away nothing. If she'd heard what people were saying she never let on. I remember that Ernesto came home while we were all still there and she offered him her cheek to be kissed, as if nothing out of the ordinary was happening.

Imagínate! Ernesto *must* have been aware of the stories circulating behind his back about Graciela and Pepe Medina Ynclan. It's not as if Palmagria was a town known for its restraint. Imperio and I decided that, because Ernesto was not a man given to hysteria, he thought he could just wait it out. And then, in his own time, he would quietly dissolve his marriage without scandal. Like a teaspoon of sugar in a glass of warm water, it would simply vanish and leave only clarity and sweetness behind.

But Imperio's husband Mario, who, sadly, often found courage in alcohol, finally told him what no one dared to say. He did it to his face and in front of everyone.

It happened while Ernesto was playing dominos outside the grocery store. He had been playing the same game with the same five men every Sunday for fifteen years. Mario walked by and saw Ernesto calmly involved in a game while the town talked about Graciela and seethed with shame for him. He stood watching for a moment, swaying from side to side, then stepped up and poked a finger into Ernesto's chest.

"Ernesto," he said in that over-familiar way Mario took on when he'd been drinking, "do something about the situation, before the rest of the women in this town start to think they can do the same as your wife and get away with it."

The other men, who loved Ernesto like a brother, just looked down at their domino tiles. No one jumped up to defend him. No one told Mario to get lost. In fact, they seemed grateful that Mario, in his drunken stupor, had done the dirty job that everyone at that table was dreading. They had all wanted to say something to him, but how do you express something like that to the most educated and honored man in town without tearing his heart out? Even Doctor Celedonio, who had been Ernesto's friend since they were boys and had delivered both his children, did not lift a finger or even raise his voice to defend him.

Mario moved on down the dark and empty sidewalk, weaving and stumbling his way home, and Ernesto was left with the image of his wet lips spitting out words like bullets.

The next morning, as soon as I heard what had happened, I ran to Imperio's house. Mario hardly remembered the incident at all. But just the same, Imperio had decided to send him away for a while, to a cousin's in Pilón. She frantically packed a bag for him while he showered.

"Por Dios," she said, "he felt terrible about the whole thing once I told him what he'd done. He wanted to go and apologize to Ernesto. But I told him he'd already done enough."

"Ernesto must have felt so alone last night," I said. My heart ached for him.

The rumor of the encounter between Ernesto and Mario grew louder and went farther faster and faster, until it was on everybody's lips. The town was abuzz with gossip. It was all they could talk about. I could hear it as I walked down the street, whether I wanted to or not.

"Pepe neither confirms or denies it —," someone said.

"Pepe's become too important to be pushed around —," from another.

"Rumors become fact if no one contradicts them —" It continued.

"If no one steps up and offers a different story it must be true —"

"The whole thing stinks of weakness and no *cojones* —"

"It sets a bad example —"

"I told my Nena, if I ever catch her, she's as good as dead; and she's taking the kids with her —"

"If it were me, I'd cut her cunt —"

Sadly, people started to look at Ernesto with anger. For the whole of the next day, Graciela was nowhere to be seen. Her house became like a tourist attraction. People walked past it to gawk, even if it took them blocks out of their way. But neither she nor her children were seen. The doors and windows remained closed. Imperio and I stood across the street, unsure of what to do.

"What if something terrible has happened in there," I said.

"Well," Imperio said, her eyes on the closed windows, "it would not have been the first time that an unfaithful wife in Palmagria found herself at the pointy end of a kitchen knife. *Por Dios,* before the Revolution, any other man in this town would have handled this situation with a swift and simple action. He would have confronted the man who brought shame on the mother of his children, and shot him dead."

"Ruining many lives in the process," I said, "most of all his own."

"*El honor es el honor,*" Imperio said, "what do we have if we don't have our honor?"

As we walked away, I thought that any other man would also

have hunted Mario down and cut his throat for speaking in front of others what was, in all honesty, none of his business. I was sure Imperio had had the same thought, so there was no need to mention it. I felt just awful for Imperio.

Fortunately, Ernesto was not the type to take someone's life with his own hands. And after the Revolution he had another choice.

The day after his much discussed encounter with Mario, Ernesto went to the courthouse and filled out countless complicated legal forms requesting an exit visa to the United States.

"Only to discover," Silvia, a clerk at the courthouse told us, "that a married man is under no circumstances, allowed to leave the country without his children."

That was news to me. There was still so much we didn't know. The constitution was being rewritten daily. Something that was legal one day was illegal the next. And sometimes, certain things would become legal again all of a sudden, and so on. But what Silvia said was true, and would remain so.

"The Revolution is not about to take on a traitor's unwanted family," Silvia explained to me patiently, as if this made perfect sense to her and should to all others.

In Palmagria, for those who dared to fill out an application to immigrate, there were very specific steps to follow, which was good in a country where everything had been turned upside down. It was also very public.

The first thing a family had to do was request an exit visa. That included complicated paperwork that needed to be overseen by a lawyer or at least a notary public. This would be followed by a thorough inventory of all their possessions.

Right after her inventory, my friend, Cuca Soto, had been so nervous that we took her to Graciela's to get her nails done, hoping it would calm her down. But her hand was shaking so much that Imperio had to go first. Cuca sat in a chair far from any door or window to the street.

"When I first went in to file, they treated me like I was trash," she said. "The immigration officials looked at me — and all the others in line — as if we were the worst people in the world. They made it seem like leaving the country was the same as abandoning a baby at the church. They didn't try to talk me out of it, but I could feel it in my bones that, from that moment on, I was despicable in their eyes."

As soon as the application was filed, three military guards showed up at her doorstep with a pad in carbon triplicate.

"They took the whole day to count and write down every piece of silverware, every ashtray, every cup-and-saucer, every item of clothing. All of our shoes," she said.

"Some people smuggle as much as they can out of the house before filing their application," Imperio said.

"Yes," Cuca said, "but if they got caught they voided everything. I couldn't risk that."

Even houses with children where items are always breaking or disappearing, had to account for everything before they were allowed to leave. The process was not just time consuming but humiliating too.

Poor Cuca Soto, a common housewife who'd never had anything to do with the military before and had never expected to, walked around nervously opening and closing drawers for men in big black boots and olive green uniforms, men she had never seen before. She showed them her closets and cupboards, let them look through her most private belongings.

"Halfway through the day," Cuca said, "they wanted *almuerzo,* so I had to treat them to food as if they were guests. They sat at my dining room table, eating and chatting like they were friends of mine doing me a favor."

Once they were gone with their long list, Cuca would spend the next few months, she was lucky, others spent years, worrying and wondering what would happen if something went missing on the day when the visa finally arrived. Because everyone knew that everything on the list had to be accounted for before they could leave the country. Once their possessions had been inventoried, they belonged to the State, and heaven help anyone who tried to sell or give anything away.

Even Graciela, whose head was always in the clouds, stopped what she was doing and paid attention. Her little brush stopped in mid-air and dripped onto the tabletop.

We had already heard horror stories about families whose visa had been denied because the exit inventory did not match the original. I had seen desperate people running around the neighborhood begging and borrowing items from friends to replace lost or broken items.

"It's a blatant invasion of our privacy," Imperio said over and over, while Graciela quietly clipped her cuticles. "*Por Dios,* why doesn't someone stand up to them?"

"Some people complained," Cuca said, "but their paperwork disappeared, and now they're stuck and outcast; neither here nor there. I'm keeping my mouth shut and my bags packed."

The people whose paperwork "disappeared" were the first people to take one-way, midnight boat rides. Before long, everyone stopped complaining. Just like Cuca said. You filed for your exit visa and kept very, very quiet.

I agreed with Imperio. It was an invasion of privacy. As soon as those military guards showed up at someone's front door, all their neighbors immediately knew that that family was planning to leave the country, and from then on, they became, depending on who you talked to, "one of us" or "one of them."

The adults in the family lost their jobs, and the vultures starting circling their houses. Admitting that you wanted to go into exile was the same as admitting that you were a traitor to the Revolution. You were excommunicated from your country. No longer a Cuban citizen, you were more like a slimy worm inching towards Hell. You waited for that visa and tried to survive as best as you could.

Cuca was understandably terrified. It could take up to five years, sometimes longer, for the visa to arrive. During this time, it was almost guaranteed that her money would run out completely. That she would go into a severe panic every time one of the kids accidentally broke a dish that had been inventoried. That the kids would suffer insults and physical violence at school and everywhere they went.

In Palmagria, when the visa finally came, it was in the form of a telegram. Not from the same mailman who always delivered telegrams, letters, and packages, but by a special messenger appointed by the State. In Palmagria, this man was Pepe Medina Ynclan, who had been a nobody but had somehow managed to get promoted after the Revolution.

"I wonder how many 'comrades' he stabbed in the back to make that jump," Imperio said.

I couldn't begin to imagine.

Pepe Medina Ynclan sailed around Palmagria on an old, black bicycle with a worn leather sack attached to the handlebars. He was the most detested and the most desired man in town. It didn't hurt that he had beautiful green eyes that ate you up when he looked at you. In a country of brown-eyed men, green eyes — or the even rarer blue — were considered a delicacy. Pepe was handsome, single, and rabidly committed to the Revolution. Like so many of the young men in our town, Pepe had gone up to the mountains to fight. It was completely unexpected because when he was younger he never showed any heroic tendencies. If he did, I never saw them. He hadn't been a particularly brilliant student or athlete, and after we all finished school, he didn't find a profession that suited him. He was at every dance, or loitering outside of a bar; whistling at girls. Something happened up there in those mountains, because when he returned, he was much more of a man. Clearly, there had been a transformation, but the real difference between Pepe and those other young men from Palmagria who went up to the mountains is that he managed to come back alive.

Now Pepe, with his bright eyes and powerful job, was fast becoming the most famous man in town. *Imaginate!* Of all the men in Palmagria, this is the one Graciela decides to have her scandalous affair with.

"How did Graciela manage to have romantic relations with Pepe under our very noses? Our noses!" Imperio and I asked each other over and over. It seemed impossible. Insane. But the rumor was too powerful, and there was no use denying it. No one knew who started it, who first saw them together, how it happened, but once people started talking, there was no way to stop them. The rumor grew and grew, passed from lip to ear until it was all anyone could talk about. It was very sad.

"There we sat week after week," Imperio said, "our hands in hers, our trust in hers, our friendship growing; or so we thought. She had unforgivably fooled us all."

Now, everyone in Palmagria and as far away as Palmas Altas, Palma Soriano, Las Palmas, knew about their forbidden romance as sure as if Pepe himself had delivered telegrams to each house in town divulging the information, confirming it in writing. Looking back, no one really remembered ever seeing them together or seeing his bicycle parked outside her house. When was Graciela ever alone? Either she was with her kids, or we were there getting our nails done. Or just visiting. It was the perfect place to spend an afternoon. When did it happen? How?

While Mario was away at his cousin's, I visited Imperio every day.

"The idea must have hit Ernesto like lightning, no?" I said as Imperio made café the way she liked it, using one of Mario's old socks for a filter, "because right after he signed his name at the bottom of each form, one for his Graciela and one for each of his sons, he went home, packed her up, and the kids, too, and walked them, in daylight, back to her father's house."

"*Dios Santo,* in daylight," Imperio said, I couldn't help notice the little smile that curved her lips.

Imperio had not been at her window that day; it would have been unseemly considering that none of this would have happened if it wasn't for Mario. But I saw it all and, sad as she was, Imperio insisted on details.

"Tell me, Caridad, what was she wearing? What does a woman wear for such an occasion?"

It had been quite a spectacle. The sidewalk was lined with people as if a parade was going by. Graciela walked in front, in a black-and-white dress, the colors of a nun. But on Graciela it looked obscene, a black skirt and a white blouse that showed every curve. And with a child holding each hand. They walked slowly, Manolito smiling at the neighbors and waving 'hello.' He was just a little boy then, maybe four years old. Ernestico, a year older and more aware of the situation, kept his eyes downcast. Graciela continued to look forward, like a magnificent lioness carved into the bow of a sinking ship. Ernesto walked behind with the suitcases; the shadow from his hat covered his eyes. People shook their heads sadly as they watched their beloved professor walk by in disgrace.

Ernesto had always been a proud and proper man who kept his dignity in spite of doing a woman's job. Year after year, he worked hard to earn the respect of his cynical and disrespectful students only to end up like this. What was Graciela thinking? All her life people had been mistrustful of her, and now she had handed them her head on a silver platter. Only out of respect for Ernesto did they refrain from hurling insults and covering her with spit. But talk they did, as soon as the family was out of earshot. They even suggested that Graciela might be pregnant with Pepe's baby.

"I guess we'll know the truth when we see the baby's green eyes," someone whispered.

Once again, her parent's house was surrounded by a curious mob; not as many as on her wedding day, but once again she was the center of attention, the cause for concern. And once again, she walked through them without saying a word and on to the front door, which opened just wide enough for her and the children to walk in and then closed behind her.

This time, Ernesto did not follow her in, but turned to face the gossiping crowd. They grew suddenly quiet, as they used to whenever he had turned away from the chalkboard to stare down a disruptive student. They shrank back under his unwavering gaze. Slowly at first, then more uniformly, they all began to disperse, allowing Ernesto to walk uninterrupted to the school, where he sat at his desk one last time and wrote his letter of resignation. This letter he read aloud at a rally commemorating Jose Martí the following Friday.

All the students were lined up in their uniforms. They sang the national hymn. Then, a little girl recited Los *Zapaticos de Rosa*, but she was no Graciela Altamira (everyone said so). And it wasn't so much that the little girl, whose name was Haydee Moreno, was untalented. It was just that even the youngest students knew all about Graciela. They knew what was happening between Professor de la Cruz and his wife. They were so curious to find how he was going to handle this enormous scandal that they hardly paid attention to Haydee's poetic efforts.

What the students and the rest of the faculty were not expecting was Ernesto's brief and painless resignation. There was no emotion in his voice, not a crack or a quiver. It took only seconds for him to read it all. After that, he went home and began the long wait for the visa, which would eventually be delivered, no doubt, by the very same man who had ruined his life.

Graciela Altamira vanished from sight after the door to her parent's house closed that day. When that door closed, so did the door to our hearts.

One afternoon, Ernestico showed up at my house with a message from his mother. *Imagínate!* Graciela wanted me to convince the girls to come to her mother's house to get our nails done.

"Tell your mother I will see her soon," was all I had the heart to say. But I knew I wouldn't. I couldn't! No one was going to go. Not me, Imperio, Cuca, Azucena or anyone else. Not anymore.

What had once just been a shabby and rundown part of town was now actually considered very dangerous. Things were going on there that no one could understand. That was the official reason. Truth is, not one of us could afford to be seen in the company of the woman who had betrayed our beloved Professor Ernesto de la Cruz.

Palmagria set a very high price on a woman's fidelity. Infidelity for women was not tolerated. *Mujeriegos* — skirtchasers were another story. Men could do whatever they wanted. It was what it was. For women it was the most shameful of acts. Even more than murder, I think. When there's a crime of passion, one person is dead, remembered only by their loved ones, and the other one vanishes to a faraway prison, never to be heard of again. But people who got caught cheating stayed around, and every time they were seen, their disgrace was remembered, discussed, used as an example.

"I don't want people saying that we knew, that we covered for her. *Por Dios*, she could bring us down to her level."

What Imperio was saying took my breath away. It hadn't even occurred to me. I had always been beyond reproach, and intended to stay that way.

"Distance," I said. "Time and distance. Discretely."

In order not to arouse suspicion, we let a few days go by before we found someone else to do our nails. But it was never the same again, never those same precise half-moons. Eventually, little by little, we stopped having our nails done at all. What for? There were no restaurants to go to. Parties were few and weddings less fancy. Even nail polish had become scarce and hard to come by. At first, we hoarded the little bottles as if they were filled with liquid gold, but eventually they dried up. All the color started to drain out of Palmagria as well, to be replaced with a dull, military gray that made even the copious palm trees our town was known for look dull.

Imagínate! the next time I saw Graciela Altamira de la Cruz, we were across from each other, divided by a fast-moving conveyor belt at a toy factory in Union City, New Jersey. I was not happy to see her. Not happy at all. But I couldn't turn my back on her, a woman alone in New Jersey with two mouths to feed and not a penny to her name. How would that look?

Chapter 6

IMPERIO

After all I've done for her since she arrived in Union City, she's still holding on to all that shit that happened with Mario back in Palmagria almost seven years ago. Seven years ago! I see how she still looks at Mario, like he's the devil. I told her back in Palmagria, and if I have to, I'll tell her again: *Por Dios,* Graciela, Mario was drunk!

I did what I could and if that's not good enough for her, then to hell with her. I never told Caridad, but I went to Graciela's house right after I put Mario on the train to Pilón. I put my own reputation at risk by going to her house and she wouldn't even let me in the door. I could see her mother standing behind her, in back of the house, towards the kitchen. Graciela just stood there, looking at me without blinking. She didn't seem one bit sorry for what she'd done to Ernesto, instead she looked like she was angry at me. What a bitch.

"Graciela, you can't blame a drunk man for saying something stupid," I said. "That's what drunk men do, everyone knows that."

She remained silent. Not that I expected her to forget the whole thing at that very moment. But I thought we could at least talk.

"Let me in," I said. I was getting uncomfortable standing there. Someone might see me. She must have noticed, I could see something in her eye begin to give. Then her mother came up, almost running, and before Graciela had a chance to say anything to me, *la vieja* slammed the door in my face. In my face!

I stood on the sidewalk *con la boca abierta,* with my mouth hanging open. After that day I didn't see Graciela very much. There was really no reason for me to go to that part of town. It was then that the whole thing started with Graciela saying that Mario had ruined her life. Not that it was that much of a life to begin with, but she certainly didn't make things any better putting *los cuernos* on Ernesto de la Cruz, and with Pepe Medina Ynclan of all people. She never said yes or no to the rumors, so naturally everyone in Palmagria, to this day, still believes that it was true. How could we ever trust her again if we don't know what really happened? Caridad and me, we couldn't just come right out and ask her. That wasn't our way.

Now, in New Jersey she acts like noting happened. Like crossing from one country to another has baptized her new again. As if I can't remember who she really is and what she did. As if I couldn't see right through her.

In the van, Leticia protected her, I could tell. I have eyes, I have ears. She let us say whatever we wanted to Raquel or Berta. But whenever we tried to get anything out of Graciela, suddenly she'd screech, *"niiñas,"* and changed the subject.

All Leticia cared about was money. She knew that if we pushed Graciela too far she wouldn't ride the van to work anymore. That Leticia had dollar signs in her eyes. She raised our fees again, and for what, I wondered, the sheer pleasure of riding in that smelly, yellow van like prisoners being taken to court? The least she could do, if she was going to charge more, was make sure Chano cleaned the inside every once in a while — I was sick of the smell — and fix the radio and get the upholstery repaired. We'd been sitting on exposed springs far too long. I'd torn several of my skirts. And do you think Leticia offered to replace them, or even an apology for the pig smell? No.

"Be careful with the springs," was all she said, as if I was a careless idiot, as if I had torn my skirts on purpose. As if I liked wearing mended clothes.

Before Graciela arrived, things were different. We were used to doing things in a particular way. For example, we took turns sitting in the front seat. And then one day, when it was her turn, Graciela decided to offer it to Berta.

"You take it, Berta," she said.

Caridad looked at me with that look I knew only too well. The look that says, *Imaginate!*

I just shrugged and got in back, as always. Contrary to what people have said about me, I'm not always in the mood for a fight. Some days I just look the other way, and that's what I chose to do that day.

"*Ay, gracias, cariño,*" Berta said and plopped her fat ass in the front seat. The following week, it happened again. And once again Berta accepted. So what could the rest of us do? Raquel was the next to offer Berta the front seat when it was her turn.

I bit my tongue for as long as I could. I even had the decency to take Graciela aside and have a words with her. During our break, not in front of the others. I'm no savage.

"What exactly do you think you're doing?" I said. And she knew exactly what I was talking about.

"I don't like to ride in the front," she said, "the way Leticia drives, I get nauseous."

"Well, then, why didn't you offer it to all of us?"

"Because Berta is the oldest," Graciela said as if this was the most logical of answers.

"Well, you're just complicating everything."

"I think you're being childish," Graciela said.

"*De veras,* Graciela?" I asked. "Because I think it's you who is being childish. Everything functioned fine until you came."

"On my day I do what I want with my seat, you do whatever you want with yours. I'm not forcing you to do anything you don't want to do," Graciela said and she left me standing there speechless. Speechless! Because, *por Dios,* it wasn't that simple. I wasn't doing it for myself, but for Caridad. Caridad loved the front seat and always looked forward to her turn. But Graciela had left us no choice. What were we going to do, be the only ones?

So I gave up my turn. The next day, Caridad finally gave in. She offered Berta the front seat. But she wasn't happy about it. For a couple of days afterwards she didn't speak a word to anyone. She sat in back quietly while the rest of us discussed the *telenovela.* For almost a week, Caridad didn't say a word.

Now, Berta crawls into the front seat every day, both on the way to work and on the way home. She rides up there in the front like she's the Queen of the Parade, always rubbing her legs and complaining. I thought it would only be that one time, maybe twice, but it was forever. The front seat, thanks to Graciela, now belongs to Berta and the rest of us ride in the back like cattle. So you can imagine how we felt when Leticia raised the fee. Not only were we stuck in the back with torn upholstery and no radio, but paid more for the privilege.

I didn't feel so bad for myself as I did for Caridad. *Por Dios,* if anyone had a right to get whatever she wanted to in this country, it was Caridad. After all she had to endure. She escaped from Cuba in a boat in the middle of the night. In my eyes that woman was and always will be a hero.

"It was just awful," she told me. "We drove through the night with our headlights turned off. And now I wonder if that was smart at all, but no one seemed to really know what they were doing. I can understand that we didn't want to attract attention, but what attracts more attention than a dark car on a dark road. But you know me, I didn't say anything. All I could do was follow Salud and hang on to my little Celeste. *Imaginate,* we sneaked out of our country like thieves in the night."

Every time Caridad tells me that story I just want to weep, or hit somebody.

I remember not long after Caridad escaped, I saw a woman in the neighborhood wearing a blouse that looked just like one of Caridad's favorites. It was orange with little pink flowers and I remember the first day Caridad had worn it, to Cuca Soto's bridal shower, and how happy and pretty she'd looked that day. So I followed the woman, keeping a safe distance, my eyes on the flowered pattern as it moved through the crowded streets of Palmagria.

After Caridad left, I had watched her house be ransacked, looted. The officials had not properly sealed it and strangers came in and took whatever they wanted. I knew that whoever the woman was, she had to be one of them, a looter, a thief. That she'd gone into Caridad's closet and taken that blouse before the house was boarded up. As I followed the woman, the distance between us became less and less until I could practically smell her perfume. I could even see the indentation the strap of her brassiere made across her back.

It was Graciela.

I hadn't seen her much since Ernesto sent her back to her parents' house like damaged goods. I followed her a little while longer, my blood boiling. And then I stopped and let her go on, because what I really wanted to do was reach out and rip that blouse right off of her. And I just couldn't do that. *Dios Mío*, what would people say if they saw us rolling around on the sidewalk like a couple of one-eyed cats? Sometimes with Graciela you just had to let her go.

"You know what it felt like after you left?" I said to Caridad one day, after we were reunited in exile. "Like you had committed suicide."

"It felt the same to me," Caridad said, "except I was still alive."

I remember the morning she left clearly. She had left the jar with the mentholated cigarettes on the front porch of my house. When I saw it, I knew she was gone. One of the best things about the United States is that we now smoke Kool cigarettes. We don't have to mentholate our own cigarettes any more.

Yes, I think if anybody has a right to sit wherever she wants in that van or anywhere else in this country, it's Caridad. But she was stuck in the back with the rest of us just because of Graciela.

"Cari," I said one day, "you know what I was thinking about? I was thinking about that beautiful blouse of yours, the orange one with the little pink flowers. Whatever happened to that blouse? I loved that blouse."

Caridad got a dreamy look in her eyes as if she was searching her mind for every blouse she'd ever owned. Graciela remained quiet and turned her face to the window, as if she wasn't even remotely interested in anything I had to say.

"Which blouse?"

"You know, the one you wore to Cuca Soto's bridal shower? Orange with pink flowers, little flowers and pearl buttons up the front."

Graciela continued looking out the window. I could see her face reflected in the glass.

"Was it like the one Esmeralda wore the day she went to visit the man she thought might be her father?" Leticia asked. Always with the *telenovelas*. I mean, I like them and I watch them, but with Leticia it's a sickness.

"No, *por Dios*, this was much nicer, you remember, Graciela, don't you? It had little pearl buttons down the front?" I met Graciela's eyes in the glass. She couldn't avoid me.

Graciela turned and looked right at me. I could tell she was hating every moment. She was so close I could feel the fire in her eyes.

"Oh, yes, that old blouse," Caridad said, "what made you think of that?"

"I always liked it, and I wondered what ever happened to it," I said, keeping a watchful eye on Graciela. I had her cornered and I knew it.

"Oh, I think I left it behind with all my other things. I told you, we didn't even bring a change of underwear to this country."

"Are you sure," I asked, turning almost completely to face Graciela.

Graciela took a deep breath and exhaled slowly.

"You gave me that blouse," she said.

Caridad turned to look at her.

"I did?"

"Yes," Graciela said, "after Celeste was born."

"*Imaginate.* I think I did. You remember, Imperio, how I always used to give my old clothes to Graciela?"

Graciela was looking out the window. She couldn't deny that we gave her our old things. She couldn't deny that even after she was married, we were better off than she was. But the most annoying part of it was that Graciela wouldn't always accept our kindness. Most of the time she'd look at perfectly good items and reject them, as if our sense of style just wasn't good enough for her. I'll bet she jumped at the chance to own that blouse.

"So whatever became of it?" I asked.

"I don't know," Graciela said. But I could tell she was lying. I was sure of it.

A silence came over the van — that silence everyone hated because it threatened to reveal our deepest thoughts. I knew no one hated that silence more than Leticia because it exposed all the sins of that van, the nauseating smell of pork, the rattling motor, the lack of music from the nonexistent radio, the sharp, coiled seat springs that seemed always ready to cause damage.

"*Niiñas,* do you think Esmeralda's ever going to find that old man?" Leticia asked, determined to change the subject. "How long is that deathbed going to hold him?"

"He won't last the week," Caridad said.

She was talking about a show called *Solo Vive El Corazon* (The Heart Lives Alone). Every once in a while a *telenovela* played that no one was crazy about — but we watched it anyway. And no matter how awful the story, Leticia was always fanatical about it. Personally, I couldn't care less if Esmeralda ever found her father, even if I did watch it every night. Caridad was of the opinion that the father was going to die before Esmeralda found him, but I knew the opposite was true.

"*Por Dios,*" I said, "in these things the girl always finds her father before he dies."

"Always," Caridad said.

The Heart Lives Alone had another thing that I absolutely hated: Esmeralda was blonde. She was as blonde and blue-eyed as the dolls we worked on. It was filmed in Argentina, where I hear blondes are quite common. But I wondered if this was a new trend, where the blonde was the heroine. And it eventually proved to be true, the slow but sure Americanization of the *telenovelas*.

Graciela and I rode the rest of the way in complete silence; neither one of us wanted to talk about Esmeralda. It was certainly not one of our favorite *telenovelas*. Then I remembered something else about the blouse. The reason I turned back. The reason I didn't stop Graciela that day in Palmagria. The reason I had trouble recognizing her from behind. It was a different Graciela — not the old Graciela with the high-heeled look-at-me attitude. Her hair was pulled tight into a thick braid, like a country girl; her back, usually so straight and tall, was slightly hunched. She held her shoulders close to her body. Even her silhouette seemed different, narrower, defeated. As I watched her walk away, I thought, 'she did this to herself, she doesn't deserve my sympathy.' I continued watching until she turned the corner and both Graciela and the blouse disappeared from sight. That was the last time I ever saw her in Palmagria.

Chapter 7

GRACIELA

As the van cut through the night and Imperio prattled on and on about Caridad's blouse, I pretended to look out the window. But I was really looking at my reflection. Am I still attractive? Am I too old? Is my life over? Is Mr. O'Reilly paying special attention to me or is it my lonely heart creating romance where there isn't any? Do I seem desperate to him? Sad? Tragic? Can he sense that my heart quickens when he says, "Buenos dias," no matter what time of the day? Can he tell I'm trying to be discreet about my feelings? Can he see Caridad and Imperio eye me like hawks?

Imperio's voice cut through my thoughts.

"You gave me that blouse," I said, just to shut her up.

Imperio was right. The blouse was beautiful, sublime. One of the most beautiful blouses I had ever seen. It was made out of Chinese crepe and it wasn't orange with pink flowers, it was pink with lavender flowers and little sprigs of green. The buttons were real pearls, which I loved, but they were difficult to keep fastened, they tended to fly open at the bosom. Caridad gave it to me, because after Celeste was born she put on a quite a few pounds and she couldn't keep that blouse buttoned, not even with safety pins.

I only wore it once. I had saved it for a special occasion and I didn't have many of those. But I knew that chatter was not about the blouse, just one more attempt to shove my past in my face.

They craved to know what happened. How did a woman who seemed to have everything risk it all for a man as undeserving and ungrateful as Pepe Medina Ynclan? How did it feel to be thrown out by my husband, a man loved and respected by everyone he'd ever met?

What was I going to tell them? That I spent the years after my separation from Ernesto practically locked away in my father's house? That I lived in agony? That I only went out for short little errands, maybe to pick up something we needed for the boys? It was a crazy time. I had married a man I didn't love just to get out of that house and had been brought back to it like a common whore. Just as my mother had predicted. They took me in because she had triumphed. And I had to change my ways. She had been right and I had been wrong. She warned me and I didn't listen. Now it wasn't just me, but also the boys. My parents didn't say a word, for I had only delivered what they had always expected of me, disgrace. From the moment I returned to that house I was a silent, dutiful slave. Everything that needed to be said between us had been said. And just like any slave, I hated my masters.

Sure, I'd had other options, I could have gone to Havana, where people could do as they pleased. But I had missed my opportunity. After the Revolution, so many wanted to go to Havana that the city had been closed to outsiders. The capital was just like a little country, you practically needed a visa to go there. I was stuck in Palmagria, and destined to die there a marked woman, a scandal.

For days after Ernesto dragged me back home, Palmagria simmered with gossip and bile. There was no one to turn to for comfort.

Pepe kept his distance from then on and I punished myself for missing him. He had been my one refuge from a strange, incomprehensible loneliness, a feeling that I suspect I had been born with. Or maybe it was the coldness of the home I grew up in. It was a feeling that I had tried to mask with fashion and makeup and even those silly recitations of poetry at school assemblies. And then Pepe, my biggest and most costly extravagance, had turned his back on me. He was determined to climb the political ladder, wasn't satisfied to deliver exit visas on a bicycle. I heard he had taken leave to go up to the mountains to teach *guajiros* to read. That had been the breaking point for us. He returned six months later, again a changed man. He returned to the bicycle but there was something different about him. Something anxious and desperate. The same way that people expected that telegram to arrive telling them they were free to leave the country, Pepe was waiting for orders from above relieving him of what he considered a menial position in the Revolution. And what had happened with me was holding him back. Time and distance would erase the error of his ways. No matter. Now he was gone from my life. Everything was gone. I couldn't even step outside because prying eyes followed every move I made.

I had lived in Palmagria all my life and I knew it was just a matter of waiting for the curiosity to die down, for another scandal to take its place.

It came a few weeks later when the police unlocked a house a few blocks away, a house that everyone believed had been vacated some weeks earlier, when its inhabitants had escaped to Miami in the middle of the night. What people were calling the one-way midnight boat rides. But the house was not empty. Inside they discovered what was left of their bodies, floating in tubs of lye. A morbidly curious mob congregated around the house, peeking through the grated windows, watching as the men from the morgue assembled the corpses side by side on the living room floor until all of them were accounted for. There was no doubt that it was them, the bones, some with flesh still clinging to them, told the whole story. There was a long one, which certainly belonged to the father, Basilio, then a slightly shorter one, his wife Viena, and the two smaller ones exactly the same size, twins girls, Maite and Lili. Everyone knew them. We not only knew their names but we knew everything about them. How old they were, what grade they were in, what they liked and didn't like. The twins hated beans, even puréed and strained, and if forced to eat them, they would throw up. It had been that way since they were babies. Other than that they were perfectly nice little girls. That was what we'd heard countless times from Viena. Basilio hated anything starched and would never wear a shirt if it had even the slightest smudge or stain on it, which kept Viena busy at the washboard. Viena hated washing and ironing but could not afford to hire someone to do it for her. She didn't mind cooking and cleaning the house, but she hated laundry. That was the sort of day-to-day information we got from our neighbors. The sort of thing that women talked to each other about when they stood outside on hot days waiting for a cool breeze. We passed the time by telling one another stories about ourselves, about our families. Of course, we never really knew each other, no one tells everything. Everybody had their secrets or else we would have known why Basilio, Viena and the twins had been murdered in such a vicious way. We were horrified.

The stories traveled from mouth to mouth, from one end of the town to the other.

"How could something like this happen and no one notices or smells it . . . ?"

"Four bodies decomposing and I walked by, day after day . . ."

"I sat on the step of the very house of death, night after night . . ."

"Drank beer, smoked cigars . . ."

It was upsetting to the core, because, up to that day, we lived under the assumption that nothing could go on in Palmagria without everyone knowing about it.

But right after the Revolution, a lot was going on that no one could explain. The stories drifted into our house, in spite of the locked doors and sealed windows.

The milkman, at sunrise, had found the bodies of two men, stripped naked and lying dead in the middle of the street. Places on the outskirts of town that had been boarded up and believed to be vacant were being uncovered as hellholes where tortures and other crimes had been committed.

On a cross-country train, a trunk leaking a foul-smelling fluid had been forced open and, inside, there were five severed human heads. Nothing but the heads. No one could remember whose trunk it was or how it got on the train. Of course, the only reason to transport a trunk full of heads cross-country was to pick up a ransom. Or to send someone a very powerful message. Who was paying for these crimes?

It wasn't just the morbid tragedies that shook us up. Everything seemed different.

The sun was not as bright, the earth didn't smell as fresh. The sea, which used to look like a restless jewel, had turned pale and complacent. Everything had changed. Now, it was dry during the rainy season and torrential at the most inopportune moments.

People known for their strong constitutions were taking ill. Fishermen were complaining that time after time, their nets were coming up empty. A virus known as *cocotillo* wiped out entire chicken farms. Everyone said it was a curse.

I thought it was a long-overdue retaliation from above. I had few illusions about my place of birth. I had seen too much, I knew too much. I knew that Palmagria could be a cruel town. It was a place where people reveled in torturing the weak, the crippled, and the insane. There were two famously crazy old ladies that generations of kids had loved to torment. One of the ladies had the affliction of walking very fast. All day long, she walked maniacally from one end of town to the other and back again. Her nickname was 'Chanclas,' and she would chase you if you called her that. Bored teenagers taunted her for sport. So, whenever you saw a red-faced boy running up the sidewalk, it was a good bet Chanclas was not too far behind.

The other crazy lady was 'Arroz Blanco,' which meant White Rice. She got that name because she was invited nowhere but showed up everywhere. Particularly weddings. People started to think it was bad luck if she didn't show up for your wedding. After the first kiss, the bride always looked towards the door of the church for a glimpse of Arroz Blanco. There she'd be, smiling her toothless smile, eyes bright with tears, happy to be anywhere. But like Chanclas, if you yelled the name 'Arroz,' she would chase you, hollering profanities. Denouncing you to God. My mother had warned that my marriage was destined for disaster, so on the day of my wedding I was so glad to see her that I gave her my beautiful bouquet. I heard she ate it. Maybe that accounted for the disasters that followed.

I never once called her Arroz Blanco. I knew her real name, it was Nena, but no one had called her that in a long time. In Palmagria, they loved to nickname people with deformities. Men liked to stand outside of bars and call out names as you walked by. If you limped, they called you 'El Cojo.' If you had a big ass, the called you 'Baul.' They would do it by cupping their hand over their mouths and changing the pitch of their voice so that, if there was a group of men, you couldn't really be sure which one was insulting you.

I'd seen them do it to retarded people, Chinese people, fat people, ugly people, people with crooked teeth, or a big head or a scar. There was a young girl named Alvita who'd been born with a huge lavender mark that covered half her face. People said it was because her mother, while pregnant, had slept on her stomach during an eclipse. Alvita was hounded whenever she left the house alone. They called her 'Mancha' — an unpleasant word for stain. If you looked closely, you could see that Alvita's eyes had shrunk back into her head from fear. She tragically died when she set herself on fire one day, but that was many years later, when she was grown and so lonely she couldn't take another day. Hard as she tried, Alvita could not develop a sense of humor about herself, and no one loved her enough to save her.

Everybody was a potential target and, a lot of times, whatever nickname you were given stuck with you for good. So that as time went on, the person actually adopted the nickname and his or her real name was eventually forgotten. There was a handyman who helped out at my father's house. He was called 'El Gago' because he stuttered, and everybody called him that to his face. It was always 'El Gago this' and 'El Gago that.' But he didn't seem to mind. His actual name was Policarpo — which took him forever to say. So eventually even he started to refer to himself as El Ga-ga-ga-go. It became his name.

They all thought they had me labeled when they started circulating that rumor about Pepe Medina Ynclan and me. What they didn't know was that I had been in love with Pepe long before I married Ernesto.

But Pepe did not want his relationship with me to interfere with what he wanted. He told me as much. Sure, he could have stayed in Palmagria and continued to rise in status, but he wanted more. He wanted a post in Santiago or even better in Havana. His dreams, he hoped, would take him even farther than that, to Madrid or Buenos Aires. He knew a wife meant children and children meant responsibility. He had seen it happen much too often to other men. He needed to stay free, or as he put it, choosing a word that reeked of diplomacy and politics, flexible. Pepe was a smalltown boy with very big dreams.

"Then what is this, Pepe?" I asked him, getting out of bed. "What are we doing?"

"That's a question you should ask yourself," he said, and turned to face the wall.

I didn't have an answer.

Pepe was the first man I laid eyes on after my horrible wedding, holding that poor dead baby. At the time I'd believed with all my heart that there was some significance to that. I had wondered why Pepe had cried that day. Was it over the dead baby or because of my wedding? I never asked him. It was enough to know that a heartless man like him could shed a tear. Funny, the people we choose to love. I know people couldn't figure out how we found the time to see each other. Imperio and Caridad in particular. Those two never missed a thing. They joked about Arroz Blanco being everywhere, but they're the ones always with their noses in everybody's business. At least Arroz had the decency to keep her mouth shut. I know that Imperio and Caridad talked garbage about me for weeks on end. I became a favorite topic for them and their friends, it gives me satisfaction that they never figured it out. Pepe and me, we found ways. Manolito was sleeping in his crib, Ernestico was at a neighbor's. I had cleaned the house, prepared myself for his arrival. I had prepared myself for love.

Like in my *telenovelas*, love always finds a way. And for me it had been love. Only love.

Sometimes, Pepe was trapped in my bedroom during one of these afternoon gatherings, when the local ladies came to get their nails done. It was quite a teeth-grinding feat trying to get them out of our house before Ernesto came home and found him.

One afternoon, Cuca Soto arrived early. I quickly closed the bedroom door and rushed to the living room to greet her. She looked very pretty in a new orange-and-green striped summer dress that looked like she had pulled out of the sewing machine just before she arrived. She had started wearing her silky black hair in a shoulder-length pageboy that flattered her curious face. She had Sophia Loren's mouth and Gina Lollobrigida's eyes, so depending on the time of day she could look beautiful or monstrous. Her figure was still as trim as it had been when she was thirteen, even though she had four children who were all under the age of ten.

"*Te gusta?*" she asked and twirled around, a blur of orange and green, hardly taking notice that I was only half dressed.

"I love it," I said, handing her my manicure box, "why don't you set up while I finish dressing. I'll be out in a second."

She accepted the task without question. I went back into the bedroom and could hear her in the dining room moving things around. Setting out my cotton, my acetone, my colorful little bottles of the most up-to-date nail polish — *Rosado Pálido,* pale-pink — which was their current favorite. They all insisted on the same color. Never red. Not anymore. Red, they said, was the color of the new regime.

Pepe was still in bed, still undressed, he looked like a long, brown, bright-eyed crocodile.

I remembered him years ago at the little pine dotted beach. There he was, a young man, just starting to show his beard, the hair under his arms, on his chest. He was dark brown and dusted with white sand. I didn't mind the flies that swarmed all around my head, or the sea fleas that were picking at my legs. I only cared that the breeze carried the smell of *guayabas* and seaweed. Pepe had been so playful that day at the beach, delicately handing me tiny seashells the size of a thumbnail, and pale hermit crabs the same color as the sand. He placed the crabs on my arms, shoulders, breasts, and their sharp little legs tickled me endlessly. Pepe's white teeth showed through an eager smile that said, "Play with me forever."

He sat up in bed and I pushed him back. He looked at me with anger, so I sat next to him and took his hand. I had to make him understand.

"You have to stay here very quietly until they leave," I said, "I'll try to get rid of them quickly, but it's going to be a while, so you might as well take a little nap."

I reached down to buckle my sandals. Pepe reached over and stroked my back.

"What if I snore?" he whispered, but even his whisper sounded too loud.

"Pepe, shhh, *cariño,* and please don't snore. Don't sleep.

Here, read this instead," I said and handed him one of the books Ernesto kept on his dresser. Pepe looked at the book as if I was handing him excrement.

"Couldn't I just jump out the window and run out the back like a real man?" he asked. My throat was dry but my hands were wet. I could hear the others arriving, Caridad, Imperio, and Azucena. They always greeted each other with loud voices and exclamations as if they hadn't seen each other in years, when in fact a day had not gone by ever in their lives when they had not seen each other at least in passing. I could hear them clearly through the closed door.

"Let me take a look at that new dress," Caridad said.

"Those are your colors, no question," said Azucena.

"*Te gusta?* It's what they're wearing in La Habana," Cuca said.

I heard Imperio's unmistakable voice, "Looks like black market material. Is that how you got it, through *bolsa negra?*"

"Imperio what a thing to say," Cuca giggled.

"I should have that idiotic woman arrested and her dress confiscated," Pepe whispered.

"Shhh," I said again.

I smoothed my dress and checked my hair in the mirror. Before I left the room I took a last look at him. My heart, remembering what had happened on that bed just a few minutes before, gave itself a little squeeze. I loved him.

On those rare, nerve wracking afternoons when Pepe was hiding in the bedroom like something out of a dirty joke, I did not talk very much so as not to encourage the girls to stay longer. I just focused on their nails, one finger after another, making sure to provide them with the high quality half-moons they expected. Then I rushed them out, which wasn't easy — they had all the time in the world. And even though they saw each other every day, they always had one more thing to say, one more inane idea to express. Even as they sauntered down the sidewalk with their newly manicured hands extended in front of them, I could hear them laughing and chattering.

The one-and-only time I wore Caridad's blouse was the last time I saw Pepe. That day all I wanted was to look special, pretty, young.

I escaped from my mother's prying eyes and almost ran to his house. I saw him through the open window. He was wearing the pants of his olive green uniform and no shirt. The olive green shirt with all the emblems was draped over the back of his chair. He was hunched over his desk, going over some papers. I looked at his broad, brown shoulders and remembered their smell, their warmth. I continued looking into that room waiting for him to turn around. Surely, I thought, he will sense that I'm here, looking at him, full of love. If he turns around, it's meant to be, if he doesn't, I will leave. I waited and waited. I set a time, five minutes, and then extended it another five, then another. Pepe never looked back. It was clear to me that he had not given me another thought. I expected my heart to break, but instead I felt as if I no longer had a heart. I backed away slowly, my eyes on the back of his neck, giving him every opportunity to turn around. He didn't. I walked slowly back to my parent's house, in my beautiful blouse that someone I once considered a friend had given me.

Chapter 8

CARIDAD

I never had much of a head for numbers and dates. But there's one date I will never forget.

We left Cuba in the middle of the night on June 6, 1961.

Imagínate!

All of Palmagria wondered why we left in such a hurry, and in such a dangerous way. We did it for Celeste, of course. There were rumors, strong ones, and behind every rumor there's more truth than anyone cares to hear. The government was going to take our children, they said. Like *brujos*. We could only keep our children until they were three years old, they said. After that they had to be turned over to *Circulos Infantiles*, state-run day-care centers. From ages three to ten they would live in dormitories and could only come home to visit their parents two days every month, and that was only if they were good. If they were trouble, they would not be allowed to come home at all.

There were stories going around that truant children were

being picked up in the streets and taken to prisons. They were saying that when the parents came to claim them the parents themselves would be imprisoned for being irresponsible. *Imagínate!* In a country where children roamed the streets at all hours happy and carefree, suddenly they were being taken away in trucks.

Like specters, Cuca Soto and Azucena Martinez appeared at my front door with clouded and frightening faces.

"What is it? What's wrong?"

They didn't even wait to be asked in, but pushed their way past me and into my living room.

"Cari, you have to sign this," Cuca said, taking a folded piece of paper out of the big pocket of her house dress. The paper looked as if it had been folded and unfolded a dozen times, pawed and turned over by countless others.

"What is it?"

"It's a pact," Azucena said. Her face twitched, her eyes filled up, and then she couldn't go on speaking. With trembling hands she motioned to Cuca to tell me.

"Sit down, Cari," Cuca said calmly. I did but only on the edge of the couch. I found the way they were behaving very unsettling, it was as if they were vibrating. I knew Azucena had a tendency towards nerves, and that sometimes she had to be put to bed in a dark room due to pounding headaches, but Cuca suffered from no such condition.

"This," she said trying to remain calm, pronouncing each and every word very carefully, "says that we will kill our children before we let Fidel Castro or any other Castro take them away."

With that, Azucena burst into sobs.

"Sign it, Cari, I beg you," she said through her tears. "It's our only hope."

"Have the two of you lost your minds?"

I tried to keep my voice soft, almost kind, but I could feel a small hurricane starting to build up inside me, the winds and rains of fear.

"It's the only way we can stop them, it's the only way we can make them see what this means to a mother."

"You can't be serious."

"We're not just serious," Cuca said, her voice rising and screeching as if her throat was being pierced with a million needles, "we're desperate."

Azucena stopped crying just long enough to say, "It's already started in Santa Clara and Cienfuegos. It's spreading east."

I looked at the sheet of paper again. There were already more than thirty names on it, written in pencil; some were already smudged from being passed around. They were names I knew very well, the names of respectable women, not just twittery birds like Azucena and impulsive women like Cuca.

And then I saw her name. Graciela Altamira de la Cruz. I was shocked that she still used Ernesto's last name! There was her signature, halfway down the page, and just as you would expect: bigger than the others, a dramatic script that took up two lines. No one had seen her for months. So more than a signature, it was a statement. I'm still here, it shouted, and I'm still me.

What would Imperio say? I wondered. She'd say it was reactionary, alarmist propaganda. She wouldn't understand. Only a mother could truly understand. And Graciela, for better or worse, was a mother.

Well, I couldn't have the whole world saying that Graciela was a better mother than me, so I signed it. I signed it with a shaking, unsure hand that acted as if it had never before held a pencil. *Imagínate!* It was the hand of a mother signing her own daughter's death sentence. And what if this document went to the wrong people? Was it evidence of a conspiracy? I could be imprisoned, and then Celeste would be alone and at the mercy of who knew what.

All night I was wide awake with my mind going a mile a minute. What sort of mother would do a thing like that even under the most horrendous circumstances? But what was I to do? Pack a little bag with her diapers and her bottle and dress her in her best dress and just hand her over? Who do I hand her over to? Who would be at my door to take my girl? Would it be women or men? Whoever it was would certainly be in an olive green uniform. And then what? Do I just go back to my life as if I never had a baby at all? What would become of my girl in the hands of strangers? Celeste was a child with very special needs.

I woke up Salud. I shook him until he was alert.

"We're leaving," I said to him. I felt as if my mouth was filling with blood. "Do what you have to do, pay what you have to pay, but I have to get my little girl out of here, and it has to happen now. Today. Before it's too late and all we have is regrets."

Looking back, it *was* reactionary, alarmist propaganda. But at the time it seemed as real as anything. I could not, just could not risk it with Celeste. She was starting to show signs that she was unlike other children. A child that fragile I had to keep close to me. What sort of monster would do such a thing? I wondered.

The waiting list for the Freedom Flights numbered in the hundreds of thousands. So we took the midnight boat. We practically ran out of Cuba. That was how it seemed to me, as if we were running away to hide. Just for a little while, just until things got back to normal. We knew it could not last. A government that crazy would soon come to an end.

I kept our plan a secret because just the slightest whisper

could ruin everything. Not a word about it to Imperio even though she was the one person I could say anything to. In my mind it was a way of protecting her. The less she knew, the better. All I could think of to do was leave the jar of mentholated cigarettes at her doorstep. I considered a written note but that could incriminate her and in those days there was no telling where a little thing like that could lead.

Talk about things turning out differently than I expected! We were rescued by the Coast Guard, and at the time I thought for sure we were going to die. I thought for sure they were going to shoot us all down and dump our bodies into the sea. That was the feeling I got when that big white boat with those tall Americans were pointing rifles at us and we had our hands above our heads.

But to my surprise the Americans were friendly, not hug-and-kiss friendly, but certainly not hostile. They towed our boat all the way to the shores of the United States. They even gave us snacks. I've come to know that very little happens in America without snacks.

Imagínate! It was completely different. Because we were *clandestinos*, and had arrived in a boat, we were treated like heroes.

That was at first. Then we were just like any other penniless immigrants in a foreign country, but I couldn't say that to Imperio when she phoned. I couldn't tell her that every morning I woke up with a towering desire to burst into tears and that this desire followed me around like a mean black dog. That even on the days when I told myself to go ahead and cry, on the days when I locked myself in the bathroom and sat on the edge of the bathtub, nothing came out. My eyes remained as dry as chalk and the heaviness of grief stayed with me for the rest of the day and into the night, and was waiting for me when I woke up again. I couldn't tell her that I had become mean-spirited towards the people I loved the most, that I snapped at my husband for no clear reason. I couldn't tell her that I no longer seemed to know the difference between fairness and selfishness, that I looked to find someone to blame for my situation, and that because it was Salud who was always there, he was the one I unloaded all my fears and frustrations on. I blamed myself for leaving my country, for allowing rumor and panic to force me to act foolishly. No one had their child taken away. I hated myself. But I couldn't tell Imperio that.

I couldn't tell her that I hardly recognized the person I was becoming — a woman who constantly complained and nagged, even at poor little Celeste who would just look at me with frightened eyes and go seek the comfort of her father's lap. I couldn't tell her that it was impossible for me to find any sort of comfort, not in my husband's lap or in anybody or anything. I couldn't tell her that the world had become as flat for me as in the days before Columbus and that I felt as if at all times I was floating towards the edge and was sure to fall off.

I couldn't tell her that if she came here she would feel lost without the flowers and the green and the language we took for granted. That she would go days and days without hearing someone yell out 'Buenos Dias' from across the street or even "mal rayo te parta." That she wouldn't hear the annoying bicycle bells of the churro vendors or the curses of the garbage man as his wooden wheels ground into the pot holes. Or smell the constant stench of the open sewers and the flies, mosquitoes and gnats that swarmed there and often flew into our mouths when we laughed. All I could think of was that back there we laughed. I would give anything to laugh like that now, even if to do so would mean I had to swallow a million bugs.

I couldn't tell her that everything we found irritating back in

Palmagria we would miss with a terrible desperation. No, I couldn't do that. For all I knew Imperio would have a much better time of it here, she's much stronger, practical — and selfishly I wanted her here. I thought that perhaps with Imperio nearby the black dog would go away and I would start to greet each morning with my usual resolve and courage without even thinking about it, the way it had been back then, back there, when I knew who I was and where I was going at all times. When I never, for one second, encountered a doubt. Where the horizon was just a beautiful, distant line where the glorious sun went to sleep each night, the sea was the mattress and the sky was the blanket and all was cozy and blue and gold.

I couldn't tell her that even if Palmagria had turned into a hopeless little town filled with strangers, it was home.

"Come," I said instead. *"Mi casa es tu casa."*

The girls in the van, they had it easy, with their apartments and television sets and the jobs at the toy factory and a van that picked them up and dropped them off. When Salud and I arrived we had nothing. Just hunger and poverty and heavy hearts and doubts that we had maybe been too hasty, had left too soon. We were sustained only by the hope that something would happen that would get us back to Cuba right away. We didn't want to make ourselves too comfortable here. There had been an invasion, Playa Giron, which everyone insists on calling Bay of Pigs, which gives you an idea of what Americans really thought about us. Playa Giron was a beautiful place and pigs were not allowed there. Anyway, we didn't find out until after it happened, when we read it in the newspapers. It was a disaster. Salud blamed the Americans.

"Their hearts weren't really in it," he said. "This has just been a pantomime."

Poor Salud was lost. In Palmagria he was practically a doctor, and here he was nothing, or less than nothing. Hard as he tried, Salud couldn't learn English. It was as if his brain had a block against the language. So going back to being a chiropodist was out of the question. Imagine how we felt when we walked around Union City and saw the signs. There were chiropodists everywhere and clearly no need for any more. As dark as it was inside my mind, I never told him because I suspected it was even darker inside of Salud's. He'd always been able to provide and now it was as if his hands were tied. So I did what I had to do.

I put on the best shoes I had and took to the streets to look for a job, leaving Celeste in his care. Every morning I looked through the newspapers and tried to decipher what the job ads said. And then I'd go to this factory or that. I was like a mute in those interviews, signaling to the foreman that I was strong and capable and always smiling. I was the sweetest girl for them. Subservient, even though my heart was breaking.

'I should be *your* boss,' I'd think as I tried to fill out the application with a small, blunt-tipped pencil.

That was the year that I became Mrs. Rodriguez. I hated the sound of that. I had my own name, my own last name, the name of my father and mother, but here I was to be known as Caridad Rodriguez. The woman I had been was gone. I would fill out those applications as carefully as possible, answer all the questions, give them all the information. *Imagínate!*

Imagine how absurd, to go through all that. It was like a slave showing up at a plantation and begging to be taken in, like offering your wrists to be shackled, only to be turned away, for no reason that I could understand. Of course, they didn't want someone who didn't speak English — why should they? I tried place after place until finally we saw an ad that had the RCA Victor logo printed on it, the little dog listening to the Victrola. It was as if a light had gone on in my head. I recognized that little dog, he was on all our records at home. And as if that little dog had willed it, that was the first place where I was treated like a human being.

The factory was big and white. So spotless it even smelled clean. It was hard to imagine that people worked there. I was taken into an office and left there, alone. The professional American woman who I assumed was going to conduct the interview rattled something in English, then rushed out. At first I thought she had gone to get a policeman. In those days I only expected the worst to happen and I sincerely thought they were going to arrest me and send me back to Cuba and I would never see my husband and baby again. I sat in the office and tried to calm my nerves by taking in the clean and organized desk with its neat towers of papers and folders. There was a telephone with many buttons on it. The telephone rang several times. I watched as the buttons lit playfully like a musical toy while the telephone rang and went off when the ringing stopped. The office smelled strongly of her perfume. I looked for photographs of her family but found none. On the wall hung a calendar with a picture of a long, wide, empty beach.

She returned with an interpreter — a Spanish-speaking man who talked a mile a minute in English and then very slowly to me in Spanish. While the man talked to me in Spanish, the American woman nodded and smiled at me, which was funny because I knew she didn't know what he was saying but was trusting that her words were being passed on correctly. What could I do? I kept my eyes on her and nodded and smiled.

When it was all over, she extended her hand to me, "*Hasta*

mañana, Señora Rodriguez," she said with an accent and I was happy to hear those words no matter how strange they sounded.

"Hasta mañana," I said while my stomach tightened because I dreaded *mañana* more than she could ever imagine. I had never worked a day in my life. Now I was to be a factory worker in a strange country and in a foreign language.

As I walked into our apartment that day I felt surprisingly victorious and triumphant. I was Mrs. Rodriguez, a woman with a job. It was a feeling that would not last for long. Everyone who worked at that factory was one hundred percent black. All black ladies. Not that I have anything against *los negros*, but I knew enough to know that in America this placed me at the bottom of the heap. Not one of them welcomed me in any way, no one said a word to me. They just looked at me like I was *bicho raro*. The foreman was the same man who had been at the interview and that was lucky for me, because I had a lot to learn. I was given a light blue smock to put over my dress and a shower cap for my hair. Then they seated me on a stool at a big white table where many other ladies were seated and each one of us had a huge magnifying glass in front of us. On the table were tiny little parts and tiny little screws and tiny little screwdrivers and the idea was to look through that magnifying glass and screw everything together.

Olvidate de eso. My hands were shaking and sweating and the screws kept falling to the floor and the black ladies kept looking at me and then looking at each other and the more that happened the worse it got but this was going to put food on the table and pay our rent so I kept trying and trying finally one of the black ladies left her post and stood next to me and placed her black hands on mine and steadied me and helped me do the first one while the rest of them watched but then my eyes started to fill with tears and I couldn't see anything and I just dropped my chin on my chest and cried and cried I couldn't stop I was so embarrassed I just wanted to die the more I cried the more my hands shook and then the Spanish speaking man came and said something to the black lady and she went back to her stool but no one was working, everyone was watching the spectacle. Me.

"*Vamos, Señora,*" the man said kindly, and he led me to the women's washroom where I threw up. Then I returned and I sat on my stool and looked through the magnifying glass and grabbed the screwdriver and the little screws and I got to work. I don't know where it came from, but I did it. When I looked up the black ladies were looking at me again and I found the eyes of the one who'd tried to help me and I smiled and she nodded like she knew.

The job didn't get any easier. Looking through that magnifying glass gave me headaches and my vision was getting worse. Sometimes I would look at my fingers through the magnifying glass, see the ravaged cuticle and the bare nails where once a glorious half-moon had existed and it just made my heart sink. I was bringing home a paycheck every week and that was the only thing that kept me coming back. Same as everybody else. It was then that I started taking a few dollars out of every paycheck to buy hand cream and lotions. I may have been reduced to working in a factory, but some dignity had to be maintained.

Yes, Imperio had it easy compared to me. By the time she arrived I had already met Leticia and switched to the toy factory where the job was much easier, even fun, and it paid better. Mr. O'Reilly had shorter hair then, and even wore a tie, one of those you clip on.

Best of all, I didn't have to take the bus any more. Leticia bought a van and she asked if I wanted a ride. I accepted immediately. Only later did she tell me there would be a fee. Every day I just climbed into Leticia's van with Raquel and Berta and pretended I didn't mind paying, but I felt like she had tricked me.

You should have seen the look on Imperio's face when she first arrived in Union City. I don't know what she was expecting, but it certainly didn't please her.

"This is where you live?" she said, sniffing around my little apartment with a look on her face like the beans were burning in the kitchen.

Imagínate! I sat her down and explained things to her. And I was very clear about everything. Of course, she denied having grand expectations, but inside of her words was an apology and I let her get away with it. Her reaction wasn't all that different from mine. The first night we stayed up all night talking.

She and Mario stayed with us for a few weeks until they could get an apartment of their own. Fortunately, it was in our building.

And they got that apartment just in time because Salud and Mario were not getting along.

Mario complained to Imperio that Salud acted like he was still a doctor when he wasn't anything like that. Imperio told me about it because she tells me everything, and I had to mediate between the two men. I'll admit, Salud tends to be a little arrogant. But that arrogance is all the poor man has now.

Mario called him "El Medico" just like everyone used to back in Palmagria, but he said it with an ugly sneer, like a *burla.* My poor husband hadn't been able to get a job and he was so successful once. He was not used to watching his wife go off to work every day and control all the money. But he was good with Celeste and I knew that sooner or later he would find his way.

"Salud, por favor, just ignore him," I said. "You know how Mario is. He's still recovering from that *Santero's* curse."

"Curse," Salud said, "what do I care about a curse. Why should I listen to garbage from a man who lost everything to a *Santero? Carajo!* I could be bitter too, but why should I have to pay for his superstition and bad judgment? While he's in my house, eating my food, he should at least show some gratitude. And he drinks too much."

"All the gratitude we need I get from Imperio," I said, and I meant it.

Shortly after they moved out, and much to Mario's frustration, Salud got a job at a hospital. He worked nights cleaning up blood, vomit and *quien sabe que,* and we hardly saw each other, but we had a little more money coming in and he was still able to watch Celeste during the day while I was at work. I was suddenly filled with optimism. I started to feel a little happier with Imperio at my side. I no longer woke up with that horrible desire to weep. I had my friend back. Together we would make it through this difficult time, until things in Cuba went back to normal, until we could return and claim what was ours. For now, it would be like old times again, if in a different language, with a different last name, and in different surroundings. I got her a job at the toy factory, and of course, she rode to work in Leticia's van. Leticia was only too glad to have the extra money. Yes, the situation was getting better. That was back when it was just us. Graciela arrived two years later, and everything started to change.

Chapter 9

GRACIELA

I never believed we were going back. I was not like those other Cubans who looked at the horizon every day with tearful eyes, who carried poison in their souls, who refused to learn English or move forward. There was nothing for me back there. But because my heart is treacherous, sometimes my thoughts drifted to a distant future and I saw myself back in Palmagria, with a soft breeze blowing through the narrow streets. And the streets full of strangers. My boys didn't figure in my daydream, they were grown and gone, most likely married, and hopefully happy.

When we first got to Union City, I made Ernestico write letters to his grandparents. I knew both my parents were furious with me, but thought that if they heard from the children, who knows, maybe it would soften them a little.

I sat him at the aluminum dining room table with a clean sheet of paper and a well-sharpened pencil.

"What do I say?" he asked me.

"Just tell them about your life here; your school, your new friends."

"I don't have any friends here."

"Well, then just tell them that you miss them."

"But I don't."

"They love you, don't you remember how nice they were to you?"

He didn't say anything. I could see memories and doubt cloud his face.

"Do it anyway," I said. "Sometimes we have to say things until we mean them."

"Isn't that like lying?"

"Just do it."

So he hunched over and created a list of lies that ended with, "we miss you very much, your loving grandson, Ernestico."

"Here," he growled, handing the sheet of paper to me as if it was on fire.

As much as he hated writing these letters, afterwards he was anxious to receive one back from them. Every day he asked me if they'd written. The answer was always no.

"Maybe it got lost in the mail," I told him. "Write another one." Which he did, this time with a little more sincerity. But when they still didn't write back, we stopped doing that. He never mentioned it again, but I sensed his disappointment, like only a mother can. Ernestico was the sort of boy who hid his feelings very deep inside, but I knew he was hurt. I could see it in his eyes.

I talked to Raquel about it because she had children too. I waited until we were in the clock-out line at the end of the workday.

"The reason you don't hear from them," she said, "is because the mail is censored."

"I think they were happy to see us go, and are happy that we've stayed gone," I said as I slid my timecard into the clock for a stamp.

After Raquel had clocked out, we walked across the parking lot and took our seats in the van.

"Seriously," Raquel said, "not one piece of mail goes into Cuba unopened."

Imperio and Caridad had been walking closely behind us and now joined in the conversation as if they'd been invited.

"They open everything," Imperio said, "every letter, every package. And if there is anything suspicious or that they think could be code for something counterrevolutionary, they burn it."

"Just the thought of those grubby hands opening my envelopes makes me crazy," Raquel said.

"It's the mail from us to them that gets all their attention. You know they take the money out and keep it," Caridad said, "and they read everything you write out loud and laugh. *Imagínate,* it's like a party there in that post office when they get hold of a letter from one of us. The more you talk about your life here, the louder they laugh. They chew your gum, pocket your money, and they laugh."

"Especially if you say you're working in a factory," Imperio said, "*Por Dios,* I hope you don't write to them about that!"

Raquel didn't say anything because that was exactly what she was doing. Writing letters that described her shabby life in Union City, and along with the twenty dollar bill she enclosed, she was also apologetically telling her relatives how hard life was here, how difficult it was working in a factory, and how she wished she could send more. I could see her sealing the envelopes with her tears.

Leticia turned the key and the motor started. While she

waited for it to warm up, she said, "I tell them I drive a big yellow van, that I eat steak every night, and that I have never been to the shoe repair. When I wear out a pair, I buy new ones. Let them eat their hearts out."

And with that, she shifted into reverse and maneuvered us out of the parking lot without looking back.

"So you never write to anyone in Cuba?" Imperio asked me.

A simple question if it'd come from anyone else.

"No," I said.

"No one?" Caridad asked. She didn't dare look at Imperio but they were dying to exchange a knowing glance. She kept her tone light and curious, as if this was just a simple question she would ask anyone.

I knew this day would come as sure as I knew my own name. They had been dying to bring it up. I could see it in every movement of their eyes, the way Imperio and Caridad's backs straightened whenever I climbed into the van. Sure, they were all smiles and greetings and happy to talk about the *telenovelas*. But I also knew there was a little topic in their minds that they wanted to discuss. And I wasn't going to let them have even a little bit of it. I had loved and lost and had no need to repeat it for their amusement.

I felt Berta and Raquel's eyes on me. What sort of heartless person was I that I just severed all connection with everyone back in my country? But of course, neither Berta nor Raquel were about to say anything. Berta rarely heard from her son in Venezuela and Raquel wanted to keep her mysterious circumstances mysterious.

"*Niiiñas*, I'm sure Graciela has her reasons," Leticia said.

Then it was like someone had sucked all the air out of the van. It wasn't that Leticia was coming to my defense. Her statement was implying something else. And it was then I knew that she knew about Ernesto and Pepe.

Of course she knew. Of course Caridad and Imperio had told her all the juicy details. I had been discussed with wide eyes and arched eyebrows. Dissected with such excitement that their lips flapped and their mouths watered.

But hearing it from them, secondhand, was not the same as hearing it from me. They had no proof.

Suddenly, the van felt hot and crowded. My arm was rubbing up against Imperio's who was sitting next to me. Now, though that would not have bothered me before. But now it made me nauseous. I moved myself away. I didn't want to be in contact with any of them. Particularly Imperio. I just wanted to get home.

I knew that Imperio and Caridad were not going to give up. That this *chismoseo* would continue endlessly. They not only wanted me to tell them what really happened back in Palmagria, they wanted more. They wanted to hear how sorry I was that I had done what I did. They wanted a confession and a repentance. They wanted some sort of reason.

They wanted me on my knees.

And this was exactly what I was not willing to do.

I didn't even want to think about it. I kept quiet for a few minutes, looking out the window, but I could sense their anticipation, as if at any moment, I was going to turn back to them and start reciting a very painful episode from my past like an old poem or the plot of a *telenovela*.

They would have loved that.

Instead, I kept my sights on the passing scenery. The bitter winter had given way to an unbelievably beautiful spring. Where there had once been nothing but dirty ice and gray pools of water, now the most incredible violets and geraniums bloomed. They were everywhere: hanging from planters on balconies, growing out of cracks in the sidewalk, filling the islands that divided the traffic.

The trees, thick with leaves, cast cool shadows on the asphalt.

Even the buildings had taken on color. All winter long they had been darkened by the damp air and melting snow, but now the gentle sunlight brought out the warm, dry tones of the russet brick, brown wood, and green patterns of moss on cement. Rows of windows reflected the blue sky.

The air outside was cool and breezy. Unlike the winter months, when people dashed from one warm place to another, they now walked the streets leisurely, the women in light, pastel sweaters, children in short pants. The men in light-colored suits of gray or tan. How was I to know that my anger towards Pepe was to be just like one of these Union City winters? That, in time, the ice would melt and that I would find myself as vulnerable and quivering as a spring blossom?

Looking back, I can see how lost I was. How trusting. He made promises and I believed him. "After the Revolution, *preciosa*," he said. "After the Triumph, *tesoro*." It was always after this happens and after that happens. And I knew how important it all was to him. But I was twenty-two and single. All the girls I knew were married and starting their families. I had seen it happen too many times, women who waited and waited and then one day found themselves gray-haired and hardened. I was not going to let that happen to me.

"Pepe, the revolution came and went," I said to him, "and what about me? What about us?"

He stroked my naked body, and I immediately forgot what I had asked him.

"Be patient, *mi corazón*," he said. "There's still a lot of work to be done."

"There's a man who wants me," I said. It was a trick and an obvious one, but I was reaching desperation.

"We'll talk about it when I return, *preciosa*," Pepe said.

I was tired of sweet words. No one made me feel the way he did. Every touch was heaven. I adored him, and climbed into his bed every chance I got. Every single time. All he had to do was signal and I was his.

But I also had to think of myself. He went to the *sierras* again to teach the *guajiros* how to read. He put them before me. He always would. I had my answer.

Months later, when he returned, I didn't have the will to resist him. I was a married lady with a good life and I made a horrible mistake. But I'm not sorry. I see no point in regrets. Maybe I'm sorry with the way things turned out. Particularly with Ernesto. But what can I do about that? When I married Ernesto, I knew that it wouldn't be easy, that he wasn't the love of my life. But I was willing to move forward, to enter a new life. I made the right choice, as if I could tell my heart how to feel. As if I could tell my soul who to love. As if I could tell my body who to desire. I can honestly say that I thought Pepe Medina Ynclan and I were over and done with. I really believed that that chapter had ended. I was so angry at him, I didn't think I would ever let him back into my life. I thought the anger would last forever, that it would protect me, hardened me to his charms.

As my wedding day approached, I had a nasty, nagging, thought that would not go away. On the morning of my wedding, as I laid out the beautiful white gown and veil on my bed, I kept hoping that Pepe would come to the church and put a stop to the ceremony. I imagined him shouting that he objected; that he was sorry, that he'd been a fool. I would throw down my bouquet and run into his arms. It was a fantasy that haunted me, and that I braced myself against.

No, I told myself, you can't do that to Ernesto. He's a good man. He's worth a thousand Pepes. If Pepe comes to the wedding and makes a scene, you must take Ernesto's arm and stand by him. You must denounce Pepe as a liar and a fool and have him dragged screaming from the church. And I knew that there were plenty of men who were willing to do just that. No one was going to let Pepe Medina Ynclan make an ass out of Ernesto de la Cruz on his wedding day. It wasn't going to happen.

All through my brief courtship with Ernesto, my mother and father endured his visits, and as soon as he left, they went into their bedroom and closed the door. But at least they were somewhat gracious to his face. It wasn't that they preferred Pepe.

Even on the day of my wedding, my mother insisted that Ernesto was a mistake.

"Maybe," I said, "but it's my mistake to make."

"You don't love him," my mother said as the boy from the bakery brought in my wedding cake. I waited until the delivery boy left. The last thing I needed was for him to go back to the bakery with *chismes*. Everyone goes to the bakery at least once a day. Letting him overhear anything would have been like putting my personal life on the radio.

"I'll learn to love him," I told her. And I meant it. But she wouldn't hear of it.

"You think I don't know you?" she said. "I know you too well. I know there is someone else. I see how you look when you come home. I sense it in you, I can smell it. All I can think of are all the babies God denied me, and you are the one he chose for me. You've been giving yourself to a man who used you, and now that you're getting older, you've chosen this unfortunate creature for a husband. A man too deep in grief and memories to know what he's doing. You will bring disgrace to your father. Ernesto is an important man, so you'd better be sure of what you're doing. I can't stop you, I could never stop you. All your life you've been willful and disobedient. So what can I expect of you? You say you'll learn to love him? *Ya veremos,* we'll see. But if you've ever had an ounce of respect for me, you'd go talk to Ernesto right now and call this wedding off. Today you can start doing what's right."

"Mamá, how can you say this to me? You're my mother. I'm getting married in a few hours."

"I had to clear my conscience. I had to be a mother."

"But you just called me a whore."

"I did not use that word," she said, "it's not a word that comes easily to me, particularly in regards to my own daughter, but perhaps you do know yourself. Perhaps you do. Only you know what you've done to yourself."

"Yes, I'll admit . . ."

"No," she interrupted, "I can't listen to your confession. Do you honestly think I can sit here and listen to the disgusting details of your life?"

"Mamá!"

She raised her hand to silence me once and for all and left the room. I wanted to tell her that I had been stupid. That I trusted a man who didn't love me. I wanted her to comfort me, to bless me, to teach me what she knew about being a good wife.

Moments later, Ernesto and a friend delivered a case of champagne. He was full of good cheer. He kissed my mother's cheek while she swallowed her tongue.

"Is everything all right?" Ernesto asked me.

"Yes."

"You seem upset," he said.

"Just a little nervous," I told him. He smiled at me and took my hands in his.

"That's only natural."

I nodded in agreement and forced a smile and he left without kissing me.

As I started to get dressed, my mother and father came into my room and announced that they would not attend the wedding. I can't say I was surprised by their decision, as a matter of fact, I would have been more surprised if they had supported me. I had cleaned and decorated the house all by myself; filled the living room with flowers by myself, set out the glasses, the plates, and the napkins by myself. The two of them had been home, watching me like owls in the daylight, their eyes big and blind; and neither of them lifted a finger to help.

"Why not?" I asked with a tired, resigned voice.

"Because we know you," my mother said.

"You don't know me," I said, "you don't know anything about me. Nothing you said earlier is true. You're wrong. You're always wrong."

"Your mother only wants what's best for you," my father said. "Think about it, Graciela,"

It was then that I started to shout.

"You think about it. You think about what it's going to be like for me to walk down that aisle without you. Think about what people are going to say."

"When did you start caring what people say?" my mother asked, closing the window.

I promised myself there would be no tears, but it wasn't easy. They backed out of the room, and I closed the door on their faces. Still seething, I slipped into my dress, pulled on my gloves, and attached my veil. I checked my makeup in the mirror. It was perfect. Not too much around the eyes, and very pale lipstick. I looked in the full length mirror behind the door, and I saw the bride I had always dreamed I would be. The sight almost made me let go of the tears I was holding back. But I didn't. I wasn't going to spoil all the work that had gone into my face. Instead I threw a pillow on the floor, carefully dropped to my knees, and prayed. I prayed to Santa Barbara to give me the strength to go on. I begged San Lazaro to help me become the person I had always wanted to be. I begged la Virgen del Cobre to help me forget Pepe, and I begged Santa Lucia to help be a good wife to Ernesto.

I had never been too fond of praying, but on that day, the prayers helped immensely, even the ones to the saints I didn't believe in. I rose from my knees with a light, clear heart. I searched my mind for the darkness and despair that had tormented me a few minutes before, but it wasn't there.

As I left my violet colored bedroom, where I had slept alone all my life, I felt free. I walked through the house, took a final look at the living room. It looked beautiful. Just right. My only fear was that my crazy mother would take it all down before I returned for the reception.

Married.

Married to a man my mother was convinced I didn't love. Would never love. As if her marriage had been based on anything other than convenience and routine. I never once saw a kiss or caress pass between them. I wondered, if the roles were reversed, if my mother had been my daughter, would I have opposed or tried to stop her marriage to my father. Would I have been so cruel? So cold? So unforgiving? Those were the kind of thoughts that ran through my mind that morning. And I had no answers.

But I was sure of one thing: she wouldn't touch a thing while I was out getting married. That would have required too much of an effort. More effort than either one of them was willing to make that day.

She sat on a rocking chair next to the front door; too exhausted to rock. With her head bowed to her chest, content to play the helpless victim — the martyr, to just wash her hands of the whole thing. I walked past her without a word. My father had sequestered himself somewhere. He was probably in the backyard puffing down a cigar. I didn't want another encounter with him. It would bring down my spirits. I wanted to put distance between us.

I stepped out of the house and into the sunlight; the breezes licked my face like a hundred butterflies. I decided to walk to the church by myself, like a crazy person; the type of lunatic who wanders the streets in a tattered old wedding dress. Except mine was fresh and white and lovely. If it wasn't for the long dress, I would have run to the church. I didn't have to walk alone. I had choices. I could have asked Imperio or Caridad to walk with me, or called Ernesto who had hired a car for the day. I could have hired a car and driver, or a horse-drawn carriage. But I hadn't thought of that. As soon as I was dressed and ready, I just wanted to get out of that house as fast as possible.

I felt beautiful and proud, as if I was floating, as if I was being carried by the gentle wind to the next phase of my life. It was a perfect summer morning, cloudless and bright. Later, it would get hot and horrible, the wind blowing as if from an oven. But, at that very moment, the day seemed blessed.

Everyone I met on the streets smiled, admired my dress, and

wished me well. That day, I took them at their word. I didn't care if they shook their heads or rolled their eyes as soon as I had passed. Further along, I met up with people also hurrying to the church. I knew all of them: neighbors, former classmates, shopkeepers; as familiar to me as my own relatives. They were all dressed in their very best and, although at first they were surprised to see me walking alone, they hugged me and kissed me and joined me. I knew they were only going to the wedding out of respect for Ernesto, but I didn't care. I gracefully accepted their good wishes and compliments. A car even stopped and offered me a ride.

"Get in, Graciela," the driver shouted.

"No, *muchas gracias,* Felo, I prefer to walk," I said. The people walking with me took him up on his offer and happily jumped into his car. Off they went — while the bride walked alone. I didn't give it any thought. I laughed as I walked. I didn't have much farther to go. I could hear the church bells ringing. At an altar just a few short blocks away, there was a man waiting for me who was willing to make me his wife. And I would be the best wife anyone in Palmagria had ever known.

All regrets were mine and mine alone. I would not air them in the van for all of them to judge. There was no possible way for me to get them to understand, not if we talked about it every day on the way to work and on the way back for the rest of our lives. How could I express what it felt like after my wedding, coming home to the house and finding all those people crowded around that ugly spectacle, and then seeing Pepe again after all that time? His green eyes expressing pain and confusion, that dead baby in his arms. How would I get them to understand that, at that moment, I gave that unfortunate baby no second thought, that all I could think of was 'so that's why Pepe didn't stop the wedding.'

They were the thoughts of a much younger woman. I no

longer harbored such illusions. I still thought of myself as romantic, I had not entirely given up hope that, one day, I would meet the right man.

Pepe had not been the right man for me. When he showed up at my doorstep a few days after my wedding, I made my first mistake.

"I have to talk to you, *preciosa*," he said.

"It's too late to talk, and don't call me that," I said, and I meant it. I didn't want to hear one word he had to say, particularly those useless ones, *preciosa, tesoro, cariño*. But he wouldn't go away, and the last thing I needed was for the neighbors to see him standing at my door. And once he was inside, nothing else mattered for either one of us.

Not one of the women who rode the van knew the first thing about desire. The sort of desire that won't let you think of anything else. The sort of desire that made everything else in the world seem unimportant. Husband, children, neighbors.

After that first time, he never knocked on the door again. One moment, I would find myself alone, wandering from room to room, going about my day, lost; and the next he was inside. And as soon as I saw him, my mind became as blank as a newborn's. It didn't matter if the neighbors saw him. It didn't matter if Ernesto came home early. I would take any chance, any risk, just to feel that skin next to mine. Sometimes I pretended that it mattered, but Pepe could see right through me.

"You can't stay," I'd say as he reached for me.

"I know," he'd answer, coming closer.

"It's dangerous. If he finds us it will break his heart."

I worried about Ernesto, wished that he was a crazy, violent man, so that it could all be settled. But I knew that he wasn't. I knew my husband too well.

"I don't care," Pepe said each time, as he guided me into the bedroom and toppled me backwards onto my carefully made bed. "Do you?"

"No," I said as I fell. But I was lying. I watched while he stood above me unbuttoning his shirt. His eyes fixed on mine, a shameless smile on his lips. I felt him reach under my skirt, take hold of the elastic band of my bloomers, and roll them down my legs. I felt his beard caress the inside of my thighs. He was lips and tongue and hands, as if a dozen invisible men had joined him, and I felt myself engulfed by twilight, even if I'd wanted to stand up and walk out of the room, I couldn't have.

The moment I started to tremble and my eyes started to water, I knew there was no turning back. He would stay and do whatever he wanted to me for as long as he wanted.

Every time he left, I thought about packing my bags and leaving Ernesto's house. I had every intention of doing just that. But it never seemed like the right time.

Pepe and I always took the necessary precautions, even in moments when we were so rushed and breathless that it seemed as if the world would end if we didn't wrap ourselves around each other. But accidents do happen. Before I knew it, I was pregnant. Nine months I waited, feeling limp and lifeless, to see what would happen. But the moment I saw that child, I knew he was Ernesto's. I remember an overwhelming feeling of relief; as if my life had been spared.

I couldn't very well take away his baby, and I wasn't about to leave my child. And so it seemed like the only thing to do was to continue dividing my time between the two men. I had the feeling that whatever it was that drew me to Pepe would eventually fade away, and I would return to some sort of normal life.

No one will ever know how nervous I was. What it felt like to be unable to look your husband in the eye, day after day after day. To speak in a normal tone and talk about ordinary things, all the while knowing that I'm counting the long, painful moments until I could see Pepe again.

As soon as Ernesto was gone, Pepe arrived and I fell into his arms as if my mind had been erased clean by the absence of my family.

How I hated washing those sheets in such a hurry and hanging them up to dry in the small backyard. Watching them flutter in the wind, casting the scent of our lovemaking to the sky; convinced that all the neighbors could smell the unbridled truth of it. But my passion had started to turn into frustration because Pepe seemed to enjoy the arrangement just the way it was. Never once did he suggest that I leave Ernesto. Perhaps if he had, I would have been more likely to make a decision. To leave, or to stay.

While I waited for Pepe to ask, I became pregnant again. But Pepe had started to withdraw, and I had stopped caring. All he wanted to talk about was the Revolution. Every time we saw each other, the sweet words he had used before were replaced with bitterness towards those who were leaving the country.

'Traidores,' he called them. Traitors. He railed against them at every opportunity, asking bitterly why anyone would choose to leave a country so many had shed blood to improve. He talked about the military officials who had taken over Palmagria with worshipful admiration.

"They've changed our world," he whispered to me in my husband's bed, as if trying to convince me.

His whispers soon turned into orations, as if he was rehearsing on me what he would say later.

"They've made the country free and every person equal," he'd muttered into my ear as he pushed my face deep into my husband's pillow. "They've chased out the crooks and the gangsters responsible for the poverty that was rotting away our society."

Perhaps he noticed my growing disinterest, because he started to make his discourses more personal.

"The woman who drowned her baby in the outhouse latrine," he said, tangled up in my husband's sheets, "is a perfect example of the madness that poverty and desperation can lead to. Do you remember?"

I remembered perfectly.

"That woman ruined my wedding," I wanted to say. I wanted to say that she had ruined my wedding not just by drowning the poor creature, but by bringing Pepe and me face to face. When I saw those tear-streaked eyes I wanted to turn back time. I wanted to go back to that church and undo what had been done. I wanted to drop to my knees in front of my mother and tell her she'd been right. But I swallowed my words.

Pepe's visits started to become less frequent. But by that time, I was so frightened all I could do was wait for the inevitable. The inevitable came from the stupid, drunken lips of Mario Santocristo. I heard all about it, the moonless night, the weekly domino game, the spiteful words spoken for no good reason. But he's Imperio's problem, she's the one who has to sleep with him. I would rather spend the rest of my life alone, at the bottom of a salt mine, than spend five minutes in bed with Mario Santocristo.

The images of Palmagria freeze and fade like the ending of a Friday night episode. "Graciela, you're home," Leticia shouted.

The brakes of Leticia's van screeched to a halt in front of my building. I looked at Imperio and Caridad, who were searching my face as if they were able to read my thoughts.

"You're so mysterious tonight," Imperio said as she moved her legs aside for me to exit.

I said nothing as I climbed past her. I only vaguely remembered when Raquel and Berta were dropped off, although I am sure they had said good night. I said a general and half-hearted "good night."

"Graciela," Caridad called out. My heart froze for a moment, I turned back and she was holding up my bag, my clear plastic bag. I took it without a word.

"Where is your mind tonight?" Imperio said with a giggle.

I slammed the door and practically ran to see my boys. Until tomorrow I was free. I didn't care how much they pried, I was not going to turn my personal life — my past, imperfect as it was — into a *telenovela* for their enjoyment.

My life was mine to live. And, as always, in answer to their questions, they received only silence. But in my heart, I knew the answer was no. I would not be writing any letters to Pepe Medina Ynclan. Particularly now that I'd caught Mr. O'Reilly's eye. Maybe I'm too romantic, maybe I watch too many *telenovelas*. Maybe my mother was right. I didn't care. Those looks from Mr. O'Reilly made me feel alive again. Suddenly, I felt free to dream again.

And as Esperanza said in the *telenovela, Mil Millas Entre Nosotros* (A Million Miles Between Us), "what is a woman if not her dreams?

Chapter 10

IMPERIO

I was furious. Furious! After the so-called "Triumph of the Revolution," it was as if a plague had swept through Palmagria, taking with it all the decent women. Caridad was gone, Cuca Soto was gone, Azucena Martinez was gone, and I had not made any new friends. *Por Dios!* There was no one to replace them, no one I could trust. Graciela was definitely out of the question. She could rot in her father's house for all I cared. She had done it to herself and now she had to pay the price. If things had been different, maybe if she hadn't been so cheap. *Quien sabe?* But the way things were, with that cloud of shame hanging over her, I knew to keep my distance. It wasn't just about me, I never much cared what people thought, but I had Mario to consider.

For a time I thought Caridad would return. How long could this son of a bitch in La Habana last? I asked myself. Everyone was wondering the same; even said as much, after they made sure all the windows and doors were shut.

"The Revolution had been a success," people had started saying, "but everything after that has been a complete disaster."

My husband, Mario, owned a restaurant at the railway station which did good business and afforded us a good life. But not long after the Revolution, the restaurant was nationalized, along with the trains and anything else in Cuba that smelled of money. No more private enterprise. We didn't feel we had much of a choice. How did it happen? How did we become like those unfortunate people that sad and senseless things happen to?

Mario didn't take it well, to say the least. He'd always liked to drink, but now he felt he had every reason. I didn't blame him, he was heartbroken.

"Let's just wait it out a little," I told Mario. "Let's see what happens with this crazy man in La Habana. *Por Dios*, somebody's got to put a bullet between his eyes sooner or later and then everything will return to normal."

But while I was waiting for Castro's assassination, Mario developed a very strange illness. A red rash about two inches wide erupted on his back and continued spreading until it circled around his chest. But rather than itch, the way rashes do, Mario screamed that it was tightening, like a belt or a snake. We took him to the doctor, who prescribed useless ointments while Mario could hardly get out of bed for lack of breath.

I took him to every doctor, looked for every possible explanation. I even took him to a specialist in Yara who looked him over and over and could find no explanation.

"This is *Santeria*," he said and I just looked at him wanting to kill him. We had traveled all the way to Yara just to be told that nonsense.

Finally, Mario's mother, Liliana, insisted that we take him to see El Haitiano, a man from Jacmel who practiced some superior sort of Santería that was said to be very effective. I had heard about him. Everybody was always talking about El Haitiano in those days. I was never the kind of woman who believed in *Santería* or any of that voodoo nonsense. My family always looked down on that sort of thing, because, truth is, those are the beliefs of the very poor, you know, the same people who play the lottery. I'm not saying we were wealthy. The restaurant afforded us a comfortable life. I didn't have to work, I had help with the house, a girl who came in to clean and do the wash. I was never the kind of person who needed fancy things, but I could buy what I wanted. We even took vacations to Playa Giron twice a year. And we did it without offerings to the saints or buying lottery tickets. It just wasn't in me to believe those sorts of things. We had what we had because of hard work. Although my mother-in-law would argue that point.

But Mario's condition got so bad that there were times when I thought he wouldn't make it through the night. He'd wake up gasping for breath and would actually roll off the bed. He would lie on the floor, his face turning colors I had never seen before on a human being, pounding his fists hard on his chest while I desperately tried to help him.

"Mario, *por Dios*," I shouted, shaking him. It looked like he was dying. I was not about to let him die and have his mother giving me the evil eye for the rest of my life.

"An ounce of faith is worth a pound of priests," Liliana said. To tell you the truth, at that point I was willing to try anything. Anything!

El Haitiano lived out in the country, off the main highway, in an area that can't be reached by car. In fact, there are no roads at all where he lived. We were told to follow the Aguadulce River to his house. Liliana arranged for a friend, Genarisimo, to drive us to the designated spot on the highway. But he just left us there, frying in the sun.

"Imperio," Genarisimo said, "I can't leave my car here in the middle of nowhere." I understood. There was a very good chance that the car could get stolen or gutted for parts. But what was I going to do? Mario could hardly walk. We had to carry him to the car and even though he had lost a lot of weight, he was still a heavy man.

To my relief a boy of about twelve, pushing a wooden gurney, met us there.

"Are you here to see El Haitiano?" he asked.

We laid Mario down on the gurney and started our bumpy walk though the sweltering foliage. I felt as if we were traveling deep into the primeval jungle. Even though it was early in the day, the heat was already unbearable. Insects of every shape and size attacked us. At times, the vegetation was so thick that the boy, whose name was Chevy, had to stop and cut through with a machete.

It was slow going, with Chevy pulling and me pushing over thick roots that grew in the footpath and then stopping to cut branches and weeds. There were parts where the soil was wet and soft and the wheels sank in and we had to lift and pull at the same time. After what seemed like an eternity, but if you think about it, was probably less than one hour from the highway, I started to hear the strangest sounds. I immediately wanted to turn around. I stopped.

"*Espera*," I said to Chevy. Wait.

I think he could see the fear in my eyes.

"*No falta mucho*," he said. We're almost there.

I looked at Mario, who hadn't said a word. His chest was heaving as if it wanted to break open. I had come this far, but what had I been thinking? What had I gotten us into? If Chevy was right, there was no point in turning back. What would I say to Liliana? I would never hear the end of it. I nodded and Chevy started pulling again and I, pushing.

Not much later we came to a clearing. All the thickness of the jungle opened up on a small, brown shack surrounded by a wire fence. The front yard of the shack was a combination of flat dirt and trenches. The trenches were full of brown water. Scattered around the holes at least a dozen crocodiles seemed to be sleeping.

I remembered Liliana mentioning that El Haitiano worked with their blood. The thought of it disgusted me.

The place had the creepy feeling of an abandoned gypsy camp; a place where anything could happen. Anything! Again, I wanted to turn right around and take Mario home, but when I looked at him, thin and pale, I knew I had to keep moving forward. I also remembered I didn't want to face his mother, who had wanted to come along. She had ranted and raved when we left her behind. But it had been a good decision not to bring her, or we would have needed two gurneys, one for Mario and one for her.

Liliana had always been a strong, practical woman. She was as firm in her Catholic faith as in her faith in the *Santeros.* But she held the love of her country above all else. She believed that Cuba, even with all its problems, was the best possible place in the world.

"This is the Pearl of the Caribbean," she liked to say.

I had never heard her say a word against Batista or any of the previous dictators. Of course, she had always been well cared for.

She got to stay home and give money to the Catholic charities and to the *Santeros,* and left the rest up to God and the Saints.

"I have no use for politics," she'd say, "Machado, Batista, Grau, Prio, Batista again — as long as they leave me alone, it's all the same to me."

Then, when Fidel Castro took to the mountains and his face started appearing almost daily in the newspapers, she took a sudden turn. One afternoon, while sitting on the front porch, she pointed at his picture.

"Look at him, Martica, doesn't he remind you of Jesus Christ?"

I will admit that, in those days, Castro's face, desiccated by months of starving and marching in the mountains, had the clear-eyed look of a hermit monk. As far as I was concerned, that's where the similarity ended. But Liliana, driven by a revolutionary zeal that bordered on lunacy, sold bonds to raise money for the Revolution, an activity that was punishable by firing squad without trial. Mario had been worried to death, because she kept the illegal bonds in her underwear drawer.

"You're insane," Mario told her over and over again, "if they find out we're all as good as dead."

Even I tried to reason with her.

"*Por el amor de Dios*, Liliana, we could lose everything," I said. "Everything!"

Liliana would just click her tongue at him and continue out the door to see how many of her friends she could embroil in her clandestine activities. Even with her legs stiff from arthritis, she'd hobble from door to door and try to get her cronies involved.

When that son of a bitch in La Habana came down from the mountains in victory, no one was more excited than Liliana. It was her own personal victory, and she savored it like a juicy mango.

"Didn't I tell you?" she chirped happily from the wooden rocking chair she kept right next to our radio. She spent all of her free time sitting on that chair, her back bolstered by a pillow, listening to the speeches of the rebels as well as the trials that were now being broadcast daily.

"He's a messenger from God, come to save the poor," she insisted, her eyes glowing with fanaticism. Even when things started to change for the worse, even after Mario lost the restaurant, she remained strong in her support of the Revolution.

It ate away at me like you wouldn't believe that she could be so stubborn. She could see, as well as any of us, that the increasingly oppressive regime was killing her only son. But she refused to see the connection between Castro's triumph and Mario's condition.

"Go to El Haitiano and see what happens," was all she said. She had heard about El Haitiano from one of her church friends and that was all the proof she needed that the man could work miracles.

So I found myself in that bizarre place full of crocodiles in the middle of a swamp with a half-dead man while she sat by the radio, happily listening to Castro's latest delusion and congratulating herself on the triumph of the revolution.

I ignored my fears and inched closer to the shack. Suddenly, the crocodiles began to crawl towards the shack as if to protect it. I could hear the chirping sounds of the jungle, the roaring of a river, the wind through the branches of the trees that surrounded us. In spite of the heat I felt cold, the sweat that was pouring out of me felt like freezing rain.

"Imperio, take me home," Mario said. They were the first

words he had said since we left. Most of the time he was coming in and out of consciousness. I could only imagine what he must have felt, lying on that wooden gurney, completely helpless. And with just me to protect him.

"Tranquilo," was all I could think to say for my mind was shutting down, my thoughts were coming to me thick and lazy from exhaustion and fear. I missed Caridad so much. She would have come with me. My mind was so weak that I even wished Graciela had come with me. That's how desperate I felt.

After dropping us off and collecting a tip, Chevy had left. I was suddenly aware that I was alone with Mario, who by now was really of no use at all. The sun began to feel even hotter on my uncovered head, and I felt a strong wave of nausea cloud my eyes.

Just then, the door to the shack opened and a small, brown man with shoulder-length hair, neatly dressed in white, was fearlessly walking past the crocodiles the way you would walk through a flowering garden.

"Bienvenidos," he said, with a strange, French accent. Welcome. It was as if he'd been expecting us. The man opened a small gate, walked up closer and glanced down at Mario, whose pale face had become flushed and alarmingly red from the heat.

"Don't worry, brother," El Haitiano said to Mario in a kind of sing-songy voice, patting Mario's shoulder. "Don't worry about anything."

With that, he looked up at me and smiled.

El Haitiano had a kind smile; it made his brown, leathery face crinkle around his eyes, but I had my eyes on the big, ugly lizards.

"You don't expect us to go in there," I said, my voice loud and strong.

"Come with me," he said. Mario struggled to get up and El

Haitiano helped me get him to his feet. He took hold of Mario from one side and I from the other. Mario's back felt unfamiliar. I could feel his bones where there had always been muscles. What will I do without you, I wondered. I'll be stuck with that crazy old woman and that voice on the radio.

Mario was wobbling, hardly able to place one foot in front of the other. His body was weighing down towards the ground, as if he just wanted to fall, as if he didn't have the strength to remain upright for one more second.

To my relief, El Haitiano directed us away from his shack, towards the river. We half-pushed, half-carried Mario. And there, on the peaceful and sunny bank of the Aguadulce, with the soft rumbling of the waters behind us, El Haitiano cured my husband. To this day, I don't know how he did it, and I don't care. As they say, if you knew what the river carries, you would never drink the water.

I watched as he took a large, smooth-edged knife and dipped it in the river. Then slowly, without actually cutting the flesh, pressed the blade against Mario's rash, creating a cross while at the same time dividing the rash in two. He dipped his finger into a small vial and dabbed at the rash exactly where the knife met the skin.

Mario let out a deep howl and tears poured out of him. But he hadn't been cut or harmed in any way, it was just the simple contact of the blood upon his skin. Still, I was alarmed. I had never seen him cry. I had heard him say horrible words and throw things across a room. Of course, he was a man, after all. But cry? Never.

"What are you doing?" I asked El Haitinao

"Shhh. . . . crocodile blood. Very powerful," El Haitiano whispered to me. "It's helping to drain the poison out of his soul."

What poison, you fraud? I wanted to say. Instead, I nodded, pretending to understand, to believe that something as common as crocodile blood had any sort of power over a man's soul. He must have read my mind, because he looked at me and said, "Crocodiles attack each other all the time. Like the humans, they are territorial. They tear each other apart, gaping wounds, missing limbs, just for a piece of land. They live in mud and filth, but they never get infections, they heal very fast. Something in their blood protects them."

"Hmmm . . ." I said.

"But crocodile blood alone cannot heal your husband," he added.

El Haitiano took my hand and asked me to pray with him. I could feel one of my eyebrows involuntarily arch with skepticism, but I prayed. I prayed like I never had before, intoning novenas and supplications I hadn't uttered in years. And then the snake began to disappear, to fade from my husband's flesh, and a few moments later, it had vanished completely. Mario opened his eyes, still weak from everything that had gone on before, and looked around. When he looked at me, he smiled. He was breathing without effort. I could tell from his face that the pain was completely gone.

"I felt it happen," Liliana said when we got home, "I was getting too nervous here in the house, so I went to church. It was empty, just me and my rosary beads, and I tell you, I felt it. I felt the release and I knew my son would survive. Look, I'm getting chicken skin just telling you!"

Later, I learned that Mario's affliction was called La Culebra. It was a common curse that can actually strangle a person to death. I had never before believed in the curses of the Santeros. I chose, instead, to believe that it was just another of the countless superstitions that abounded in Palmagria, supported by tales made up to frighten ignorant people and to keep their lives in the hands of others.

But that morning by the Aguadulce River opened my eyes.

I was more than impressed by El Haitiano's miraculous abilities. If anyone could bring people back to life, I said to myself, this is the man.

As we were leaving, he took me aside and told me to pay very close attention.

"While I was working on Mario I had a very disturbing vision," he said. "*La Culebra*" is the work of bad magic, someone is trying to harm you."

"I don't have any enemies," I said, "who would do something like that?"

He looked away, "There is a way out, but you're resisting. Mario could get very sick again, and maybe the next time, he won't be so lucky. Sometimes even the crocodiles can't help."

I searched my mind, but could think of no one. Truth is, there were people who didn't care for us, but not to such extremes. Just recently, we'd had a bit of a struggle with our next-door neighbor over the building of a fence between our properties, but that had been settled somewhat amicably. And Mario did have the tendency to tell people the truth when he'd had a few drinks. But that sort of thing went on all the time with lots of folks. People loved Mario. They loved him! When word had gotten around about his illness, many stopped by the house with gifts of eggs and cheese and to offer their help.

Except Graciela. Could Graciela be the one behind this curse? Or her crazy mother?

I asked El Haitiano before we started back for the road.

"It could be a woman," he said, "or a man."

It was one of those infuriating answers that most irritated me about *Santeros*.

"What do you suggest I do?" I asked, but never imagined I would get such an answer.

"You must get out of Cuba."

"Leave Cuba? *Nunca!*," I said. Never. "I will not be run out of my own country. And do what, go clean toilets for American tourists in Miami Beach?"

Grateful as I was to El Haitiano, I was shaking with anger. How dare he put those thoughts in my head.

I admit, I had voiced my opinions here and there, but I never, in my wildest dreams, ever expected that one of those people, those idiots, would try to do us harm. I have learned over the years that desperate people are capable of anything.

I didn't know what to believe. I felt my world turning upside down. And I no longer had Caridad to talk to. She was gone for good. Vanished in the middle of the night without a word. All she left was a jar of mentholated cigarettes and they were gone too. What was left of our friendship had gone up in smoke. In smoke!

I couldn't blame her for being secretive. No one knew who to trust anymore. And it was clear that we had to protect ourselves too. There no longer was a place for us in Cuba.

Mario would never be the same again. It took some time for him to get back on his feet. Something had been taken from him. But as soon as he started feeling stronger, we began to plan our escape.

Truth is, we didn't plan to be gone very long, convinced that Castro's hold on the island, gained through lies, couldn't last. He had captured the imagination of the people, not just the very poor, for those people anything would be an improvement, but also the working class and the middle class. People like us had the most to lose, because our money had not been handed to us. We had worked for it day after day. So, we decided to leave until someone knocked him out of power. It wouldn't be long before the American government or the American Mafia stepped in. I knew it was just a matter of time.

I asked for a sign and I got it. And I'm not a big believer in signs, but how else do you explain the letter from Caridad? She had been gone for months with no word. And then the letter arrived. It had been opened and read and then sealed back again with scotch tape. Whoever opened it at the post office was not very subtle about it, the letter had not been carefully steamed open, it had practically been ripped and then stuffed back in the envelope. It was a miracle that it had reached me at all. The message inside was very simple.

"*Aqui tienes tu casa,*" it said. You have a home here. And then an address and phone number. I was impressed.

"She already has a telephone," I said to Mario.

I called her immediately, but it took two days for us to be connected. And it was sweet as sugar to hear that voice again. She sounded like she was right around the corner.

But she was in a far away place called Union City.

Liliana wouldn't hear of it. We sat her down and tried to explain the situation to her. We told her about the Freedom Flights. She sat on her rocking chair but she didn't rock. She kept the chair steady, both feet planted firmly on the floor.

"But we want you to come too," Mario said.

Liliana stood up, her face turning red with anger.

"I'm not leaving my house or my country," she said and started for her bedroom.

"Liliana, are you crazy? What are you going to do here all alone?" I said. I was ready to wring her stubborn, wrinkled neck.

Mario started to follow her, but I held him back. Mario didn't know what to do. Does he follow his wife or stay and protect his mother?

"*Mira,*" I said to him, "we go first, and then we send for her. A few more months here and she'll beg us to get her out."

Liliana stopped, turned and looked at me with hatred.

"Freedom Flights," she said and spat on the floor, "that's what I think of your Freedom Flights."

A few months after we had left Cuba, Liliana wrote to us that El Haitiano himself was the one who had moved into our house. But by then it was far too late. He had kicked her out of her own house, those were Fidel Castro's rules. "A little old lady doesn't need such a big empty house," they said. "Give it to someone who needs it, someone with children and in-laws."

It never crossed my mind that the whole thing had to do with our house. The idea that someone would put a curse on a family just to get their house was just crazy! *Por Dios,* it was just a simple old house. Sure, it was in one of the nicest parts of Palmagria, but it was still in Palmagria, which was like being the prettiest girl in an ugly contest.

Liliana had to pack up her radio and go live with relatives in Palma Soriano. If you ask me, she got what she deserved.

Chapter 11

CARIDAD

I wouldn't dream of telling others how they should raise their children. No one knows better than me how difficult it is. It was just that I worried. Graciela left the boys alone at night to fend for themselves and went who-knows-where. *Imagínate!* What sort of mother is that?

She said she was going to school; she said she was studying English and Fashion Design.

"Por Dios!" Imperio said, "She'll design the 'easy to undress' dress. For ladies who need to take it off and put it back on quick before the husband comes home."

Those kids of hers were growing up wild! Ernestico looked like a little thug. There was something angry about him, something hidden, as if he was waiting for just the right moment to do something crazy. And in this country children his age did crazy things all the time. How could any right thinking person trust him? There was something about him — he wouldn't look you in the eye, and he answered all questions with a shrug, like he cared not one bit about anything in the world. I kept my Celeste away from him.

Imperio predicted a problem.

"That boy's going to end up in juvenile detention," she said.

But Graciela didn't seem to notice that anything was wrong. And if she did, she never mentioned it. Nothing. It was like the three of them had a secret pact. Some sort of family agreement that no one could figure out.

I was not prying, I was worried.

Manolito was still too young to be left alone, even if it was with his older brother. Who knew what two boys could get up to, alone in an apartment?

Don't think we didn't mention it to her.

"*Piensalo bien,* Graciela," Imperio said. Think about it.

"I will," Graciela said, but there was an airiness to her words, as if they came just from her mouth, not her mind. We knew she just wanted to shut us up.

It was a closed subject with her. The curtain came down as it always did when she did not want to listen to reason.

She shut us out, after all we did for her. We were the ones who gave her a hand up, as we have with all the other exiles that came after us. With Graciela we made an extra effort; after all we'd known her forever — and we knew what she was capable of. Graciela could dig herself into a hole faster than anyone I had ever met. So we tried to guide her, to protect her from herself.

But no, Graciela will be Graciela until the day she dies.

"A palm tree that grows crooked stays crooked forever," Imperio said. And I had to agree.

Still, we did all we could, foolishly thinking that in this country she could turn a new page, make a fresh start. First, we got her out of that horrible hotel room, found her an apartment, and helped her out with furniture. We introduced her to Leticia so that she could get a ride to work, and we got her boys enrolled in school. And how did she pay us back? As Imperio said, "You can paint the stripes off a zebra, but she will never be a white horse."

Imagínate! After months of giving me the cold shoulder, she showed up at my apartment as if we were still the best of friends.

"I like your new furniture," she said.

Little by little I'd been buying furniture. On credit, which made everything so much more expensive. But what else could I do? My apartment was Mediterranean. The new living room set was dark blue with scalloped cushions, and I painted the walls light pink to remind me of my house in Palamagria. Of course, it will never be as beautiful as that house. There were no portraits of my family to hang on the walls, we had to leave all that behind. The new lamps were much nicer than what I had in Palmagria but, still, I missed the old ones. I missed them every single day.

"Mil gracias," I said, and sat down on my new couch. Graciela remained standing. I could tell she was charged up about something. She had on a full face of makeup, and was wearing a knitted black dress that showed her nipples as if she was standing naked in my living room. Well, what could I do?

"Come in, sit down," I said. Why is she here, I wondered. After all, I have to see her at work every day. But I acted as nicely as I could. I even offered to make her some coffee, which she refused. She said she didn't want any and I could understand why. She didn't need it. She was already over-stimulated enough. You could see it in her eyes — an excitement, or was it desperation? I never can tell with Graciela. I went ahead and made coffee anyway, just to keep moving.

She followed me to the kitchen and stood in the doorway, which seemed too narrow to contain her.

"I'm starting a little business," she said.

I was glad that I had my back to her or she would have seen the expression on my face.

"Oh, how nice for you, Graciela," I said, but I thought, she is crazy! This woman had lawn furniture in her living room because real furniture was beyond her means. No store would give her credit, and she thinks she can start a business? Everyone knew that Ernesto ditched her and the kids as soon as they got to the states; shipped her to New Jersey while he stayed in Miami. We heard that in Miami she stayed with Ernesto's cousins and made their lives miserable. That she tried to turn Ernesto against his own family. As far as I was concerned, Ernesto was a saint, he should have had a monument raised in his honor. After what she put him through, he brought her here. He saved her from a life of darkness and disgrace. Because Palmagria does not forget or forgive. Forever she would have been Graciela The Whore, or Tarros. But she can be ungrateful and selfish. We heard that in Miami she would not lift a finger to help around the house. That Ernesto's cousins, who already had their hands full with the old man and his cancer, could not wait to get her out of their apartment.

I'm willing to wager that Graciela noticed not one bit. She just sails through life on her own winds. And the winds were blowing full force that night she came to see me.

"And what kind of business is this?" I asked her as I walked past her with my little cup of *café*, the frozen smile on my face was starting to melt.

I wished Imperio was there with me, because I knew that when I told her she was not going to believe what happened next.

Instead of answering, Graciela ran out to the hallway and returned with a huge plastic bag that she plopped down on the floor. She was breathing hard. Her heart must have been going a mile a minute. She dug into the bag and retrieved what looked to me like a big fur rug, and lifted it over her head and it hung on her like a Mexican poncho. Then she dug into the bag some more and pulled out a hat made out of the same sort of furry, rug material and she put it on and stood there looking like *el Doctor Chivago.*

"You know I'm taking fashion design classes," she said with a serious face, a face made out of cement, "at the Junior College."

Her eyes danced on mine as she waited for my reaction.

"I thought it was just that one course," I said, "I thought you were concentrating on learning English."

At that moment I wanted to cry and I wanted to slap her. I forced myself to remain calm. I could sort of understand that she needed to learn English, even if it meant that her children stayed at home unsupervised for hours on end. But this frivolous undertaking was much too much.

"My English is very good now," she said, "now I'm concentrating on design and cut. That way I can start earning extra money right away."

I don't know if she saw the look on my face. I was trying to control my expressions but it was useless and exhausting. All I could think was WHAT?

I took a moment trying to think of the best way to advise her. I mean, she wasn't thinking clearly.

Not that she ever had.

A person doesn't just become a fashion designer after a few classes at a junior college in New Jersey. This much I knew, and it was depressing that this wasn't obvious to her. It would be one thing if she was designing, say, pretty dresses or something practical. That I could almost understand. I could almost forgive that effort, that sacrifice.

But this?

This is why she leaves the boys alone at night? I could have strangled her right then and there.

"Graciela," I said, the tiny coffee cup feeling heavy in my hand, "if you need to make a little extra money, why not start doing our nails again, like you used to?"

She stared at me for a long time.

"No, I don't do that anymore."

Imagínate! I was offering her not just my hands, not just a way to make money, but forgiveness. I was telling her I was willing to put the past behind, to forget her indiscretion, but she showed no interest in that. Not one bit. I had to sit down after she left. She really knocked the life out of me with that one. I wanted to be helpful, not unkind, but as I explained to her, "Yes, New Jersey winters are very cold, but I can not walk around looking like that in that thing."

I said it as gently as I could, but of course it was not the reaction she wanted. She wanted me to throw that thing on and go parading up and down Bergenline Avenue as if I was a trendsetting mannequin. She frowned at me for a moment, then nodded her head.

"You're right, it might be too high fashion for you," she said. With that little insult — don't think I didn't get it, don't think I didn't grasp it — with that little insult she let me know that she considered me too much of a peasant to ever understand her. She thinks herself so sophisticated, Graciela. She said not another word and neither did I. Without any hurry, she took off her furry poncho and hat and packed them back into the plastic bag.

Her movements were much slower than when she arrived. She took forever to leave, carefully folding her furry things, turning the plastic bag this way and that, all the while avoiding my eyes.

As Imperio said when I told her the whole story, "*Por Dios, Caridad,* why are you surprised? Graciela's always been selfish. And now she can be selfish in two languages."

Her English was a constant source of embarrassment for me. *Imagínate,* she was taking classes three nights a week, and after a few months considered herself an expert. At work I overheard her laughing and talking to the Americanos during a break, and I just cringed. I mean, without abandoning my family at night to take lessons, I probably knew as much English as she did, but I dared not speak it. Especially in front of the Americanos. The way Graciela mangled their language, I was surprised those people didn't just laugh in her face. She talked to everyone, black and white, even the Puerto Ricans, who would have cut off their tongues rather than say two words in Spanish to us.

She became particularly friendly with a black woman named Cloretta Johnson. Cloretta was not only fat, she was tall, too. Tall and fat, a giant of a woman.

One day we arrived for work and were standing in line to punch our cards, and there was Cloretta in front of us, a mountain of cheap fur. She was wearing not just Graciela's poncho, but the hat as well. Imperio and I pinched each other to keep from bursting out in hysterics. We were choking.

Graciela, who had been standing behind us, jumped ahead and she and Cloretta started admiring one another. Cloretta made turns like a model, and all the others, even the men, came up to them saying ridiculous things like "gorgeous" and *"preciosa."*

Imperio and me just punched our cards as fast as we could

and ran to the ladies' room where we almost cried from laughing. I got a pain in my stomach from laughing so hard.

"*Que ridiculo,*" Imperio said.

"Poor Cloretta," I said, "and nobody will tell her the truth."

But who could? Who dared? We didn't know what we were going to do about Graciela. Other than the time we spent together in the van, we really tried to keep our distance. But I must confess, I did enjoy discussing the *telenovelas* with her. Thank God we had that in common, or the drive to work would have been torture because you really can't count on Raquel or Berta for stimulating conversation.

It was right around that time that poor Berta started dropping things at work. First her legs stopped functioning properly, then her hands. What next? At least she wasn't falling down in a faint anymore. But something was going on. Even Mr. O'Reilly noticed, he asked her into his office and had a talk with her. She was slowing down production and she had called in sick way too many times. Even when she was there she did half the work all the others did. Dolls went by her on the conveyor and arrived at the other end missing an arm or a leg. So we had to run to the end, past the stares of the blacks and the Puerto Rican girls, rescue Berta's doll and fix it.

"Berta, you better shove new batteries up your ass," Imperio told her, "you have to wake up or you're going to get yourself and the rest of us fired."

Berta just looked back with that long-suffering look she liked to give you. Every single day we sat in the van with the motor idling while we waited for her to slowly make her way to us. And then of course she went directly to the front seat.

"It's bad enough," Imperio said, "that we have to spend eight hours in that place, I don't want to spend an extra fifteen minutes, unpaid, sitting in the parking lot waiting for you."

In spite of Imperio's harsh words, I knew that she cared deeply for Berta. It was always Imperio who was there whenever Berta had to go into the hospital. And it was happening more and more frequently. Imperio got Mario to pick Berta up each and every time she was released. And it was no easy task, what with the wheelchair and the bags. But Imperio also knew that if she was soft with Berta, she would not take her health seriously. So she said what she said, and her words set Graciela off.

Graciela rushed to defend her. Graciela *La Santa*.

"Imperio, would you talk to your own mother like that?" she asked.

Imperio just ignored her, she has the ability to make her point with silence. One of the many things about her that I admired.

Raquel said nothing. *Esa es otra.* She's another one. Getting more nervous and skinnier and stranger every day. On a Monday morning she got into the van and we were shocked at how much weight she'd lost over the weekend. She looked skeletal.

"*Por Dios,* Raquel, what do you eat?" Imperio asked her. "I think you're sending all your money to Cuba and starving yourself."

"Chá," Raquel said. "I eat." But we didn't believe her. Her skin told the whole story. She was too thin and her face was covered with angry red pimples, and she stunk, but she covered it with perfume. *Imaginate!* There was something wrong with the van and gasoline fumes seeped in through cracks on the floor. That, mixed in with the ever present smell of pork, and then Raquel, with the stench of armpit and perfume! It was unacceptable.

"You ever hear of soap?" Imperio asked her. Raquel didn't say anything. I started to use a little cough when she got in the van just to let her know she was overdoing the scents, but she didn't seem to notice. With Raquel you couldn't be subtle.

"Roll down the windows," Imperio always said as we approached Raquel's apartment building in the morning. No one had ever been inside that building, let alone inside Raquel's apartment. We teased her about it.

"Raquel," I said, "ask us over for at least some water and crackers."

But Raquel was as unsocial as they came. Other than at work, no one saw her. She rarely visited anyone, except on special occasions. It was very un-Cuban and naturally we were suspicious. The few times we had been to her apartment, she seemed nervous and uncomfortable, as if she was hiding something.

Imperio said she suspected that Raquel had joined those militants in Alpha 66. That in her desperation to get her husband out of Cuba she had become part of that crazy bunch that is always trying to overthrow Castro with no success.

"It wouldn't surprise me one bit," Imperio said. "If anybody is unnaturally attached to Cuba, it's Raquel."

"Alpha 66? Raquel!" I said, "I would find that very hard to believe. I mean I know she lives and breathes her family back in Cuba but the militant type she is not, and she never pushes any pamphlets on us, you know how pamphlet-happy those freedom fighters are."

I knew only too well. They had already approached Salud and I warned him, "You stay away from them. Did I come to this country to watch you go back in a boat and die in some swamp like a dog?"

Raquel remained a mystery. What did a woman do every night and every weekend, alone, without a husband, just her and those three little girls? Every day she interrupted our conversation with some new political report. We let her have her say so we could get back to talking about the *telenovelas*.

"So now everybody in Cuba can read and write," Raquel said one day, "but what's the use if you are told what to read and what to write? They're going through all the libraries and removing books that they think send the wrong message. You can't find Jose Lezama Lima. People pass to one another tattered copies of books from these authors who we should be proud of instead of abusing, silencing or deporting. Eventually all books will vanish from the island. Journalists are going to jail all the time for daring to write the truth. What's the point of being a journalist if you can't report what you see, what you live?"

"Let it go, Raquel," Graciela told her with that fake compassionate voice of hers. "You're making yourself too nervous. Why don't you come to my house for dinner tonight?"

"What are you going to serve?" Imperio asked, "one of those frozen dinners?"

"I'll make her an *ajiaco* that will bring her back from the dead," Graciela said and the rest of just went into shock.

Raquel never accepted Graciela's offers, so every few days Graciela brought her a little jar of leftover food for her lunch.

Graciela had left us no option. So every few days either I or Imperio brought a little something for Raquel.

"You better eat it," Imperio told her, "or a strong wind is going to blow you into the river."

Raquel said, "Chá," as she took the food.

Graciela was changing in front of our very eyes. *Imagínate*, she was cooking. No more frozen dinners for those poor boys of hers. It had tortured me no end to think of them picking through those frozen vegetables and cardboard chickens. She seemed more mature, more responsible. Imperio and I exchanged looks, thinking, who knows, maybe she will finally grow up.

Just when we were starting to believe that all the time, effort, and prayers we had invested in Graciela were beginning to pay off, she did it again. *Imaginate!*

It started as a rumor and I'm not one to listen to rumors but behind every rumor there is always some truth. And I was right. I got all the proof I needed when Imperio told me that she'd heard from Leticia that Graciela was "seeing" Mr. O'Reilly, the hippie foreman.

"And by seeing I mean screwing," Imperio said.

There was no doubt about it. And it made everybody in the van very uncomfortable. Well, I can't speak for everybody, but Imperio and I were shaking with outrage. We didn't know how to bring it up, not even Imperio who had been shocked into silence. Graciela just sat there, she said nothing. *Nada.*

We had no proof, but we knew there was something going on. We didn't mention it, of course, after all it was not our concern.

Fortunately, a new *telenovela* called "Apasionada" had just started. It was about a girl, Rosalinda, who was in love with her boss. So we called Graciela "Rosalinda" behind her back, and every time we talked about it in the van, everyone knew what we were talking about, except Graciela, who thought we were really talking about the *telenovela*. It was the nice thing to do.

Chapter 12

GRACIELA

If smells had colors the lunchroom at the factory would have looked like a rainbow. Tuna fish and mayonnaise, mustard and bologna, Pepsi-Cola. That's what the Americans ate. They brought square, crustless sandwiches wrapped in wax paper, tucked in a neat brown paper bag — sometimes a kind note was discovered, from a wife or a child, like the fortune in a cookie. The Cubans ate ham and butter sandwiches. The ham we brought in huge chunks and sliced at the table, the stick of mostly melted butter was passed from hand to hand, the bread we broke off, then dug into with our fingernails to get the soft *masa* out of the center, like gutting a fish. And we licked our fingers between bites, and talked with our mouths full. All but Caridad, who always worried about the Americanos.

"They're going to think we left our country so we could stuff ourselves with ham every day." she said.

"What do you care, Cari?" Imperio asked. "We're here for the ham and we'll eat ham until we choke. Pass the butter, it goes down easier."

That afternoon I could feel their eyes on the back of my neck like blowtorches. Because I didn't sit with them. Because I would not touch the ham. Because I was sitting with Barry O'Reilly. who now found me more interesting than a science fiction novel. The novel was there, on the tabletop, next to his sandwich, both untouched. On the cover of his book was an extravagant pirate ship sailing through a starry universe, towards a distant, orange planet.

"How?" he asked me.

"Airplane," I said and put my hands together and moved my fingers up and down to simulate wings.

He smiled and said, "Escape?"

And I said, "No, many papers."

"Red tape," he said. I didn't know what that meant, so I just said, "yes."

He nodded, his blue eyes fixed on mine, but gently, so gently that I could have made him look away with a shrug. But I didn't. My English was so limited that looking and being looked at was all we had. We talked to each other like Tarzan and Juana. I wanted to tell him about the drive to Havana, the flight to Miami.

I made myself a promise to tell him someday.

Our drive to Havana was bad from the start. Ernesto hired the worst possible driver, but there weren't many to choose from. Very few people in Palmagria had cars that could make it all the way to Havana. The driver's name was Agustin Garcia-Mesa, but everybody called him Garcia-Mesa, as if they were talking about a government building or a patriot.

As a young man, Garcia-Mesa had gone to the United States to study music. He had a passion for the piano and had been blessed with perfect pitch and long slender fingers that could majestically perform even the most complicated runs and chords. Even though he was probably one of the most arrogant citizens of Palmagria, one of those who never attended a dance and looked down on everyone just because he was the master of a classical instrument, he was still considered a local treasure.

All of Palamagria celebrated his acceptance into an academy in New York City, and throngs went to the port to see him off. But people said that when he arrived in New York, he discovered that the money he had saved, in pesos, suddenly shrank to nothing. Even though back then the peso and the dollar were almost equal in value, New York City proved to be expensive beyond belief.

It was a tragic, frightening story García-Mesa was only too willing to tell, in minute detail, to anyone who ever rode in his car. What happened to him in Manhattan was enough to make anyone never want to leave Palmagria.

To make ends meet, he offered himself as a piano tuner for the Academy, for which he had a natural talent. He soon became quite popular as a tuner and easily made the second semester's tuition. Before long, his services were being requested by music lovers all over Manhattan Island.

"There's this Cuban fellow," people would say during breaks at recitals and cultural salons, "who does unbelievable work. Perfect pitch! I'll give you his number."

Garcia-Mesa suddenly found himself in great demand, but once again he held himself above the rest. He had made no friends in school or in his building. He loved New York, particularly riding the subway trains, engulfed in a thick overcoat and knitted scarf, to the better neighborhoods of Manhattan, to the Upper East Side and the Upper West Side, to Sutton Place and Beekman Place. To buildings where red-cheeked doormen ushered him in with gloved hands. He loved the spacious lobbies dripping with crystal chandeliers and the shiny marble floors that echoed with his footsteps. He loved the spacious apartments where he became acquainted with women with musical voices who dressed in velvet and insisted he call them by their given names: Violet, Lillian, Gertrude.

Then, one day, while lying on his back beneath an antique Steinway in the home of a Park Avenue dowager everyone called Babe, a string, weakened by a microscopic speck of rust, suddenly snapped, severing the tips of three fingers of his right hand, ending his musical career forever. The errant wire had just barely missed the eye that his hand had instinctively shot up to protect. The blood gushed as if from a spigot, darkening the red and gold Persian rug. Babe rang bells that day and an army of servants rushed him downstairs and into a waiting taxi. During that taxi ride to the hospital, his hand wrapped in a thick and monogrammed towel, he saw that ahead lay a life of waiting tables and sweeping garbage for the same people who had once insisted he call them by their given name.

Garcia-Mesa returned to Palmagria without fanfare and with just enough money to buy a car, and dedicated his life to making everyone he came into contact with as miserable as possible. As miserable as himself. He was a gushing fountain of pessimism which he administered with unrestrained brutality, along with the sad story of his glory days in New York. People liked to joke that it was a shame that it hadn't been his tongue that had been sliced off

Ernesto rode in the front passenger seat of Garcia-Mesa's car, and if he was having second thoughts about this venture, he never said a word. I sat in back with the boys. Manolito, who had never been in a car before this, suffered from severe carsickness. Garcia-Mesa kept complaining because we had to make stops every time Manolito said he felt like vomiting.

I stood by the side of the road and held Manolito's shoulders while he leaned his little body over and coughed and gagged, then looked up at me with watery eyes and shook his head no. Every time, it was a false alarm, which was driving Garcia-Mesa crazy. Manolito made us stop half a dozen times and, even with the full encouragement of everyone in the car, never did vomit. I lost count of how many times Garcia-Mesa cautioned us.

"He better not do it in my car," he said again and again, "that's all I've got to say."

I was quite proud when Ernestico, who'd been sitting quietly in the back, enduring his brother's condition, finally said to him, "It would be nice if that *was* all you had to say."

Sometimes children can speak your thoughts better than anyone. Neither Ernesto nor I dared say anything for fear that Garcia-Mesa would turn his car around and take us back to Palmagria for good. You only get one opportunity to leave Cuba. You miss that flight, you stay forever.

I had never been more relieved than when we finally approached Havana. It was my first, and perhaps last, opportunity to see that city. I had no illusions that I was ever coming back.

I was looking forward to seeing all the people in the street, the bright flags, the tall buildings. They said La Habana was as beautiful as Paris. I wanted to see this jewel of a city. I asked if we could take a fast sightseeing drive through, but Garcia-Mesa immediately started to complain and Ernesto said that we had already wasted enough time with all of Manolito's unscheduled stops.

I felt the time in Havana slipping away from me, like water through my fingers. I longed to see Old Havana, El Vedado Park, the world-famous Malecon seawall, the ornate buildings. I just wanted to take a moment and inhale that magnificent old city I had heard so much about. But Garcia-Mesa took us straight to Varadero Beach. The Freedom Flights were taking off from that legendary beach instead of Jose Martí International Airport. I saw nothing of the beach, just a dirt road that led to a dirt runway. The airport was much smaller than I had imagined. Just a small, gray building. Behind it I could see the waiting airplane, big and white. Its propellers were already spinning, a giant bird anxious to take flight. I gathered the children close to me while Ernesto took our suitcases out of the trunk. Then Garcia-Mesa surprised us by giving us each a tearful embrace.

"*Cuidate, Gracielita,*" he said as if he was the loving older brother I never had. "Take care."

While Ernesto and the boys took our luggage inside, I stood still for a moment, breathing the salty air mixed with jet engine fuel, and watched his car vanish in the distance, back to Palmagria, which at the moment seemed like a prehistoric, mythical land.

"That poor Garcia-Mesa, he drinks happiness and misery from the same cup," my mother said whenever she saw him pass by.

Flights to the U.S. had been closed for three years, since the Missile Crisis almost brought us to the end of the world, almost the same amount of time I had spent at my parents' house. Almost the same amount of time since I had last seen Pepe. But now, in 1965, the flights had miraculously reopened and people were pouring out of the country as quickly as they could get a visa. We were to be on one of the very first flights out and I wondered how much Pepe Medina Ynclan had to do with it. Had Pepe intervened on my behalf? Did he want me gone so badly?

He knew I was leaving. To the very end I expected to see him, a glimpse, a wave goodbye, just a little gesture to let me know that what had happened between us had been real, that the risk and it's consequences had been worth it. But he did not appear.

The boarding area was packed with people. Some chatted amiably, laughing too loud. Others sat solemnly, clutching their few belongings. Some prayed while others paced, nervously glancing at the wall clock. A glass partition separated those departing from the ones who'd come to see them off and they talked loudly to each other across the glass that divided them, making promises and plans. Swearing unending love. Vowing never to forget.

"*Volveremos,*" they shouted. We will return. And fingers went to pursed lips in a warning of silence, that word was counterrevolutionary, that word could have kept them from getting on the airplane.

There was no one there to see us off. We were on our own, a strange little family at once together and divided, just like the country we were abandoning. I treated Ernesto with as much respect and courtesy as possible. I didn't talk to him much and he, as usual, didn't have very much to say. There were years of bad blood between us, but for the boys I was willing to make this sacrifice. A rumor that Castro was going to put all children in a concentration camp had kept me up nights, although nothing had come of it. But you never knew.

While Ernesto was providing the officials with document after document, I had to run Manolito to the ladies' room, which was just as crowded as the boarding area. While we were waiting for one of the stalls to vacate, Manolito vomited violently all over the floor. All the women in there gave me sympathetic eyes, but not one of them offered to help.

Fortunately, he didn't soil his clothes, and I held him over the sink to rinse his mouth and cool his forehead with water. Afterwards, I held him tight, wondering what more I could do to protect him; feeling as if I wanted him back in my womb. He was convulsing with hiccups and I rubbed his little back gently.

Someone must have complained, because suddenly there were two armed guards at our side yelling at me to clean up our mess. Ernesto walked in, against the ladies' loud protests, to see what was delaying us.

"They're beginning to board our airplane," he said.

One of the guards placed a hand on his revolver and barked at him to wait outside. The airport was so small that I could actually hear the sound of the propellers through the thin walls.

"You're not leaving until you've cleaned up this mess," he said to me. I had no choice but to obey. So my last moments on Cuban soil were spent on my knees mopping up vomit off the granite floor of a public restroom.

When I was done we rushed out of the bathroom, practically knocking people out of our way. We made it to the gate just as it was closing.

"We're here, we're here," Ernesto shouted, which should give you an idea of his desperation because he never raised his voice for any reason. We were the last ones on board.

The airplane was completely full of Cubans and the mood was more cheerful than I had anticipated. People were talking openly and with optimism for the first time in a long while. They all had big plans for their new life. They were strangers now united by this short crossing from one shore to another. Optimistically, they exchanged phone numbers and addresses, and compared notes on what they knew about life in the United States. The women were excited but terrified that they would need to learn to drive, something that, outside of Havana had been as masculine a task as peeing while standing. The men mostly talked about food. They all planned to eat a big ham sandwich every day for lunch. When the attendant brought out glasses of red wine, everyone made a loud toast.

"*Abajo con Castro!*" "Down with Castro!" they sang out, flushed with wine and freedom. At last, the words that had been singing in their hearts could be shouted.

"*Abajo!*"

Others stood up and made little speeches that always ended with "*Volvermos!*"

"Don't get too comfortable over there," one of them said, "this is just a temporary interruption. We will be back soon, sooner than we think."

"*Mira, chico,*" the solution is simple," another one said, "but that president — who they called LBJ, *no tiene cojones.*"

While those two were solving the political problems that plagued the greatest minds of the world, the rest were in the mood to celebrate.

"*Volveremos!*" they shouted again.

Only the stewardesses remained removed, they were not on the brink of freedom or any such thing. They would be returning to Havana that very same day. On an empty airplane.

Just them and the pilots.

When the passengers tired of celebrating Cuba and wishing the politicians ill, they started celebrating the country that was so generously taking them in.

"To our big neighbor who has given us what our own country has denied us, *jamón y libertád!*" Ham and freedom.

"*Viva Jorge Washington!*" people shouted. "*Viva Abraham Lincoln!*"

Then they went crazy, shouting out the names of any famous American they could think of.

"*Viva el Tio Sam!*"

"*Viva John Wayne!*"

"*Viva El Norte!*"

I tried to join in and even took a sip of wine, but it tasted like rusty water to me.

Earlier, during the car ride, I had noticed Ernesto becoming slightly irritated with the children's behavior, and he was getting worse on the plane. He had not spent any time with them during our separation, even though he only lived a few minutes away. The children were now taking full advantage of having a father again and constantly chattered to him about their concerns.

"Is it true that in the United States children can have all the toys they want?"

"Is it true that in the United States they have color television?"

"Is it true that in the United States Coca-Cola comes in a can?"

"Is it true that in the United States you can buy a box of crayons with one hundred different colors in it?"

"Is it true that in the United States children can make enough money delivering newspapers to buy a car?"

I could tell his head was spinning from their questions. Manolito eventually exhausted himself and fell asleep on Ernesto's lap, and it was nice to see them together. They resembled each other so much that it almost made me cry when I looked over at Ernestico who carried Ernesto's name, but was nothing like him. For better or worse, he was a lot more like me.

The flight lasted thirty-five minutes but seemed endless. The conversations and the toasts never stopped. Everybody was too nervous to be quiet, to sit still. They kept the noise going just to distract themselves and it went on and on. Then, suddenly, we were landing. We were there.

Miami.

The lunchroom had started to empty out. The smell of food faded and was replaced by the smell of industrial soap as a cleaning woman mopped the table tops. Barry O'Reilly was so close to me, I thought he was going to kiss me. Right there in front of everybody.

"You came straight to Union City?" He asked.

"No, Miami." I said.

"Ah, the Cuban Plymouth Rock."

"What?"

Not everything he said made sense. I was trying had to understand.

"Nothing." He smiled at me the way a man will smile at a pretty girl who isn't very smart. Give me time, I prayed.

"*Vámos,* Graciela, put your tongue back in your mouth," Imperio said. "The dolls don't wait for nobody."

I could have killed her for talking like that in front of my boss. But I was grateful, too. I didn't want to think about Miami. I got up and followed them back to the assembly line. The long afternoon stretched ahead, the line of dolls seemed endless. But it was Friday and I just had lunch with Barry O'Reilly in front of everyone. And I would see him again tomorrow, privately, far away from the factory, far away from Caridad and Imperio's prying eyes.

I didn't want to think about Miami.

Chapter 13

IMPERIO

Por Dios! If I'd had a mother like Graciela, I would have gone to the nearest orphanage, banged on the door, and demanded that they take me in. She was the worst mother ever. She left her boys on their own all night long.

What were they, eight, nine years old? Too young to spend so much time alone. Sometimes I thought that what she needed was to have those boys taken away from her, maybe returned to Ernesto. They couldn't possibly be worse off with him than with her. Graciela was a problem. A problem! She had always been only concerned with herself and hopelessly irresponsible, but at least she gave the impression of being a good mother. Now, not even that. Why was Graciela taking a fashion design course? And spending good money on material to create those awful coats — what did a Cuban know about coats? Was she part Eskimo? That was time and money she should have been spending on her children. But what was the use?

There she was, in the lunch room, swimming in his eyes, hanging on his every word, talking to him in English, and not very well. What does he see in her? Well, with Graciela, men have always been more than willing to see only what they want to see. And she's always been more than willing to show it to them.

In the new *telenovela*, "Apasionada," Rosalinda's boss was married. Fortunately for us all, and I mean all of us, Mr. O'Reilly wasn't. *Por Dios,* for all I knew, Graciela and Ernesto had never divorced, so I didn't know what to think. I seriously considered taking her aside and asking her what in hell she thought she was doing running around with that man. I needed to know what was going on in that crazy head of hers.

Graciela and Mr. O'Reilly were seen together at the drive-in movies, I heard that they steamed up the windows and drank so much beer that she had to go to the ladies' room several times. What could she possibly have been thinking? Who behaved that way with a man she hardly knew? With a man she worked for? What respect could he possibly have for her when he saw her at the factory the next day? He must have thought we were all like Graciela. Didn't she realize that her behavior affected us all? That she was bringing all of us down with her. Again. I shuddered to think what Mr. O'Reilly thought of us. All American men tended to think Cuban women are whores. Before the Revolution they flocked to Cuba for cheap sex. It took a lot of effort to maintain our dignity in this country. Why Graciela found that hard to understand was a mystery to me. And not only because she was behaving inappropriately, but because she flaunted it. There was never a speck of modesty about her. Not even at work. Never at work. There was a very serious policy about employees having romantic entanglements. *Prohibido.* Forbidden. And it was Mr. O'Reilly who was supposed to enforce it! So at first they were discreet — or so they thought. Sitting together at lunch was not enough. Sometimes they would go off in his car. They would be gone the whole hour. What did Graciela do with a man, in a car, in daylight! She always returned to work, not a hair out of place, and looked us right in the eye, as if daring us to comment. What she didn't realize was that all the comments happened while she was gone. People talked.

Por Dios, she brought him into the Cuban market in Elizabeth, which was ten minutes from Union City, and spent an hour parading up and down the aisles, showing him the different products on the shelves; laughing like they were at a sideshow, as if a can of black bean soup was the funniest thing in the world.

"This is called '*frijoles*,' she said to him as if she was teaching a baby to speak. "These are called '*plátanos*' Can you say '*plátanos?*'" And then they laughed and kissed and kissed again. In front of everyone she was doing this! On a Sunday afternoon no less, when everyone does their shopping. I'm grateful I wasn't there. My face would have hit the floor with shame. They had left by the time I arrived to do my weekly shopping, but the store still simmered with gossip.

It's not like when I first arrived and there were only a few Cuban families around. By 1967, Elizabeth, New Jersey, was full of Cubans. They were pouring in from all over the island and the center of our new society was right there in that little store. When I got there, the old ladies were cooling their faces with cardboard fans with the picture of *La Virgen de la Caridad*, they were still talking about Graciela, calling her '*Juana La Loca*,' like the crazy queen of Spain. And that's not all — they were also imitating her walk, the way she tossed that long hair, and the silly way she talked English to Mr. O'Reilly.

"*Mi amor*, this is called a *platano*, can you say platano?" one old lady said, pushing her lips out the way Graciela does, and the whole store burst out laughing. Laughing!

Graciela should have known better. That place was always full of old ladies with big bellies, *panzonas* with nothing to do but fan themselves, cash their welfare checks, and talk *mierda* about other people.

When they talked about Barry O'Reilly they wrinkled their noses as if he smelled bad. What was Graciela thinking, taking him to that place where she knows all people do is gossip? I did my best to ignore them, but they kept trying to pull me into the *bonche.*

Graciela and I had been to that store together many times. You'd think that knowing she was my friend, they would have had the decency to not talk about her to me or at least in front of me. But they were having too much fun.

"*Esta loca?*" they asked me. Has she gone crazy? Others suggested that maybe she was drunk. Drunk!

"*Tu amiga es borracha?*" they asked.

They called her my friend, and they put a little eyebrow movement into the question. I didn't know what to answer. I certainly wasn't about to stand up for her. "If you only knew," I wanted to say, "how far back this river flows."

Instead I kept quiet and picked up my items, paid for them, and got out of there as quickly as possible. I wasn't going to join their little gossip group, but I also wasn't going to defend her. Why should I care? She was perfectly capable of ruining her life all by herself. After all we've done for her. I knew Caridad was going to be very upset when I told her. And she was.

I met up with her at the hospital. Berta fell again and this time no one could get her up. There was the usual running around, but a little fanning and a cup of water didn't do it this time. She was taken away in an ambulance. I got to the hospital as soon as I could. There she was hooked up to tubes, intravenous liquids, and a dialysis machine, fighting for her life and losing the battle. Caridad and I stood on either side of the bed, looking down at Berta. It was then that I told Caridad what had happened at the market, and for a moment I thought I'd have to check her into the hospital, too. All the color drained from her face.

"How can I ever face those people again?" Caridad asked.

"It was horrible," I said. I kept my voice low even though there was very little chance of Berta hearing anything. She was drifting in and out of consciousness, mostly out.

"*Por Dios*," I said, "now they're going to think we're just like her. You know how those people are, *dime con quien andas . . .*"

Caridad motioned with her eyes and I followed her out to the hallway.

"*Imagínate*," Caridad said, "those old ladies with tongues long enough to reach back to Cuba."

"They're vicious, but they're right," I added because I was still seething. "Graciela has gone too far."

"If only she'd stayed in Palmagria." Caridad continued. "If only we'd kept our distance."

And of course, at that moment, who came running in, breathless and dramatic? We could hear the clickity-clack of her high-heeled boots. Caridad heard it too.

"Don't look now, but here comes 'Rosalinda." she said. We braced ourselves.

Graciela kissed us both on the cheek, very quickly. She was breathless, as if she'd ran all the way to the hospital.

"How is she?" she asked. No "*buenas noches.*" No "how are you?" Nothing.

Caridad and I stood there for a moment like we'd been

turned into statues. We didn't know how to react. We were both furious. But it wasn't the right time to bring anything up.

I looked Graciela up and down. Her hair was a mess. It looked like she'd just fallen out of Mr. O'Reilly's bed.

"Go see for yourself," I said.

Graciela started for Berta's room and stopped with her hand on the door handle. She stood there for a moment, very dramatic. Very *telenovela*. With an exaggerated swing of her hair, she turned to face us.

"Is she in a coma?" she asked.

"Do I look like a doctor?" I said. Graciela made a funny little face, as if I had hurt her feelings. She raised her eyes to the ceiling as if searching for divine intervention, let out a little sigh and without another word, she went into the room.

"That was awful, Imperio," Caridad said. But I could tell she was trying not to laugh.

"I'm just so furious with her," I said.

Graciela stayed in Berta's room for a very long time while Caridad and I smoked a Kool in the waiting room. We never, ever smoked a whole cigarette any more, we always shared it. Caridad took a puff and I took a puff. It was less harmful that way.

"What is she doing in there with Berta all this time?" Caridad asked. "You can barely get a reaction out of her anymore."

"She goes in and out," I said, "but mostly out."

When Graciela finally came out of Berta's room, she was red-nosed and teary-eyed.

She can be very sentimental *cuando le conviene,* when it's convenient for her, when it's to her advantage, when she wants to get attention, when she wants to make everyone think she's a saint who walks the earth.

.   .   .

Graciela remained oblivious to the affect her selfish behavior was having on the rest of us. While Berta was still in the hospital she went off to an anti-war demonstration with Mr. O'Reilly. One of those hippie events where people got so high on drugs and so worked up that they had to call in the National Guard.

That night, for the first time ever, the *telenovela* was interrupted by a news program. One moment we were watching the real Rosalinda struggling with her conscience, and the next we were watching a world gone mad. Ambulances were sent in to remove the casualties, armored wagons and policemen with shields to remove the more violent protesters. *Por Dios,* they were burning the American flag. The American flag! Never, not even during the worst days of the Revolution, did someone think of setting the Cuban flag on fire. Most of them were young, long-haired, and completely out of their minds. They screamed, and waved peace signs as they were forced into paddy wagons; some vomited, or tore at their own clothes. Others were carried on stretchers screaming and scratching at their own arms.

I immediately phoned Caridad and, of course, she was watching.

"*Imagínate,* Imperio," Caridad screeched into the telephone, "she's in there with those people!"

Caridad came running down the back stairs and into my apartment. We watched together for a while, united by our horror. There were hundreds of them, greasy, and glassy-eyed. You couldn't tell the men apart from the women. And then we saw her, or at least we thought it was her. The camera moved away so quickly it was almost as if it hadn't really happened. But it must've been because both Caridad and I let out a yelp. Caridad's hand went straight to her neck and stayed there as if she was feeling for her own pulse.

"What is Graciela doing in such a place?" I asked, "making a spectacle of herself. One minute I'm watching the real Rosalinda and the next, it's her! We should be supporting the war in Vietnam, not protesting it. Once the Americans get the communists out of there maybe they can do something about Cuba."

"Why is Graciela always on the wrong side of every fence?" Caridad asked sadly.

Por Dios, I saw it coming. She looked so different now. Her hair was now down past her shoulders. Long hair is for girls, not mature ladies like us. She kept getting thinner, and her hair kept getting longer. It offended me. I pointed it out to Caridad, who told me to pay close attention to the skin around her eyes and her mouth.

"She's starting to sag a little," she said. And she was right. But Graciela didn't seem to care. She'd practically stopped wearing makeup. Gone were the long, extravagant eyebrows and eyeliner, the garish lipstick. Without the overdone cosmetics she seemed at once more delicate and even more defiant. At first, we couldn't believe it, but she had also stopped wearing a *sosten.*

"*Por el amor de Dios Santisimo en las Alturas,*" I said, "she bounces around the factory like it's nothing. It's indecent, the mother of two boys behaving like that."

"What did she do with her brassiere? Burn it?" Caridad asked me. "Did she throw it in with the flag?"

"She's been in this country three years and thinks she's an American," I said.

Our concern was not just about how Graciela's recklessness

affected us, but also how it affected her boys. Her boys! She was so busy with her crazy romance that she didn't see what was happening in her own house. Every Monday morning she got into the van and didn't say a word. Not a word. We asked her, "How was your weekend?" and she always said, "*Divino.*"

Of course, *divino!* While visiting one day, Leticia found overwhelming evidence against her: a man's razor in her bathroom, and shaving cream, and Brut aftershave lotion. Mr. O'Reilly was spending his nights there. Leticia saw it.

"Niñas, I came out of that bathroom shaking," Leticia said. "It was like discovering a penis in her medicine chest."

"Maybe it's for her legs," Raquel said. "Or Ernestico's."

"Raquel, wake up and smell the aftershave lotion," I said.

"But Mr. O'Reilly wears a beard," she said. "I don't know . . ."

But her wispy voice was no match for me. I jumped on her like a detective. "He shaves his throat, and his cheeks. Look at him again."

"She's right," Caridad said, "it's a very handsome beard."

"Chá," Raquel said, and for the moment the subject was closed.

Dios Santo, Graciela was entertaining a lover on that sofabed while the boys were sleeping right in the next room. The thought was too horrible, Mr. O'Reilly's bearded face between her legs, the moans, the groans, words of passion wildly mispronounced. I was sure the boys could hear every little thing, the walls in this country are so thin. And yet Graciela continued her pantomime. She continued to get into the van day after day, as if nothing was out of the ordinary. Truth is, we didn't know what to do about it, but no one wanted her in that van any more. From what I saw, it wouldn't be a problem for long.

Clearly, Mr. O'Reilly was shamelessly spending the nights at her apartment, and if that wasn't bad enough, he was also teaching her to drive! I was on my way to the hospital with Mario, to see Berta, who was not getting any better. A car passed us by, and I thought the driver looked familiar. Well, at the next red light, there I was, face-to-face with Graciela of all people. She was behind the wheel of Mr. O'Reilly's car. He was in the passenger seat and her two boys were in the back seat jumping around like they were on a carnival ride.

I'm sure my mouth was hanging wide open. Wide open!

Well, Graciela just looked at me, smiled, and waved as she drove by.

Mario said I went absolutely white. I was furious with Mario for smiling and waving like a fool, only to be humiliated when the light turned green and she took off like a rocket. With the kids in the back seat making faces at me and showing me their middle finger. Graciela did nothing to stop them. How could they know the proper way to behave when their own mother was running around all over town like a disgrace? I couldn't blame the boys.

Of course, by the time we arrived at the hospital, Graciela was already there. I did not comment on her driving because I knew she wanted me to. She kept jiggling the car keys. But I said absolutely nothing. Nothing!

Mr. O'Reilly said hello very seriously, which was exactly what he should have done. I was glad that he had come to see how sick Berta had become. That way there would be no questions about why she hadn't come to work and why she needed her disability insurance payments.

Meanwhile Ernestico and Manolito were kicking the vending machine. Those two could wake anyone out of a coma. I hoped they would wake Berta. Her time outs were lasting longer and longer.

"Did I tell you both of her kids were in the back seat?" I said to Caridad later. "Ernestico is starting to imitate Mr. O'Reilly, his hair is long, his clothes are sloppy. Of all the examples to bring home. An earring isn't far behind. *Por Dios,* won't Graciela ever do anything right? I don't know about you but I've just about hit my limit."

"Well, you know she's going to buy a car," Caridad said with a sigh. "*Imagínate,* taking food out of her children's mouths. Well, at least we won't have to go through the trouble of asking Leticia to tell Graciela that she really shouldn't ride with us anymore. All we have to do now is be patient and she'll be gone soon enough."

"Those poor *niños,*" I said. "Manolito seems nice enough. I think he has his father's sense and dignity. But in her hands, and now with that gringo in the house, they will ruin him, too. I just know it."

"Should we call Ernesto?" Caridad asked.

"Ernesto has suffered enough," I replied.

Caridad made a gesture as if she was swatting away a fly with the back of her hand, as if dismissing Graciela from thought.

Chapter 14

CARIDAD

Imagínate! Graciela came for work one Friday wearing a big plaid hunting jacket, blue jeans and carrying a rolled-up sleeping bag and a backpack that could hardly fit in the van. I was in the front seat, but I watched as Imperio and Raquel scrunched over to make room. After Graciela had tossed the sleeping bag in the back, she sat down as if nothing was out of the ordinary. We were halfway to work before she simply said, "My boyfriend is taking me camping."

"Cubans don't go camping," Imperio said and in a very nonchalant voice Graciela replied,

"Cubans should mind their own business."

She said it as cool as spring rain. Even with all that going on, Graciela decided to flaunt her new boyfriend, as she now called Mr. O'Reilly, in our faces.

I looked at Imperio, and Imperio looked at me and then we just stared straight ahead. Is she taking the boys? I wondered. I prayed she wasn't leaving them alone in that apartment for the whole weekend! But I kept quiet because I knew that if the conversation went any further, Imperio was going to turn ugly and strangle the life out of her.

You would think she had learned her lesson. You would think Graciela remembered how much she owed us. It was so sad to watch her trying to reinvent herself in this country, but making no real effort to change. Maybe she could fool Mr. O'Reilly. But we remembered. We remembered only too well Pepe and Ernesto and all the trouble she caused. We remembered her poor parents, hiding in that house, afraid to show their faces. Ashamed. Disgraced. *Imagínate!* a woman with two growing boys carrying on like she was a schoolgirl.

"How could she be so thoughtless?" Imperio asked me during our coffee break — those ten precious minutes they granted us when we had to gulp down a cup of café while it was still scalding hot and run back — and heaven help us if we were just one minute late getting back to the assembly line. Not that Mr. O'Reilly ever said anything to us, but we could just feel it. Who knew what sort of ideas about us Graciela was putting in his mind.

Graciela, of course, was always the first one back from break. Always on time, always prompt. She no longer drank her coffee with us, instead she went off somewhere, "to read," she said.

We followed her to find out just exactly where she was going "to read."

"I wouldn't be one bit surprised if we find her in a broom closet with Mr. O'Reilly," Imperio said.

She was in the back of the factory, near the shipping dock. First we saw her legs sticking out from behind a low wall, nylon stockings and the high-heeled shoes she now wore to work. The rest of us wore flat, comfortable shoes. But Graciela had started to dress for the factory the way others dressed for an office job. At first, just once a week or so, then more frequently. Now every day, except to go "camping." She looked nice, but I wondered how much she was spending on clothes and shoes. I never asked, because even if others don't, I still have manners.

That afternoon, we slowed down as we approached, almost tiptoeing past her.

"Pretend you're looking for empty boxes," Imperio whispered.

Graciela was hidden behind an open newspaper. Newspapers, that's what she read. Why on earth would a woman like Graciela need to read the *New York Times?*

"To impress her American boyfriend, of course," Imperio said.

Graciela didn't see us. We watched her for a moment. She held the folded paper right up to her face because she needed glasses but was too vain to wear them. There she was, her fingers grimy from the ink. She probably couldn't understand one word she read. It was just an act. Some sort of attempt to look smarter than she actually was.

"With her it was always just a great big show," Imperio said. "Like when she was little and used to recite those José Martí poems during assemblies. It was cute at first, but as she got older, it wasn't so cute anymore. It was just obscene. She'd stand there, with an air of schoolgirl eagerness, her hands clasped behind her, looking innocent, but even then I knew she was doing it just to show off her chest."

I remembered all too well. All eyes, both male and female, wandered up and down her body as she recited that poem. I remembered with a little bit of envy her narrow, circular waist, straight shoulders, long neck, slender legs firmly planted, her feet arched. I often thought her recitals had little to do with the poetry.

So Graciela had not changed at all. None of the women in the factory read during breaks, and certainly none of us read *The New York Times*. But there she was, in her gray skirt, pale pink sweater, and high heels, looking like a secretary, poring over the newspaper, her lips hardly moving. All the men who walked by either glanced at her or worse they stopped and asked her questions.

"What do you think of Stalin's daughter defecting to America?" they asked. "She turned her back on the commies, that one. How do you like that?"

Instead of answering, Graciela just looked up, still holding the paper in place, and shrugged her shoulders.

"I could answer that damn question," Imperio whispered to me. "I can talk Russian politics and I don't even read the paper."

"Poor Graciela," I said, "has no idea what's going on in the world."

"Poor Graciela?" Imperio said. "Poor Graciela is just planning her next move. A woman like that is never just sitting, she's never just reading the newspaper. She always has something going on just below the surface."

Imperio had been asking about Mr. O'Reilly and rumor had it that he smoked marijuana, and probably used other drugs. She found out he had a five-year-old daughter, but was never married to the mother, and had been taken to court for child support violations more than once. That was the kind of man Graciela was getting herself tangled up with. I thought we should try to talk some sense into her, but Imperio said it would be a waste of our time.

"Just sit back and watch it unravel," Imperio said. "It has happened before and it will happen again."

I tended to listen to Imperio, she was the practical one. But in spite of everything, I was sick with worry.

Graciela was away camping on the day that poor Berta died, so it was left to us to take care of everything. We had to contend with the ugly side of death.

It happened on a Sunday, the day when we always visited Berta at the hospital. Imperio and Mario picked me up at two o'clock that afternoon. It was May, and summer had started too soon. Union City was empty and quiet. The air was thick with diesel fumes and the smoke from the refineries. The sun looked big and dark through the haze, and cast the sort of ugly, brown light that made me nauseous. Mario stayed out on the sidewalk to finish a cigarette.

Inside the hospital, it was air-conditioner cool, but it still felt humid and sticky. As soon as we got to her room, we knew. Berta's bed was empty.

The first thing I felt was that the ground had gotten soft under my feet. It was like standing on cushions. Then the walls began to stretch and bend and a strange nausea attacked my insides. Then I felt Imperio grip my arm, her hand dug into my forearm like a claw.

"*Por Dios,* Caridad, don't faint," she said and she said it sternly, with a tone she never used on me before. She talked to many people like that, but never to me.

"Look at me," she said. I raised my eyes to her and they were on fire.

"Hold onto me," she said, "we have a lot to do now. We have to get through this together."

For the rest of my life I would be amazed at her strength. Her character. Call her what you will — cold, heartless — but to me she was strength. Together we walked to the nurse's station.

"When did it happen?" Imperio asked the Puerto Rican nurse.

The nurse checked a sheet of paper on her desk.

"Last night, a little after eleven," she said.

"And no one called?" I asked.

The nurse glanced at the sheet of paper again.

"It says here," she said, "that the attending nurse placed a call to Graciela Altamira, but there was no answer. Do you know who she is?"

We both nodded.

"I am Graciela Altamira," Imperio said. "I was out last night." I was impressed with how quickly Imperio lied, and more than a little disturbed to hear her call herself Graciela. No two people were less alike.

"Can we see Berta?" I asked, hoping to divert the nurse's attention.

"Miss Altamira can," the nurse said, her eyes on Imperio.

"It's ok," Imperio said, "she's with me."

"But first, I need to see some I.D.," the nurse said.

"*Que?*"

"Identification."

"I left in such a hurry," Imperio said quickly and without hesitation, "that I forgot my purse."

"Isn't that your purse right there?" the nurse said, pointing at the brown leather purse clearly hanging from her arm.

"I meant my wallet," Imperio said. She was like lightning.

Imperio locked eyes with the nurse. Angry tears were now flowing down her cheeks. But the eyes of the nurse remained unmoved. In all the time I'd known her, which was all my life, I had never seen Imperio even remotely close to tears.

"*Vamonos,*" I said. Let's go. I took Imperio by the arm. She let me lead her away, while the nurse looked at us and shook her head as if we'd tried to do something horrible.

We went to Berta's apartment. We needed to find her son's telephone number. The super let us in. And even though Berta was miles away, the place already smelled like death, like dead flowers. Her apartment was immaculate, Berta being a decent Cuban woman, after all. I expected no less. It was a very small apartment, just one room. She used her bed for a couch, and there were so many little pillows on it that you had to sit on the edge.

"All those pillows are a sure sign of a lonely woman," Imperio said.

"What ever happened to her husband?" I asked.

Imperio gave me a funny look.

"There never was a husband. Her family sent her to work here when she was a young girl because she got pregnant. They sent her here to live with relatives, who I guess are dead by now. And they never let her go back to Cuba. Not even for a visit."

"Who told you that?"

"Nobody, I just figured it out. I mean, look around, it's obvious."

"Imperio," I said, "that is how rumors get started."

She gave me a funny look and said, "Only if you repeat it. I know you won't tell anybody."

"Poor Berta," I said to change the subject.

"It's too late now for laments," Imperio said, "Berta lived her life the way she wanted to, and she was lucky to have friends like us. Friends who didn't ask too many questions, or judged her no matter how crazy and irresponsible she had been in her youth."

"*Claro que no,*" I said. Of course not.

Imperio smiled and we continued our search. We were good people doing a good deed for a dear friend.

We finally found the address book in a drawer by the telephone. The problem was that we never did know Berta's son's name and we were terrified of calling the wrong person. Berta had always referred to her son as just that, "my son." "My son this and my son that," and "his wife" and "my grandchildren." It wasn't as if Berta's telephone book was perfectly organized like her apartment was. Even the countless bottles of pills and ointments, the rolls of gauze she used to bandage her legs, were neatly lined up next to the bathroom sink.

Her little telephone book was quite the opposite, with things listed as just one name, like Bebo, for example. And then several numbers scribbled under it. Other addresses were just on scraps of paper tucked into the pages with no logic whatsoever. Some had numbers that we recognized as Cuban because they were only four digits. But there were several of those — which one was in Formento?

Some were for people here in Union City, or scattered over other parts of the United States. We even saw our own names. Just our first names and our telephone numbers. No address. When we finally located her son's number, there was no denying it because all it said was Venezuela. It was not under the V's, it was under the E's.

His name was Eladio, and he didn't live in Caracas, as we had always imagined, but in a place called Maracaibo.

I was too nervous to dial myself, so I got Imperio to do it. And it just rang forever. Meanwhile, poor Berta was cold and alone in a hospital morgue.

"Let's try again later," Imperio said. And so we waited, sitting in that apartment and getting more sad. We didn't want to go to our own homes to call because now that Berta was dead, the telephone call would be free.

"Let the phone company try to collect after she's buried," Imperio said. And she went into the kitchen to make some *café* for us and soon the smell of dead flowers was replaced by the smells of coffee, and the smoke of our Kool cigarettes.

All over the walls hung pictures of the man we needed to reach. There were pictures of him alone, at different stages of growth. There were baby pictures and childhood pictures. Pictures of a teenager with bad skin and wild hair. There were also pictures of him as a serious adult, a wedding picture, and pictures of his wife and his children.

"So we can see him," Imperio said, "but we can't reach him."

There was only one photograph of Berta in the apartment. It had been taken a very long time ago. It was a studio portrait of Berta, when she was very young. She was pretty in a unique way, with a very provocative look on her face — the sort of look that had been getting Cuban women in trouble since the sons of Isabel of Castilla first met the daughters of the Taino Indians. Her shoulders were bare and smooth, with a pronounced beauty mark on the left one. Around her neck hung a lovely necklace made of black stones, probably onyx — *el azabache* — that we make our children wear to ward off the evil thoughts of others. An *azabache* is always only one stone, but Berta had a whole string of them around her neck. She must have felt she needed the extra protection. A woman alone in the United States with a little boy, *que lastima.*

Imperio moved to the most recent picture of Eladio. He was a middle-aged man now, but the expression on his face had not changed.

"He doesn't look anything like her," Imperio said. She was right. The man in the pictures must have resembled the missing father. He was very distinguished, his face serious, even arro-

gant. He had thick black hair greased away from his wide forehead, a big mustache, and the eyes of a killer.

"He looks like a real son-of-a-bitch," Imperio said.

"Imperio, his mother is not even cold yet," I said.

Well, I didn't know what sort of place this Maracaibo was, but
it took us all night to reach him. A complete waste of time. When
someone finally answered the telephone I was told to wait while
they went to get him. It took a while.

"They must have gone to get him out of the devil's ass," Imperio said.

When he finally got on the line, he talked so slowly it was like
pouring oil through cheesecloth.

"Look, *señora*," he said, very respectfully, as you would imagine, under the circumstances. "I can't possibly go to New Jersey
to bury my mother. Do you know where Maracaibo is?"

I wanted to tell him that I didn't even know *what* Maracaibo
was, but I simply said, "No."

"Look, *señora,* Maracaibo is a ten-hour bus ride away from
Caracas in good weather, and it has been raining here like you
wouldn't believe. Bridges between here and Caracas have washed
away. And Caracas is where the airport is, *así que se la van a tener
que arreglar.*"

Imperio was next to me, straining to hear the other side of the
conversation.

"What's he saying?" she asked.

I held my hand over the mouthpiece and told her. Imperio,
she grabbed the telephone away from me.

"*Por Dios,*" she said to him, her voice rising, "what sort of son
are you? After all the sacrifices your poor mother made for you."

She was beginning to scream, so I took the telephone away

from her. She walked to the other side of the room and it looked to me as if she was going to start pounding the walls. I knew this had little to do with Berta and her son and a lot to do with Mario and his mother, so I just looked away and tried to be as gracious as I could with this Eladio on the phone.

"Look, *señora*," he said again, getting a little less respectful, as you can imagine, because he thought he was still talking to Imperio, who had been less than respectful to him. He didn't know that the telephone had been handed back to me, that Imperio was in a corner ready to take one of his photographs and smash it on the floor.

"I feel terrible that my mother has died so far away," he continued. His voice got tight. There was a long pause and I knew he was crying. When he spoke again I could detect a vague Venezuelan accent. "I have begged her to come live here with us for years, and she has always refused. She said she didn't want to live here with the Indians. She said she preferred the Americans. So there you have it. If my mother died alone, it is because that's the way she wanted it. I don't know what else to say to you or what I can do for her."

"Well, your mother is not alone," I said, "but there is the matter of money. Funerals are expensive in this country."

Imperio was nodding her head, her curly hair bobbing.

There was a silence on the other end of the line. Somewhere in Venezuela an orphan was weighing his options.

"Look," he said, "certainly I can send you a little something, but it's not like I'm made of money. I work in the oil fields here and I have children to support."

"Well we're not made out of money either," I said, "we just work with her, so anything you can send will be an *alivio*." A relief.

"I'll see what I can do," he said. Then he hung up without so much as an *adios*. We never heard from him again, not by telephone, and not by mail, and we didn't see a nickel from him. I remembered Berta always saying, "In Cuba families stay together." Maybe it was just poor Berta drifting into a fantasy. Never in my life had I met a woman so alone in the world. Not only had her family back in Formento turned its back on her, but now, so had her one-and-only-son. I wondered what sort of woman Berta had been in her youth. Probably the type that's out dancing every night. There are plenty of that type in Cuba. Which would explain a lot. Particularly her aching legs.

Chapter 15

IMPERIO

Early the next morning we knocked on Graciela's door. Caridad wanted to talk to her about Berta and I wanted to see if we could catch Mr. O'Reilly sneaking out of her apartment. But he wasn't there. Graciela opened the door immediately. The boys were still sleeping, and she looked like she hadn't slept in weeks. In weeks! Her eyes were red and the skin around them swollen. She was already dressed and I could smell coffee and boiled milk. The place looked decent enough. The lawn furniture had been replaced by a small, burgundy sofa, the kind that turns into a bed, and a wooden coffee table. The dingy white walls had been painted light blue and the kitchen bright green. The blue was nice, but a green kitchen? *Por Dios!* Just looking at it made me nauseous.

"Raquel told me," Graciela said as soon as we stepped inside, "I've been on the telephone with Berta's family. You know how it is, it takes all night to place a call to Cuba."

"What family?" Caridad and me asked at the same time.

"Her family in Formento," Graciela said.

Caridad went into the kitchen and got *café* for both of us. Graciela chattered on about how at the hospital Berta had given her all sorts of instructions and information.

"She knew she didn't have much time left," Graciela said. "She had a vision."

Dios Santo. A vision. And she tells all this to Graciela but purposely leaves me and Caridad in the dark. It just didn't seem possible.

"If Berta knew she was dying," I asked, "why didn't she tell us? We were the ones at the hospital every damn day."

If Berta hadn't been dead already, I would have strangled her, I was so angry. Now I was furious with Graciela and with good reason. I gulped down the tiny cup of *café.*

"If Berta told you she knew she was dying," I said, "why the hell did you disappear for the weekend?"

Graciela took the empty coffee cup from my hand and took it to the kitchen sink. We followed.

Graciela kept her back to us. She washed that little cup so thoroughly I thought she was going to rub off the paint.

"She told me to go," Graciela said, "I told her I had planned a camping trip, that I had the feeling Barry was going to propose, and she said to go, that the visions had told her it wouldn't be for a few days. I knew she was ill, but I've also seen her be ill before, and I've seen her come back from it like nothing happened. So I don't understand why you're so upset, Imperio. It was a simple miscalculation."

"Did that man propose to you?" Caridad asked. Personally, at that moment, I couldn't have cared less. I was growing more and more furious with Berta, dead or not.

"I don't want talk about that now," Graciela said, and walked past us and into the living room. Again we followed.

"So he didn't." I said. And from the way she held her jaw and her head bent down just a little, I knew I'd hit my target. That man, I was convinced, was never going to marry her. Never!

Graciela couldn't understand why we were so upset. Of course, Graciela can never understand *lo que no le conviene,* what she doesn't want to understand. She was talking about Berta's visions and marriage proposals just to confuse us. Berta didn't have any visions. Of that I was convinced. Graciela went camping because Graciela always does *lo que le sale* — whatever she wants.

"We talked to her son and it was the hardest thing we've ever done," Caridad said. "He's washing his hands of the whole thing."

"In Maracaibo," Graciela said, as if this was a commonly known fact.

"Yes," I said. *"Por Dios,* that son of Berta's is a cold bastard. Cold! Good thing Caridad grabbed the telephone, or he would have gotten an earful from me."

"Did he tell you what she wanted?" Graciela asked. "Did Eladio tell you about the arrangement?"

She knew his name! Graciela said "arrangement" slowly, savoring each letter in her mouth. We just looked at her because from her tone we knew something was coming. And she took her time, took her long sweet time and we were not about to beg her for an answer.

"Eladio did not mention any arrangements," I said.

"Well, maybe he doesn't know," Graciela said. "He's been feuding with Berta because she refused to go live with him in the oil fields. I don't know how often they talked or how often they wrote to each other. Berta wanted him to come here and bring the grandchildren, but Eladio kept saying he didn't want to arrive in this country without any money, so he stayed there, where he could make a comfortable living and I guess the years passed and he got used to it. You know how it is. But Berta suffered because of it. She only met one of her seven grandchildren. You know what she always said: 'In Cuba families stay together.' Well, not any more, as we all know too well. I mean, look at us."

And when Graciela said 'look at us,' her eyes welled up and we could tell she was on the edge of a big scene. It was suddenly going to be all about Graciela, her loss, her grief, how hard she was taking this, and how lonely and far from her loved ones she was. As if we didn't know she couldn't wait to get as far away from her family as she could. As if we didn't know that she never writes to her family, that they haven't seen a picture of the boys in a very long time, if ever.

I could almost see the curtain going up on the theatrical stage that has always been Graciela's life.

Caridad had had enough. I could see all that lady-like patience of hers coming to an end.

"What did she want, Graciela?" she said firmly.

"She wanted her body shipped back to Cuba." Graciela said. "She doesn't want to be in New Jersey for all eternity."

I didn't have to think about it twice.

"*Por Dios*, she must have been delirious," I said. "She's lived here most of her life."

"*Imagínate*," Caridad said, a hand over her mouth.

"Was she out of her mind?" I asked. "*Por Dios*, Graciela, was she delirious? What exactly did she say?"

"Just what I told you, that she didn't want to spend eternity here. That she had already been here too long. Those were her exact words, may she rest in peace. I guess she never mentioned it to you. I guess you didn't know."

Apparently, there was a lot we didn't know. For one thing, we didn't know that Berta and Graciela were so incredibly chummy, that they were practically *comadres.*

"But not so chummy," Caridad later said, in her slow, measured tone, "that Graciela didn't strap on a backpack and leave her friend's deathbed to go frolic in the woods with that man."

The clear and senseless selfishness of it all came to light when Graciela reached into a drawer and took out the letter. We had no idea that Berta had given Graciela written instructions, which she was only too happy to wave in our faces. The letter was addressed to Graciela, handwritten and signed by *la difunta* herself.

"*Mi Queridísima Amiga Graciela . . .*" it started. My dearest friend. Singular. So there was no mistaking that this letter was intended for Graciela and no one else. What about us? We were the ones at her side when almost to the moment when she took her last breath. And then it went on about the evenings they had spent together and what an *alivio* those times had been for her. A comfort!

"What is this, about the evenings she spent with you?"

Graciela took the letter from me and looked at as if seeing it for the first time, as if she'd missed that part.

"She came here to watch the *telenovelas* sometimes," she said, her eyes welling up again.

"What's sometimes, Graciela?" I asked.

"I don't know, two, three times a week."

"*Imagínate,*" Caridad said, "I had no idea."

Suddenly, it was clear to me.

"Did Berta cook for you?" I asked.

"Sometimes, whenever she felt like it, she said that she hated cooking just for herself. It was mostly on nights when I had school."

So that's where all those leftovers came from that Graciela was so generously offering to Raquel. What a little conspiracy the two had going. With Berta cooking for Graciela, and Graciela giving the front seat in the van to Berta, and both of them quiet like little mice about the whole thing.

"You let that old lady come here after dark?" Caridad said.

"Ernestico walked her home," Graciela said without a note of apology. As if it was the most normal thing in the world to send your son out late at night in Union City with an old woman and let him walk the streets alone.

The rest of the letter was about Berta's money, which apparently she had plenty of, in a savings account.

"She saved whatever Eladio sent her from Maracaibo because she didn't want to be a burden to him when this happened," Graciela said.

"He sent her money?" I said. "No wonder he sounded so upset this morning."

The letter went on, very specifically, about how the money was to be used to buy a coffin and to send her body back to Cuba in the event of her death. She even had the name of a mortuary in Miami that specialized in that morbid business of transporting bodies from one country to another.

I stood up and looked Graciela in the eyes, practically backing her into a wall. I saw Caridad's eyes grow wide, as if expecting me to grab Graciela by the hair and pull her to the ground. Don't think it didn't cross my mind.

"You realize this is crazy," I said, almost spitting in her face, "don't you? You know what they do, don't you? The government steals the coffins, and throws the bodies into wooden crates so they can use the fancy American coffins when one of Castro's cronies dies. You know that, don't you? She can rest right here in Union City. What difference does it make now? Just because Berta went a little crazy from her illness, doesn't mean we have to carry out this crazy wish of hers."

"Not us, me," Graciela said. She slapped her chest with her hand, but it felt like a slap in my face. She was trying to squeeze us out, take it all for herself. Graciela the Hero, Graciela the Saint.

"Look," she said, a little softer, "I know you loved Berta, we all did, I need your help and your support, but what Berta wanted is what she's going to get. I don't care what I have to do to get her back there. I've already talked to her family in Formento and we're all in agreement. They have a family plot there, and that's where she should go. Not here all by herself in this cold, foreign ground. She'll be miserable here. Her spirit won't get any rest."

And then she stopped, bit her lips as if to stop them from trembling, and said, "*Por favor,* don't fight me on this."

I looked at Caridad, who only shrugged helplessly. We had no way of knowing if Graciela was telling the truth about a family plot in Formento. And we couldn't prove that she was lying, either. She had to have been, of that we were convinced. But no one could stop Graciela once she set her mind on something. *Por Dios,* shipping a body back to Cuba! We had seen bodies in the news being shipped back to America from Vietnam. Coffins covered with the American flag and filled with men hardly old enough to shave. Is that where Berta got her crazy idea? Should we cover Berta's coffin with the Cuban flag? Or would that be just a little too much? One thing was certain, Graciela was determined to send Berta back and there appeared to be nothing we could say or do to stop her.

Fortunately, Graciela was able to talk to Mr. O'Reilly and get us excused from work. *Dios Mio*, what Berta put us through that week. She had been very little trouble in life, but in death, she was nothing but. I don't know where Berta got her information, but there was no such thing as sending bodies to Cuba. The place in Miami did not exist. A child answered the phone and told Graciela that his parents were not home.

"What kind of a funeral home is that," I asked, "that has children answering the telephone?"

"Are you sure you dialed right?" Caridad asked.

Graciela tried calling again later while we stood around her like idiots, a coffee cup in one hand and a mentholated cigarette in the other, our hearts pounding with anticipation. We wanted Graciela to fail. We wanted her to give up, and put Berta in the ground, in New Jersey, where she belonged. At first there was no answer, the telephone just rang and rang. Graciela avoided our eyes, the receiver to her ear for an eternity. An eternity!

And then finally someone answered. Graciela spoke in English, holding the telephone firmly, using a professional tone of voice I had never heard before.

"Good evening," she said. "We are calling to arrange the shipment of a body to Havana,"

From the frown on her face we could tell what she was getting from the other end of the line was not good.

"I knew it," Caridad said as soon as Graciela hung up.

"Didn't I tell you this was crazy?" I said, and meant it. "*Pien-*

salo bien, Graciela. Berta was not in her right mind when she wrote that letter."

But Graciela would not listen to me.

"I don't know why you keep saying that," Graciela said, with no small amount of irritation in her voice, "Berta never seemed crazy to me. Certainly, not any crazier than anyone else I know."

In the silence that followed, she looked at me, and then at Caridad, and I can't speak for Caridad, but I felt insulted.

"*Bueno,* that's that, there's nothing else we can —" I said, but didn't get to finish.

"We'll have her cremated and send the ashes by mail!" Graciela said as if it was the most brilliant idea anyone had ever had.

As much as we tried to talk her out of that absolutely insane plan, Graciela forged ahead. It was as if Berta's body now belonged exclusively to her and she could do whatever she wanted.

Exactly two days later, Berta was delivered to us in a waxy box. That was it, all that life, all that pain, all those men, all that dancing, was burned down to a box of ashes. I didn't want to touch it, not that Graciela would have let me. She took possession of that box and carried it around ceremoniously, like it had the crown jewels in it, her face flushed with a look of accomplishment, even excitement. Gone was the sad, worried look of the past two days. Graciela had set her grief aside so that she could properly carry out Berta's wishes and claim victory over common sense. *Por Dios,* it was almost as if she was happy to do it. Happy.

Graciela had crazy plan. She had scissors, string, boxes, tape, and plastic bags all set out on her kitchen counter. We reluctantly sat at her kitchen table and helped her distribute the ashes into four clear plastic bags. Graciela used a soupspoon while we took turns holding the bags. It was like dismembering a person. For all I knew her face was with her feet — the thought of it made me queasy. The air in the room filled up with Berta's dust. We were breathing her in, and Caridad sneezed so many times she had to go sit in the living room. I stayed and helped Graciela place the plastic bags in small boxes. We taped them shut, wrapped them with string, and addressed them all to Berta's aunt, a certain Niurca Gomez Castillo, in Formento.

I knew those little boxes were never going to reach any such Niurca. The post offices in Cuba are much too suspicious of little boxes, particularly four of them coming from New Jersey and addressed to the same person. Berta's ashes were most likely going to be mistaken for some sort of drug and flushed down a toilet. Or worse, mistaken for Russian flour, which tends to be gray and lumpy, and baked into a cake.

But I was through trying to talk Graciela out of what she was determined to do, as sacrilegious as I felt it was.

When we were finally done, Graciela placed the boxes in a shopping bag and we walked into a cold wind and headed to four different post offices to mail the boxes.

"This way," Graciela explained, like she was the smartest person in all New Jersey, "we're sure that at least a little bit of Berta will reach its destination."

"Let's just get this awful business over with," Caridad said, and shivered.

Graciela led the way. It was as if she had suddenly appointed herself the Cuban mastermind of clandestine activities. She was determined and forceful, and all we could do was follow. She was dressed in tight, black slacks, a revealing, low cut sweater, and white, high-heeled shoes. I was greatly relieved when everything but the shoes vanished under a brown, loose-fitting trenchcoat.

Leticia, smart woman that she was, wouldn't have anything to do with it. She refused to drive us even though we offered to pay.

"No," she said, "I've had enough with the stolen dolls, the no paying, the insanity. I'm done with crazy people. I've worked too hard and too long to get the little I have and I'm sick and tired of putting it all in danger. From now on it's going to be different. No more stealing, and I want your payments in advance."

There was nothing else to say. She had made herself perfectly clear and after she left all I had was a growing desire to vomit. So we climbed from dreaded bus to bus all over New Jersey. We dropped off parts of Berta in post offices in Union City, Newark, Elizabeth, and East Orange.

In spite of the bitter cold, Caridad and I waited outside of the final post office, the one in East Orange. While Graciela stood in line inside. I pulled my overcoat tighter, and wrapped a scarf around my head. A horrible sadness had come over me. I was exhausted from all the walking, from waiting in endless lines, and the effect it all had on my nerves. *Por Dios,* what if someone asked to see the contents of one of those little boxes. How would we explain it?

I looked through the glass door at Graciela, who had just handed the last of the boxes to the woman behind the counter, to be stamped and thrown in with all the countless letters and cards of good wishes and regret that flood Cuba every day. I watched all the people standing behind her, a long line of *Americanos* patiently waiting their turn. Not one of them pushed or shoved or fought to go ahead of the other. No one talked, gossiped or complained, no one had brought their dog. There were no children crying, running around knocking things over or asking impertinent questions. There was none of the heat and sweat that is common in our small, crumbling post offices, none of the constant chatter of neighbors who, for better or worse, have known each other all their lives. No one shouted to a friend across the street. Maybe Berta had a point, I didn't want to be here for all eternity either. It had not been in my plans.

"What do you miss the most?" I asked Caridad. She knew exactly what I meant because she answered quickly, without thinking too much — maybe it was something she thought about all the time, too. I could see her mind drift swiftly back to Cuba, to Palmagria, in particular.

"I miss the stars," she said. "Every night there were just so many of them. Everything important that happened to me back there happened under a dark sky full of stars. Not like here in Union City where the sky is always milky, blurry and low."

I knew exactly what Caridad meant. I hated that sulfurous haze that constantly hung in the gray air. It came from the smokestacks and refineries that we drove past every day.

"The first time I made love to my husband," Caridad continued, "the birth of my baby, the night we escaped, all took place under that black, diamond-dotted sky of Palmagria. What about you, Imperio? What do you miss the most?"

Caridad's eyes were shining from the cold wind and the memories. I looked through the glass door once more. Graciela, having completed her task, was walking back to us, and quickly, before she could hear me, I said, "I miss people like us, and look, here we are, in a post office in New Jersey, mailing one of them back."

At that very moment we heard the familiar horn and there was the yellow van. Leticia kept one hand on the steering wheel and with the other she waved to us. The three of us got in without a word. And Leticia drove us home.

Chapter 16

GRACIELA

Barry encouraged me to read the newspaper. *The New York Times* was too complicated and full of big words, but I found the local paper a little less overwhelming. On June 13, 1967 a cease-fire between Egypt and Syria dominated the front pages of the *Jersey Journal.* Also in the papers of that long, hot summer were stories about the Soviet space program, Israel's army, the taxicab industry, heart transplants, the Vietcong, and something I was quickly learning about, racial tensions. Far from the front pages, on page 8, between an add for White Horse Scotch Whisky and a book by Norman Vincent Peale titled *Stay Alive All Your Life,* was this small news item;

CUBAN ASHES FOUND IN POST HERE
By J. Neil Sheehan
Newark, N.J> — Three boxes containing what officials believe to be the cremated remains of a human being

were discovered at three separate post offices in New Jersey including one on Bergenline Avenue in Union City. Union City has a rapidly growing Cuban population, second only to Miami, Florida. The boxes were addressed to Formento, Cuba. Authorities have tried to contact persons at that address but so far have been unsuccessful. Detectives in charge of the investigation suspect the ashes are part of a rite of Santeria, an ancient Afro-Cuban religion. A flood of Cuban exiles have poured into N.J. since President Batista fled the beleaguered island in 1959. An investigation is ongoing. At the moment authorities say there are no known suspects.

I was at peace with myself. I did everything I could, because it was what Berta wanted. You have to honor the dying wish of a friend, no matter how insane it may sound. How could I ignore her request? Of course, the newspapers made it sound as if it had been the act of a demented *Santero*. My only consolation was that they only found three of the boxes, which meant that my plan worked, that a little bit of Berta would rest in Cuban soil.

Maybe not in Formento, as intended, but somewhere in Cuba.

At first, Imperio and Caridad were strongly opposed, but they went along with my plan. Reluctantly. I think they wanted to be there just to watch me fail. After the newspaper article came out they were full of regret. The morning it appeared, they got into the van with worried expressions, as if a federal agent was going to jump out of a tree. And of course, they were more than willing to let me take the blame.

"*Por Dios,* Graciela," Imperio said, "we must have been crazy to go along with your plan. It won't be long before you have the FBI knocking at our doors. At our doors!"

"*Imagínate*," Caridad said, "all they have to do is check the hospitals to find out when a Cuban woman died and they're going to track down everyone who knew her.

"Prepare your lies," Imperio said, "because they're coming, and it's going to be a nightmare. Worse than anything we'd ever face with the G-2. *Dios Santos*, they will probably deport us."

"Can you imagine the faces if we show up back in Palmagria?" Caridad asked. "Tossed out of the U.S. for doing something so foolish."

The panic started again. I started to question my actions, my decisions. Had I placed all of us in terrible danger?

And then Leticia said, "*Niiiñas*, do you think that's all the FBI has to worry about? I wouldn't give it another thought. It's not like you were mailing boxes of explosives. I'm sure they realize that it was just a sentimental gesture. I wouldn't worry about it too much."

I talked to Barry about it later that night. There were nights when everything looked worse than it really was. I could tell this was going to be one of those nights.

But Barry agreed with Leticia. We sat in my living room watching "Apasionada." He liked watching my *telenovelas* with me. He had his arm around me, but my heart was beating too fast. I kept shifting and moving. So I told him what we had done.

"Baby, I wish you hadn't done it," he said, "but don't worry, this isn't Cuba with big brother looking over your shoulders all the time. In this country people mail marijuana to each other all the time and nothing comes of it. And to the Feds, that's a real crime."

He took my face in his hands. The look of terror in my eyes made him smile.

"If you had told me," he said, "I would have shown you how to avoid the dogs. We could have wrapped that old Berta in so much plastic and tin foil, no dumb dog was going to sniff her out."

"I was afraid to tell you," I said.

His smile faded. His voice remained soft, but it was very serious.

"No matter what you do," he said, "whether it's mailing a friend back to Cuba, or even just taking another class at the college, I'll always be on your side. You understand? Please, baby, don't ever be afraid to tell me anything."

And I had to kiss him. I kissed him for such a long time that I don't know how the episode ended that night. For all I knew Rosalinda got her kiss and I'd missed it.

Barry's was unlike any man I had ever met.

I couldn't believe how wrong I'd been all my life. About men, I mean. I never thought I would enjoy walking barefoot through a cold pine forest or sleeping in a tent on top of sleeping bags in the arms of a kind man. I guess that was the most amazing thing about Barry O'Reilly. He was kind, and he looked at me with such love and admiration. And I let him. How could I not? I had not told him very much about my past, and he didn't seem too curious. I also didn't know very much about him. He once said "that's what coming to the big city is all about, baby, letting all the past just go away."

Later that night, after we made love on my burgundy sofabed, Barry lit a marijuana cigarette and stood next to the open window, exhaling into the warm summer air. I had asked him not to smoke around the boys, but they were fast asleep in the next room. Personally, I liked that Barry had such an exotic vice. Of course, I knew that if Imperio and Caridad found out about it, they would have called the FBI, the CIA, and the KGB. The thought of the FBI knocking on my door like Imperio said had been keeping me up nights.

"Baby," Barry said, inhaling deeply, "let it flow down the Hudson to the sea."

I loved the things he said, they made so much sense to me. I loved that he called me "baby," that he was gentle and thoughtful. He returned to me and held me close.

"Close your eyes, baby," he said. "Imagine all that garbage they say about you is floating down the Hudson, to the Atlantic, let it get lost at sea. Can you see it, just floating away, past the waves, into the horizon?"

I did. I closed my eyes and tried to imagine all that stuff floating down the dirty river and on to the dark blue ocean and beyond, until it met up with the turquoise waters that surrounded my island. Farther and farther to the shores of Palmagria. I sent it all down, got rid of it all. Pepe's betrayal, Ernesto's anger, my mother's disappointment, my father's shame and silence, Berta's death, Imperio's judgments, Caridad's accusing eyes, all those fingernails, polished and half-mooned to perfection, and of course, Miami.

From the airplane, Miami had looked shockingly clean and orderly. The airport, with its bright white floors polished like a mirror, had the tallest ceilings and the brightest lights I had ever seen. I remember thinking that it looked like a palace from another planet, a futuristic place where dust, hunger and inconvenience did not exist.

Ernesto's cousins, Marco and Marinela Fonseca, were there to meet us, and they greeted Ernesto with hugs and kisses while the children and I stood by, smiling like idiots. Finally, Ernesto introduced us, but there were no hugs for us, just a twisted smile from Marinela and a slight nod from Marco, who turned on his heels and led us to the parking structure.

Marco's car was beautiful, clean, and fast. We traveled along wide, perfectly paved avenues. Enormous buses passed us by, as well as police cars flashing red and yellow lights and sounding their loud sirens. Palm trees — but not like ours, for these were thick and almost unnaturally green — decorated the sky, and the sky looked just like ours used to look before the Revolution: baby blue and abundant, with cotton-candy clouds.

We moved into Marco and Marinela's small, crowded apartment. Two bedrooms, a sofa bed and a little fold-out cot we call a *pim-pam-pum*. I slept on the sofa bed with the boys on either side of me, Ernesto slept in the *pim-pam-pum*.

I can't even begin to describe how strange I felt that night, brushing my teeth and getting ready for bed with my husband just outside the door. I knew that with a little time it would become routine, that all would pass. I was determined to make myself useful, to make everything all right, if only for my boys.

I tried, I really tried, to be as nice and accommodating as I could, but everyone treated me like a scarlet woman and the kids as if they had a contagious disease. Marinela avoided my eyes and I constantly felt as if I was in her way. She wouldn't let me do anything.

"*Deja eso*," leave that. She'd said it every time I tried to do the dishes after dinner. "*Deja eso*," when I tried to make the beds or scrub the tub. It was clear that she didn't want me getting too comfortable in her house, too settled.

When she finally got tired of my protests, she said "You're a guest." She didn't say this with the slightest hint of sweetness.

She said "you're a guest." And with those words she put me in my place. She moved her wide body in such a way that I had to step out of her way.

So I did nothing for weeks. Only to have Ernesto pester me about it.

"Give her a hand," he said as Marinela cleared the table by herself.

I took a deep breath and went outside for a while until it was late and time to go to bed again.

Everyone called Marinela's father 'Pápo.' He lived with them and was only sixty years old, but he looked twice that age.

Four years before, right after they had all arrived in Miami, Pápo had been diagnosed with throat cancer. He had a tracheotomy that had left him speechless and very depressed. Or, as Marco said, "a useless burden."

Pápo refused to do anything for himself and was constantly asking for help. He sat on the couch all day long and if he needed assistance and no one was around, he would fly into a rage, clapping his hands loudly to get attention. All that hand-clapping was thought to be bad for him, since he could only breathe through a little hole in his throat which had to be vacuumed with an enormous contraption. After one big clapping ordeal, they found him seething with frustration and drowning in his own phlegm.

To ease the problem, Marco gave him a bicycle horn that Pápo kept by his side at all times. Whenever he needed something, a glass of water, his medicine, or to change the channel on the television, he honked the horn repeatedly. I found it funny, sad, and horrifying all at the same time. He kept Marinela hopping with that horn.

One day, Manolito borrowed the horn while Pápo napped

and was playing with it, running around outside honking the horn, the way any child would.

I had been outside chatting with one of the other Cuban neighbors when I heard her. I rushed in to see what was the matter.

I found Marinela screaming at him. You'd think he had committed a horrendous crime. She was about to hit him but I walked in just in time. How she felt about me was never more clear than when I grabbed her raised hand, and stopped her cold.

"*Deja eso,*" I said, turning her own words on her. I took my child outside where she couldn't touch him.

I tried talking to Ernesto about the situation. His face went slack, as if he'd been faced with circumstances he simply couldn't comprehend.

"How could you be so ungrateful?" he asked slowly and evenly.

"I have put up with more from you than anyone could ever imagine," he said slowly, beads of perspiration erupted all over his forehead.

The fires of hell came unleashed. Everything he had kept bottled up inside came pouring out.

"You have deceived me, betrayed me, ridiculed me, ruined my life, my career. It's because of you that I had to leave my country, it's because of you that I now have to beg for a dish-washing job in a foreign country. You were never my wife. You put a stink on that word, on the memory of Josefa, on all that I have tried to do with my life. And now you're here, complaining, demanding. Who do you think you are, Graciela? How much lower do you intend to drag me? How much more can a man take?"

Marinela and Marco were standing nearby. I didn't know where to look, what to do. I had no answers for Ernesto, he was right. But one thing I knew, we could not stay in that apartment any longer. As long as the truth had stayed unspoken I could pretend that everything was fine. Now it was out in the open and I could start taking responsibility for my own life and the life of my children.

Marco and Marinela lived in a busy neighborhood that some were calling Little Havana. A lot of new immigrants were making their home there. A woman named Esperanza, who lived next door, took it upon herself to enlighten me. I was sitting outside to get away from the uncomfortable air inside the apartment. Ernestico and Manolito were playing on the sidewalk and I remember I was on the stoop just watching, trying not to think about anything in particular, when Esperanza sat next to me. "Marinela is saying terrible things behind your back," she told me.

"I don't want to hear what Marinela is saying," I said. "I didn't come all this way to fall into the same sewer of gossip and betrayal that I just left behind."

"Listen," Esperanza said, "why stay where you're not wanted? Why put up with the malicious chatter of that woman? It's not good for you or for your children."

"I don't know what else to do, where else to go." My words came out with a choking spasm of sobs.

I wished with all my heart that I had stayed back in Palmagria. Leaving with Ernesto been a horrible mistake. One that I would never recover from.

But I couldn't go back. How big a fool I would seem if I went back to Palmagria? What sort of reaction they would have to me, a deserter, a traitor, coming back with my tail tucked between my legs like a frightened dog? I knew I could survive anything, but I wasn't going to put the boys through the torture that was sure to follow.

"Here," Esperanza said and handed me a small piece of paper. "It's an organization called Our Lady of Perpetual Help. They're *Catolicos* and I heard that they help out exiles with children and no husbands."

I took it and put it in my pocket without even looking at it. I just continued watching the boys play. I was in no mood to talk to Esperanza or anyone else. She sat there for a while and then stood up to leave.

"*Bueno,* that's about all I can do," she said and stood up. "Use it if you want to."

She started walking back to her apartment and I followed her.

"Esperanza, wait," I said, "*Mil gracias,* I really appreciate your efforts to help me."

"*Yo hago lo que puedo,*" she said. I do what I can.

After she was gone I looked at the scrap of paper. Our Lady of Perpetual Help sounded like someone I could relate to. She sounded busy. Hopefully not too busy for me.

The next morning I left the boys with Esperanza. They promised to behave, and I promised not to be gone very long. All three of us broke our promises. I walked all the way, not trusting buses.

"You get on the wrong bus," Esperanza warned me, "and you don't know where you'll end up. This is a very big country."

I had expected the building that housed Our Lady of Perpetual Help to be a beautiful cathedral; a place lit by votive candles and sun streaming through stained-glass windows, where people talked in hushed, reverential voices and a chorus of nuns, perched on the choir loft, softly sang *Ave Maria*.

Instead, I entered a suite of stifling hot offices filled with ringing telephones, crying babies, and sweaty, hostile workers who looked like they'd rather be anywhere else. They asked me my name and entered it at the bottom of a long list.

I waited for hours, my panic rising with each horror story I heard from the other Cubans sitting around me. They told me stories they had heard about mothers whose children had been taken away because they couldn't afford to feed them. They said the children had been put in places called "foster homes," which meant they had to live with strange American families chosen by the state.

It started to feel very hot in there. I had not eaten anything all day. I didn't dare leave the reception area and lose my place in line. I was feeling as if I was about to faint. Wherever I looked I saw black spots.

I was walking towards a water fountain when I heard my name. I forgot all about my thirst, took a deep breath, and went in.

I was taken into an even smaller office where two American men, Mr. Ross and Mr. Jacobs, (who seemed to share one desk and spoke Spanish with heavy American accents) listened to my story. The first thing I did was lie to them. Growing up in a country full of Catholics but ruled by *Santería* had taught me that honesty afforded you absolutely nothing. With a seriously distraught look on my face, which I didn't have to work very hard to achieve, I told them my husband beat me and the children. That ever since arriving in this country he had turned into an animal. That I was afraid to go home. That the Revolution had turned him bitter and angry. I touched my shoulders as if feeling painful bruises beneath my blouse.

We were interrupted more than half-a-dozen times by telephone calls and an irritable and haggard-looking secretary who constantly opened the door without knocking and asked questions in English, or brought in papers for them to sign.

I had to start my story over and over again after each interruption until I was completely confused, but I held steady, answered calmly, kept insisting and explaining the unfairness, the urgency, and the absolute tragedy of my situation. I did not want to present myself as a hopeless victim but rather as a lost pilgrim who only needed a kind soul to guide her back to the road.

I was sure they could see through my complicated web of lies. They asked me questions based on something I had just said, and I had to stop and rethink my answers while I felt their eyes burrowing into my skull. An annoying little voice in my head kept reminding me that I had been caught lying before with disastrous results.

"No es facil," I said. It's not easy.

"No es facil," Mr. Ross repeated back to me, but in a different tone. He was nodding his head in sympathy.

Surprisingly, not only had they heard, but they had understood every word I'd said. Ross and Jacobs sat talking to each other in English while I said prayers to Our Lady of Perpetual Help. The next time they talked in their funny, slurry Spanish, they asked just one simple question — which in turn changed my life forever.

"Are you willing to live in New Jersey?" Mr. Ross asked soberly.

"In New Jersey," Mr. Jacobs added with a strange smile, "there are better paying jobs than in all of Florida."

They waited, looking at me as if they expected me to take my time, to think it over.

I didn't have to think twice. It was probably a little inappropriate the way I jumped up and kissed them both on their cheeks, but I was so excited and relieved. After disentangling themselves from me, they called in their haggard assistant, who introduced herself as Sue and stunned me by speaking fluent Spanish.

From that moment on, I was in Sue's hands and she took care of me in a way I will never forget. (Sue, wherever you are, I thank you with all my heart).

Ernesto didn't try to stop me or talk me out of it. He said a tearful (and, it seemed to me, slightly insincere) farewell to the boys. Ernesto never had much of an interest in children. He didn't deny them to me, but he'd always been a solitary man. If Josefa hadn't died, he would have gone on with his life as it was. He was somewhat relieved to see us go, we were messy in his eyes, children who fight, a woman who cheats. If it hadn't been for the government restrictions, he would have left Cuba without us. He had no use for us and we had no further words. Whatever had to be said had been said.

As I walked out the door, Pápo sounded his little horn, a sentimental little send off. I did not turn back. I left that apartment with my head held high. I was on my way to a new life in a place called Union City.

As the bus made its way north, the weather started to grow colder. It was only October, but already the coming of winter was announcing itself.

I had never seen so many trees with no leaves before. They looked like the long, skinny arms of the dead sticking out of the cold ground, their spindly fingers reaching in desperation towards the gray and cloudless sky.

A back wave of fear gripped at my heart. I was terrified of the trees. I remember thinking, trees never lose their leaves in Cuba. This is an evil place. My mother was right, God has sent me here as punishment. I had not fooled those people back at Our Lady of Perpetual Help. They had given me exactly what I deserved. I would have burst into tears if the children had not been seated next to me, their big eyes getting used to the new surroundings. I had to be strong for them.

People could say what they want to. I couldn't afford the luxury of listening, of caring. I set my course, and stuck to it. I worked hard to become a stronger person, a better mother.

Day after day I did what Barry suggested. I pushed all my bad thoughts down the river until the bad dreams were vanished. One day I woke up and realized I hadn't had one in weeks. Eventually I began to feel a sense of well being that I had not felt in a very long time. I felt as if I was growing, tall and proud like the palm trees of Palmagria. I let my heart fill up with the sweet memories of the people I had loved, Arroz Blanco, Chanclas, El Gago and poor Alvita with her beautiful face stained by the moon. All the outcasts of the cruel little town I thought I'd left so far behind.

All the while, Barry had an arm around me and I could feel his heart beating against me, his easy breath coming and going. Funny that the person who would finally understand me would be a man so different from anyone I had ever known before. A man who'd grown up speaking a different language, whose childhood had taken place so far away, in a land of snow storms, fireplaces, and camping trips. Barry didn't have a tropical bone in his body, and yet he was the warmest person I had ever met. He adored everything about me, my dark skin, my funny accent, my spicy cooking, my music. He even liked the way I dressed, and my love of the *telenovelas*.

After we first made love, he said, "Wow, baby." Those were the two sweetest words I'd ever heard. And while we made love his eyes remained open, fixed on mine, and I could see all that love inside. He snuggled up closer and held me and we whispered to each other until it started to get light outside. He didn't slap my ass and jump out of bed like it was on fire, like Pepe used to. Or turn away and start snoring, leaving me feeling more alone than I had ever felt before, like Ernesto used to on those very rare occasions when he acted like a husband.

A few nights after Berta died, I told Barry I wanted to recite a poem from my country for him. We were in bed together and it was warm and safe there.

"Yes, baby," he said, "I want to hear it."

"It's about a rich girl named Pilar who gives away her new shoes to a poor dying girl."

"Heavy," he said, and sat up on the bed.

"It's in Spanish," I cautioned.

"That's all right. I wanna hear it."

"Hay sol bueno y mar de espuma," I began, as I have done countless times since I was very little, since I was Pilar's age. *"Y arena fina, y Pilar quiere salir a estrenar su sombrerito de pluma."*

I recited the long poem, verse after verse, and his eyes stayed on me, on my lips, reading them the way a deaf person would. I knew that in his own way, he was understanding every word and, most importantly, that he understood what this moment meant to me.

The first time he talked to me, other than to give me work-related orders, was when he saw me studying my English as a second language book. He didn't make fun of me; instead, he encouraged me. After that, every time he saw me, he would ask me how my classes were coming along. Little by little, he won my heart. And one day I realized that no one had ever won my heart before; that my love for him was pure in a very special way.

The boys liked Barry. From the kitchen I could hear them

over the gun-play on television. They liked to watch the F.B.I. programs, and I liked the sound of the boys talking to Barry in perfect, rapid-fire English.

"Barry," I shouted over the noise, "you don't have to entertain them."

Sometimes they teased me about my pronunciation, "*Beree*," they'd say, "*ju don haf tu ennertain dem.*" And I just laughed because I could never tease my mother. She considered it disrespectful, but I didn't.

Now, I had to decide if I wanted to start over again. Barry had asked me to marry him. In New York City!

New York City had always been the big city across the river. Almost every day I caught a glimpse of it, glittering in the distance. To me, it was a frightening place. It was the city where Agustin Garcia-Mesa had lost his finger. New York was the place where his life had been ruined, where his promising career had ended underneath a Steinway piano, where his friends had turned their backs on him.

I was a little nervous as we boarded the train. Barry held my hand gently as we sped over tracks, through tunnels. I was surprised at how quickly we got to our destination. I followed him up the stairs and into the warm night. I wanted to be taken by the thickness of it, the people, the traffic, and the height of the buildings. I wanted to become a part of what had for years been only a postcard.

But I looked around and it was dark and dingy. Instead of glistening glass towers there were old buildings, mostly two-and-three stories tall, with rickety fire escape ladders crisscrossing their worn façades.

"Where are we?" I asked like a child.

"Baby, we're in Little Italy, the most romantic corner of Manhattan," he said, and placed his arm around my shoulders, holding me close as we walked. As I looked around, I saw other couples walking, hand-in-hand, I noticed all the Italian signs on the shops, *trattoria, zeppole, chianti.* The narrow cobblestone streets took on a charming glow, the sweet smells of garlic and basil intoxicated me.

As I walked, my heart kept beating the same refrain: you found him, you found him, you found him.

There was something beautifully different about Barry that night. He was like a child, his step was light, his eyes shined. He led me into a restaurant called Il Palazzo. And there, in this dim, musty, palace, in a red-leather booth, Barry took my hand and said, "Graciela, *casate conmigo.*"

He spoke the proposal in Spanish, so I knew he meant it. He had taken the trouble to look it up in a dictionary. His eyes were misty, and in his face was a funny look, as if he was afraid I would say no.

As Caridad would say: *Imaginate!*

Of course I said yes! I said it in English, and I said it in Spanish. My heart did all the talking for me that night in that Italian restaurant, in New York.

The confusion came later — when I was alone.

I didn't know what to do, it was almost too soon. But I did know. I wanted to be with him — and someday I wanted to take him back to Palmagria and show him the horrible little town I came from. I wanted to return with my husband and my children with my head held so high they'd have to jump up to see my eyes. But I couldn't help worrying. It wasn't as if I hadn't made mistakes before. Big ones. Barry wanted to get married right away. I told him I had to think about it. That I needed a little time to get used to the idea. Most of all, that I had to discuss it with my boys. And I had to get a divorce from Ernesto, but that wouldn't be a problem. He'd had very little communication with us. He once wrote to tell me that he was working in a library, in a place called Coconut Grove. He sent a twenty-dollar bill with the letter. Hardly enough, but I didn't care. I was glad that Ernesto was in a place where he could be at peace. He always felt safest among books and silence. The only problem, if I could call it that, was buried within my own soul. This love, this happiness, was overwhelming me to the point of insanity. Just the thought of it made me want to take all my clothes off and run naked, screaming down the streets of Union City. Yet it all seemed so right, like it was the work of all the saints and the virgins I prayed to. Even the ones I never believed in.

"Send me the right man or take away my desire to find true love," I had prayed again and again. And they sent me Barry O'Reilly.

Who was I to say no?

Chapter 17

IMPERIO

Dios Mio, Rosalinda was the *only* topic of conversation for weeks. *Las Niñas,* as Leticia still insisted on calling us (even though there wasn't one woman in that van who wasn't on the slippery side of thirty), chattered faster, louder, and longer than ever. Too keep from thinking about Berta, if you ask me.

I must admit, the *telenovela* was definitely heating up. It was the best one yet, and I'm not easy to impress. Rosalinda's boss, Salvador, had left his wife and confessed his love to her, but she refused to let him near her until after the operation. If she regained her sight, she would be his. If not, she made him promise to go away forever. Only a complete moron would believe that Rosalinda would not see again. The question that had everyone worked up was: When will Rosalinda and Salvador kiss?

Caridad, who now sat in the front seat once again and for all times, (Graciela knew better than to even mention changing the system), insisted there would be a surprise ending.

"Imagínate," she said, "Rosalinda isn't just going to regain her sight, but she's also going to come to her senses. Don't expect a wedding."

"Caridad, what makes you think Rosalinda's not going to marry him?" Leticia asked.

"What would that girl want with such a rich man?" Caridad said. "If Rosalinda marries Salvador she will be miserable. People should marry people like themselves. If all your life you've been someone's maid, even if in fact you are the true heiress of the plantation, the man you marry will always look at you as if you were the maid. When the honeymoon is over, and we all know that honeymoons don't last forever, he's going to see her for what she really is. The maid."

Everyone disagreed with her. Even I disagreed with her — which is something I never do, not in front of the others. If I have a problem with Cari, I always discuss it with her in private. But we all wanted the happy ending. Why not? Even Berta, in a strange way, got hers. One of the little boxes made it to Cuba — and even if the authorities there opened it up and flushed her remains down the toilet, at least it was a Cuban toilet.

But Caridad wouldn't leave it alone. Ever since Berta's death she'd been nervous and grumpy. Even I saw a big change in her. She was always so kind and gentle. Too kind and too gentle if you asked me.

The other day she said, "Women should not marry men who are unlike them financially, and most importantly, they absolutely should not marry a foreigner."

We all held our breaths because it was a loud and clear attack on Graciela. But Caridad was not done.

"Because you never know how often they bathe," she added.

It was a really cruel thing to say, all things considered, coming from Caridad who always smells like she slept on a bed of roses. I thought it was damn funny, but no one dared to laugh. The words hung in the stuffy air of Leticia' van.

"Chá," said Raquel with a sympathetic look to Graciela.

Graciela didn't say anything at all. The discussion ended right then and there. As the van continued moving towards the factory, a very deep silence descended. Thoughts of Berta were inevitable, no matter how loud we talked, no matter how hard we laughed or quarreled.

Graciela kept her distance from us that week. But Caridad was obsessed.

"Can you imagine his *ya tu sabes*?" Caridad said to me one day, after we dropped Graciela off. Her hand went to her chest, as if to feel her own heart beat, but her eyes remained fixed on mine.

I knew exactly what she meant. *Santo Dios*, it's no secret to us that American men have their foreskin trimmed off when they are babies, like the Jews. And I couldn't imagine. None of us could imagine having that big pink head looking at us all the time. At least our men have the decency to cover it up between rounds, like God intended.

Another night, on our way home, we were talking about the *balseros*, the countless Cubans arriving in Miami on rafts, and how short the distance between Florida and Cuba really was.

And then Graciela crossed a line. And I know these were not her words, it was the *Americano* talking. I would bet my life on it. It was raining that night, hard, gray, rain that made it so loud inside the van that we almost had to shout to hear each other. And we are not women with soft voices. But on that night we had to make an effort to be heard.

"Have you noticed," Graciela said, "when you look at a map

that Cuba looks like a vagina, a horizontal slit quivering in the warm blue sea, and that the Florida peninsula looks like a big, hard, throbbing penis just waiting to . . ."

Graciela stopped and looked at Caridad.

"Waiting to *ya tu sabes*," she finished, but her voice was mocking Caridad, who's always had trouble voicing intimate body parts and functions.

Leticia almost drove the van off the road. The rest of us were mortified. We would never be able to look at our little country the same again.

"Graciela, how do you come up with such things?" Raquel said. Raquel was now always dressed in blue. In her desperation she had apparently turned away from Alpha 66 and now was asking *La Virgen* for help in getting her husband out of prison. But Caridad said it was a just a smoke screen to cover up her affiliation to Alpha 66. And it made sense to me because not once before, in all the time we'd known her, had Raquel even hinted at a spiritual life. But for weeks she'd been wearing that horrible blue dress she made herself, and a medallion. During the coffee breaks she disappeared somewhere, "to pray," she claimed. But I suspected other motives.

"You can't see it? A penis, and a vagina," Graciela asked looking at each one of us. "Who knows, maybe it's destiny, maybe it's just a temporary squabble, a lover's quarrel. Maybe someday they will kiss and even make love."

"Well," Raquel said, "if you want to look at it like that, I will admit that Cuba is no virgin. She's been penetrated by Americans before."

"Exactly," said Graciela, as if she was suddenly a professor of world history and geography. Two subjects I remembered very well that she didn't quite get in school.

"And by the Spanish," Raquel added as if a brilliant thought had just occurred to her. "And the Russians."

Caridad looked at me and I knew what she meant. Raquel's blue promise was just a farce. No true disciple of *La Virgen* would ever entertain such a thought.

"*Niiiiñas,* can you talk about something else, please? Graciela, you too," Leticia shouted over the pounding rain. "I won't have my country insulted in my van. I won't have her talked about as if she was a bitch in heat. I may be far away, but she's still my country."

Silence followed. We drove along with just the rain, and a strange sadness. I knew these were the filthy thoughts that Mr. O'Reilly was putting in Graciela's head. Perverted pillow talk. For me it just brought a picture of their sex life that, frankly, I would rather not have to think about. It just made us even more uncomfortable with that relationship. I couldn't stand it much longer.

"Tomorrow they will kiss," I said.

"Too soon," Leticia said, "Rosalinda's still bandaged. It will happen on the day when the bandages are removed and you know it's going to be blurry at first, it will take some time for her to see clearly."

We had all watched enough *telenovelas* to know that she was right. The next few weeks would be blurry because we would be looking at the world through the watery eyes of a formerly blind girl. And then the image would get clearer and clearer until the end. Until that kiss.

No matter how we felt about Barry O'Reilly or how big our hints to Graciela, she was determined to go ahead with her plan, her crazy, crazy plan. She was like a little bird chirping. Her happiness was so annoying it was giving me headaches.

But just the same, that Saturday morning, we all had to put away our differences, and put on our best outfits. We tried to make the best of a very uncomfortable situation.

At first, I didn't want to go. It felt as if I was betraying the entire community. But I'm not one to rain on the parade of others, so I clenched my teeth, took four aspirins, and got dressed.

Of all the days in the year, Graciela had to pick July 14, a day when the blacks of Newark had decided to set the city on fire. Leticia picked us up in the van, except it was her husband, Chano, behind the wheel. And the van was fresh that day because Chano doesn't do deliveries on Saturdays and I guess he took the trouble to clean it out. The last thing I needed was to arrive smelling like raw pork. Leticia sat in the passenger seat, where Berta used to sit. And once again, it was very quiet in there. It was the first time that we'd had men in there. Mario, uncomfortable in a suit and smelling too strongly of cologne, sat next to me. Caridad came alone. Salud, as usual, stayed home with Celeste.

Leticia wanted to talk about the new *telenovela* they were advertising, the one that will follow Rosalinda. It was to be called *"Amor Perdido."* Love Lost. It would be the first *telenovela* shown in color. A *todo color!* Of course, none of us had a color television, so we'd have to settle for watching it in black and white. But every time Leticia started to talk, her husband, Chano, interrupted her.

"Shut up about those stupid telenovelas," is what he actually said!

And Leticia just kept quiet. She just backed down. Leticia who was always in charge. *Por Dios,* what kind of a marriage is that? I wondered if he beat her. If Mario ever dared to talk to me like that I'd smack him with a frying pan so hard he'd never say another a word again without drooling. But I didn't say anything. We just traveled in silence. It would have been nice to be able to talk to the girls about Rosalinda, the way we always did in the van. But having those two men in there made everything different. All they wanted to talk about was what was going on in Newark. I wanted to tell Leticia's husband that we had a right to talk about anything we wanted, but I chose not to because the last thing I need is Mario getting all worked up. He'd already had a couple of drinks before we left and had been ranting about the treatment of *los negros* in this country.

So we had to sit there quietly while the men tried to solve all the problems of the world. At least our husbands were *Cubanos*, for better or for worse. We didn't go running off with an American like Graciela. We didn't sell ourselves to the foreigners. As Caridad said, "We still have a sense of decency."

It was the strangest wedding! *Por Dios*, who gets married in a city park? On a Saturday. During a riot? Shouldn't a wedding take place on a Sunday, in a church? But we all showed up with our presents. Caridad and I were shocked that she wanted us to be her matrons of honor, but how could we refuse? For better or worse, we'd known her all our lives, and that first wedding of hers was such a disaster. I looked around, almost expecting to see Arroz Blanco standing there waiting to give her blessings. If only she were here, I thought, for this union certainly could use a good luck charm, even a tarnished, toothless, demented one like Arroz.

"Of course," Caridad said, smiling through clenched teeth, "she only asked us because her *comadre*, Berta is dead."

"This is such a mistake," I replied.

"What's one more stripe to a tiger?" Caridad said, looking up at the smoky skies.

So we went along. *Por Dios*, Graciela didn't even tell us ahead of time. Probably with good reason. If we'd had time to think about it, we probably would have refused, made up some sort of excuse. But Graciela, in spite of all her endless blunders, was not stupid. Just seconds before the ceremony, she ran to us and, in that breathless way she has.

"I can't do this alone," she said. "I'm so far away from home. I need you two to stand with me."

We knew exactly what she meant. *Por Dios*, we all felt like orphans in this country. We pretended it wasn't a problem, but deep down inside, everyone felt adrift. So we let her take us by the hand, and we gladly gave her away.

Gladly.

Graciela was wearing something made of white gauze. A wedding dress, sort of. She designed it herself, and it showed. Mario said she looked like a mummy from a horror movie. The wedding took place at sunset, and there were lots of people from work. Cloretta was there, big and black, in a floral gown and a big, wide hat. She was at a wedding while her entire neighborhood was going up in flames. In flames! She was all smiles and good wishes. I kept an eye on her, though, and I noticed that every time a siren sounded, she stiffened.

Some of Barry's family members were there. He has two older brothers, and one of them looked a little *afeminado*, if you know what I mean. A tall, skinny man with long hair just like Barry's, he was looking at that strange wedding dress of Graciela's as if he wanted to be the one wearing it. But no one seemed to take notice except Caridad and me.

The only person missing was Raquel, who had taken a bus to Miami the week before to join her husband, who was waiting for her there.

"What did I tell you?" I said to Caridad when Raquel told us she was leaving. That was all she told us and I was surprised that she didn't just disappear. She could have, for as much as we ever saw of her except in the van and at work.

Caridad just looked at me with that look I know so well.

"It's just as we suspected," she said, "Raquel must be Alpha 66. How else do you explain a man getting out of jail and making it to Miami? He was rescued or paid for. I have no doubt of that."

Raquel had packed up her blue dresses, her little girls and their headless dolls, and off they all went to live in Miami.

Leticia drove her to the bus depot, and we all went to say our tearful goodbyes and to wish her luck. It's what we always do. We show up for our own, no matter how misguided their decisions.

As Raquel climbed the steps to the bus, Caridad put a hand on her shoulder.

"*Oyeme*," she said with the best intentions. Listen. "If things turn out different than you expect, come back. Remember, prison changes a man, you haven't seen him in a long time. You don't know who he is any more."

"*Cha*," Raquel said, with a twist of her orange lips, and without a look back, she got on that bus.

"Leave her, Caridad," Graciela said. "The promise to *La Virgen* worked for her. She's going to be all right."

Graciela, always so naive about the simplest things. This had nothing to do with the virgin or the saints. It was politics, plain and simple. But there she stood, crying and waving as the bus pulled away with a big fart of black smoke.

I had the feeling Raquel would be back. From the sounds of it, her husband was trouble. Real trouble. I didn't know him or anything about him, but I had a strong feeling that something was wrong. I mean, for a man to be rescued out of jail, he must be in with someone. And who that someone was I would rather not know. In my heart I wished her my very best.

But at least Raquel didn't have to be at that wedding. She may have been headed for heartache, but at least she dodged that bullet. And Leticia already had two new women lined up to fill her seats. One of them is named Flor and the other Orquidea. They seemed nice enough — Cubans, of course. But they were not assembly line, like us, they were part of the janitorial staff, and they smelled like it, believe me. But as long as they paid on time, I don't think Leticia cared. We may need to have a little talk with her.

The smoke from the riots in Newark darkened what little sun there was. The brown clouds seemed to struggle with the blue and the effect was that of an enormous bruise. But Graciela didn't seem to notice. Graciela, nervous and excited, stood between Imperio and me, and pledged eternal love to a man she hardly knew — and will probably never know very well.

Although her English *had* improved.

She didn't even have a Catholic priest there. No priest would have been caught dead at such a spectacle. The ceremony was performed by a stuttering friend of Mr. O'Reilly's from the shipping department. He looked sort of Jewish to me. He had long hair, like Mr. O'Reilly's, but brown, and big, round eyes. He read from a wrinkled sheet of paper, but he could hardly be heard because of the patrol car and ambulance sirens blasting on their way to and from Newark.

Graciela's boys were very well behaved. Ernestico seemed a little dazed, probably wondering what life would be like now that there was another man in his family. I wondered how his father felt about the whole thing. Poor Ernesto, our teacher of so long ago. From what I understand he was more than happy to divorce. Just like I'd said ten years ago, that marriage never should have taken place. And I didn't want to be a cynic, but I had serious doubts about this one, too.

Manolito read a poem he wrote himself. It was like being back in Palmagria and watching Graciela. He seemed to have all of his father's best qualities. He read the poem with a clear and serene voice, not in Graciela's dramatic way. Those words seemed to have come directly from his heart.

And Mr. O'Reilly, well, *El Americano* wore his long blonde hair loose and flowing. I thought he'd have the decency to at least get a haircut. But no, his hair was as long as Graciela's. *Y de contra*, a tear rolled down his cheek during the ceremony. *Dios Santo*, a grown man who cried . . . in public . . . I predicted a problem.

Chapter 18

CARIDAD

I would never begrudge anyone their happiness. Just the same, I tried to skip the reception. And all that business with *los negros* in Newark had me nervous, very nervous. All those sirens and helicopters! Celeste didn't like loud noises, any commotion could set her off. And even though she was home with her father, I had no idea what I would find when I returned.

I just wanted to go home and lock the door. But Graciela wouldn't hear of it, *"Por favor,* Cari, you have to stay until we cut the cake," she said.

Imagínate. She had changed out of her wedding dress and into something even more inappropriate. This dress was made of blue denim with white ruffles around the low-cut neck and more ruffles at the hem. She looked like I don't know what. But you would think she was wearing silk the way she strutted around in white high-heels. As high as you can imagine.

The party took place in a rented hall off Bergenline Avenue.

I asked if this was the same place where Castro used to hold his fundraisers back in the '50s, but no one knew what I was talking about. Personally, I wouldn't have been at all surprised that Graciela would pick that particular establishment for her wedding reception. Graciela has a tendency not to think things through.

There was a very loud American band playing the most horrendous music. You should have seen Graciela on that dance floor, shaking in directions I didn't know the human body could go. She was the life of her own party, that one. I knew it would just be a matter of time before she jumped up onto that stage and grabbed the microphone away from the singer, if you can call him that. The music was too loud, if you want to call it music. I called it noise, and the worst sort of noise. It was all electric guitars and a big drum set, the sounds seemed to be aimed directly at the most sensitive part of my brain.

I sat at the table as long as I could. Leticia and Imperio kept me company, but we could hardly hear each other. We just sat there, our purses on our laps, while Mario and Chano continued the tiresome conversation they had started in the van. We watched Graciela on the dance floor making all sorts of indecent moves. She swayed her hips like a rocking chair and shook her shoulders so that her breasts went this way and that. It was embarrassing. Leticia, Imperio and I didn't know where to look. And Graciela just wouldn't stop dancing. Typical, when you think of the spectacle she used make at school assemblies back in Palmagria. She hadn't changed one bit, that one. Not one bit.

She danced with Barry, of course. That crazy band actually knew a slow song and I have to admit, Barry and Graciela looked good together. Who knows? Maybe they *were* in love. They were alone in the middle of the dance floor and it was like they were lost in a dream. "Wake up," I wanted to shout, but I decided to stay out of it. I knew it would be useless. Graciela was off and running. What else could I do but wish her luck? And then the music picked up again and she danced with both of his brothers. First the normal one, and then with the other. With the other, she danced twice.

I watched Graciela go up to the band and I thought, here we go, she's going to sing. But she just whispered something to the singer and he smiled big and nodded and then he said something to the band and what do you know, they started to play something that sounded a lot like *Guantanamera. Imagínate!* But of course they knew that song, I said to myself, the Americans own Guantanamo.

Then, happy as if she was listening to the Cuban national anthem, Graciela started going from table to table, pulling people to their feet. Cloretta didn't need much encouragement; no sooner had Graciela asked her than she was shaking her big body like the world was coming to an end. *Imaginate,* Cloretta was going home to smoke and ashes, but there she was, dancing the night away. I had never seen Graciela laugh so much, she could hardly stand from laughing. Is that what happiness looks like? I wondered. Like insanity?

The band played *Guantanamera,* the singer *machacando* Jose Martí's legendary lyrics, for what seemed like forever to me. Over and over the same little tune, over and over again the same few lines of the poem, for of course, the Americano didn't know all of them, just *Guantanamera, guajira Guantanamera* over and over again. But Graciela didn't seem to mind, Graciela was delighted.

More and more people poured into the hall with shouts and

kisses for the bride. The Cuban population of Union City was growing. We now had a *panaderia* right there on Bergenline Avenue, not far from the hall, and from the looks of it, they had made the cake for the wedding. It looked just like a Cuban cake, pink and white merengue with a little plastic couple on top. There was a table full of *choripan, pastelitos, croquetas, bocaditos.* A real Cuban feast. It seemed to me Graciela hadn't met a Cuban in Union City she didn't invite to the party. The new girls, Flor and Orquidea, were there, smelling of detergent but laughing and dancing *como si nada.* Even the *panadero* and his wife were there. What were these people thinking, opening a business, do they think we're going to stay in the U.S. forever?

The cake sat there and I could tell that Graciela had no intention of interrupting her dancing. I waited as long as I could. I was so nervous. I kept waiting for the F.B.I to show up because of all that business with Berta and the ashes.

"This is going to turn ugly," I said to Imperio. She knew exactly what I meant. Graciela couldn't possibly have a wedding without a tragedy. I just knew they were going to show up and arrest us all. The longer we sat there, the more nervous I became. I almost wished the F.B.I. would come and get it over with. The longer they waited, the more irritated I became. Had they given up the investigation because Berta was a Cuban? Didn't we matter? Or had the riots in Newark distracted them? I didn't know what to think.

Finally, I just couldn't take one more moment of it. I thought it best to just sneak out, to pretend I was going outside for fresh air and then vanish. I would walk home if I had to. I just wanted to get home and wash the whole crazy affair out of my hair. So I grabbed the flower centerpiece, nudged Salud and discreetly said goodbye to the others sitting there. Imperio looked at me with a horrified face.

"You're going to leave me here?" she said and started gathering her things. Leticia followed. Of course, with everyone at our table suddenly jumping up, I couldn't make the clean getaway I had planned. As we reached the door, a sweating, panting Graciela ran up to us and hugged me like I was her sister. *Imagínate*, after all these years, that's what she had become.

"So soon? We're just about to cut the cake."

"Leticia isn't feeling well," I said. But what I really wanted to say was, "How could you be carrying on like that with Berta dead only a few weeks. Don't you care about anyone but yourself?"

Graciela turned to Leticia and it was obvious that there was nothing wrong with Leticia at all. Leticia did not confirm or deny. She just stood there, paralyzed and probably hating me more than ever for putting her on the spot like that.

Thank God the men took over. Suddenly they were all hugging and kissing Graciela, congratulating her and wishing her a happy life. Even Mario, who by now was, basically, drunk. Graciela accepted his embrace and good wishes, but I could see her face over his shoulder and I could tell from her expression that she was full of doubt.

"Wait here," she said to us. It wasn't a friendly, happy Graciela who said it. Not the Graciela who had been tearing up the dance floor just a few moments before. This was Graciela with a posture like a knife and eyes that could see right through you. Imperio and the men went to the van. Imperio and I waited while Graciela walked to the a table where people had placed their presents and she returned with two little, delicately wrapped packages with bows and everything.

"For my matrons of honor," she said. Her voice was low and for a moment I thought she was going to burst into tears. We allowed her to draw us close to her and felt her embrace. She was hot and moist from dancing. I could feel the warmth of her body, smell her perfume, made more potent by her frantic dancing.

For that one moment, at that instant, I loved Graciela, in all her infuriating imperfection. The feelings surprised me. Graciela kept clung to me, and, finally I had to pull away. She had no choice but to release me from her suffocating embrace.

Smiling, she handed one little package to me, and the other to Imperio. We dropped them in our purses and practically ran to the waiting van.

I waited until I got home to open the little present. It's not polite to open a present in front of the giver. What if I didn't like it? You'd see it in my face. It was wrapped with shiny white paper that had little wedding bells and lovebirds all over it. On top of the box was a little white bow, the kind that Americans glue on because they can't be bothered to do the simplest things, like use a piece of ribbon and tie a decent bow.

I immediately telephoned Imperio.

"Did you open it?" I asked.

From the silence on the other end, I knew she had. Inside the little box I had found a doll's head. It was pink and shiny and had that awful frozen smile that looks more like a grimace. Was this Graciela's idea of a joke? And then, I knew exactly what it meant. I grabbed that doll's head and I threw it hard against the wall but it didn't break. It bounced back at me. Suddenly, it all made sense. Graciela had married our boss. I couldn't believe Graciela was going to be our supervisor.

Chapter 19

GRACIELA

Rosalinda is a red rose, with sharp, deadly thorns. The kind of thorns that cut deep to the blood. She's not like the girls in the previous *telenovelas*. She isn't a delicate white rose, or blushing pink. Her love for Armando is hot and furious. She doesn't tip toe around waiting to be noticed, she wants him and doesn't care who knows it. When she sees Armando, she quickly unbuttons the top two buttons of her blouse. Whenever he talks to her, she stands as close to him as she can. There is no doubt she wants him and she's going to get him. In this *telenovela*, the blonde isn't just the fiancée, she's Armando's wife. And Rosalinda is determined to break up that miserable marriage. Blind as she is, Rosalinda stomps around their mansion like she already owns it, and the wife almost trips over her own fancy shoes to get out of her way.

I was well aware of what Imperio and Caridad were up to and it just made me laugh. I pretended I didn't know that when they talked about me, they referred to me as "Rosalinda." I knew all about it. I considered it an honor. And I enjoyed that they didn't have the courage to say it to my face. Little cowards.

"Baby, they fixate on you," Barry said, "to keep from looking at themselves."

He was right. Imperio had her own very serious problems at home. Her husband, Mario, had a tendency to disappear. I knew all about it, because Leticia told me.

"Imperio showed up at my apartment in tears," she said, "because Mario hadn't been home for three days."

Leticia had to take Imperio driving around in the van from bar to bar all over downtown Union City, for free. Imperio begged Leticia to stay double-parked outside each and every bar. Leticia had to sit and wait while Imperio ran into bar after bar to see if her husband was inside. Every time she returned alone and more frightened.

"I had never seen her like that," Leticia said. "She seemed ready to break into a million little pieces. I could have taken her apart and put her together, like the dolls at the factory."

It turned out Mario was in jail for being drunk in public, and for fighting. And it wasn't the first time. Mario Santocristo had always had a huge problem with alcohol, practically since birth. Imperio could pretend the accident didn't happen, or that she didn't remember, but there was a young man in Palmagria missing an eye due to Mario's drinking. The way I heard it, the whole family had gone to a new restaurant in the outskirts of town that was known for making really good blood sausage stew. Mario, as usual, had had too much to drink and, on the way back, his favorite nephew, Felipe, had wanted to sit on his lap and pretend he was driving. Against Imperio's protests, Mario indulged the boy, who at the time must have been about eight years old. Of all his nephews, Mario loved Felipe the most. He was a smart, goodlooking little boy. Then, of course, the inevitable happened. Mario's car smashed right into a palm tree and the boy went flying through the windshield. I remember the neighborhood was very quiet the week that poor child was in the hospital.

Imperio insisted that Mario's problems were all due to some curse a neighbor put on him back in Palmagria, and I wondered how a curse could have followed him all the way to Union City. He was a drunk, he always would be. He was drunk the day he ruined that little boy's life, and he was drunk the night he almost ruined mine. What business did he have telling Ernesto about Pepe? I saw no point in bringing it up, ever. The damage was done and in this country we had to learn to coexist. But I remembered. How could I not? An accident could happen to anybody, but Mario in Union City was the same Mario as before. He'd been given plenty of opportunities, it seemed to me, and he continued to lose job after job because of his big mouth and his hot temper. Everybody who came to this country had to start at the bottom, but not Mario. Soon after he starts a new job at a restaurant, washing dishes or bussing tables, he wants to tell the owner how to run things.

"In my restaurant, we did it like this," he'd say, or, "in my restaurant, we did it like that."

Nobody wanted to hear it. It would have been like me going to Barry and telling him how to run the factory. How long would any of us last at a job if we behaved that way? And all that talk about Mario's big restaurant back in Palmagria. It was a sandwich shop at the train station. I'm sure they did good business, but to hear him talk, he ran a five-star restaurant in the center of town. I remember that place, it was a *timbirichi*, nice for Palmagira, but hardly five stars. It was no stars, and why Mario and Imperio choose to remember it differently, I can't understand.

Everyone knows that Imperio's trying to scrape money together to send for her mother-in-law, Liliana, who last I heard was a fire-breathing Communist, but suddenly is desperate to get out of Cuba. From what I heard, officials back in Cuba wanted her to go back to work. The law was, *"El que no trabaja no come."* He Who Does Not Work Does Not Eat.

That was the new motto of the Revolution.

"Liliana is too old to cut sugarcane all day," Imperio said. "I promised her we would send for her, but time is passing and we can't get the money. Now she sends horrible letters telling us we abandoned her. *Por Dios,* she could have come with us when we left, but she refused. She was so enamored of Fidel. Now she's making it seem like we don't want anything to do with her. We do want her here, at her age she could collect welfare, and we'd have a lot more money, believe me."

Caridad also has her share of problems. She refuses to admit that Celeste is seriously ill. No one knows what exactly is wrong with her, no one ever mentions it. Celeste has to be watched constantly because, when she entered puberty, she became very sexually aggressive. She did crazy things. She attacked the superintendent of their building. I heard that Celeste went out of control and practically raped the poor man. Salud had to pull her off of him. If left unattended, she masturbates in public or shoves things into her vagina. No cucumber or banana is safe around the girl. She has to be watched constantly.

Caridad says it's a normal reaction to the hormones they give her. She gets hormone injections because her face tends to get hairy, the poor thing was starting to look like a monkey. Salud and Caridad can't afford a private hospital. Someday, Celeste will have to go into an institution for the rest of her life. Caridad lives in terror of what could happen to her daughter in one of those places. So they keep her at home. Salud quit his job and they have less money than ever. But Caridad continues to smear herself with expensive creams — how she affords them I don't know and I don't much care.

Salud was always a pompous ass. He thought he was a doctor. A doctor? He was a chiropodist, and not much of one at that. All he did was treat calluses and ingrown toenails. But the way he cocked around Palmagria wearing pressed white shirts and an air of superiority; it was like he almost expected you to call him 'doctor.' Now he stays home all day, all night. Caridad says she needs him to watch Celeste, but where was he when Celeste attacked the super? I think he uses this obsession with Celeste to stay home and not do anything at all.

So Caridad is up to her ears in debt. Her paycheck barely covers her rent and the payments to creditors. She was often on the wrong side of Leticia because she can't always come up with her monthly fee. She claims that all her money goes to the special care of their daughter. But everyone knows that Celeste gets a welfare check every month.

Leticia loves her money. She puts up with anything in the van, bickering, theft, or if one of us has one of those mornings and is running late. She'll wait patiently as long as every week we hand her the cash. She has absolutely no tolerance for moochers. None. But Caridad wants to live as if she's still the pampered wife of a successful man instead of the factory worker she really is.

One morning, some months ago, when we stopped to pick up Imperio and Caridad, who always wait outside of their building together, Leticia pointed her finger at Imperio and said, "You, get in," and then she looked at Caridad and said, "but not you."

I almost died for Caridad. She stood on the sidewalk not knowing what step to take.

"She doesn't ride, nobody rides," Imperio said, and she stood in front of the van.

Leticia turned off the engine, jumped out of the van, and slammed the door.

"Get out of the way," she shouted at Imperio. But Imperio crossed her arms and wouldn't move.

"You think this is easy for me?" she then shouted at Caridad.

"Leave her alone," Imperio said, moving to the sidewalk and putting her arm around Caridad.

Caridad started to cry, her hands cupped over her face.

"*No puedo más, no puedo más,*" Caridad said between sobs. I can't go on.

"See what you've done, you greedy pig?" Imperio shouted.

"She's taking advantage," Leticia shouted. "I've put up with it, but it's been months. What am I supposed to do? I still have two years of payments on this piece of shit van. And her with her lotions and her new furniture. Do I have new furniture? Look at my hands, do I have fancy creams?"

Leticia held her hands out for inspection. They were red, chapped, and shaking with rage.

Caridad continued sobbing to the point I thought she was going to choke. Imperio was looking at Leticia like she was going to drag her by the hair. They were like the washerwomen back in Palmagria, fighting in the street. People who walked by slowed down to watch. The spectacle of a group of Cuban women screaming at each other in public.

I stayed in the van with Raquel. Through the windshield, like watching television. Imperio kept swinging at Leticia, trying to get at her. Leticia kept moving away just in time. It was like a cockfight. Just as Imperio was about to make contact, Raquel jumped out of the van and stood between the two of them.

"*Chá!*" Raquel said, and it was a powerful *chá* that forced everybody to listen. "Let's try to solve this like friends."

Leticia got back into the van and sat there, her red hands tight on the steering wheel as if to calm herself down.

"They don't know," Leticia said so softly I barely heard her, "what I have to put up with at home when I come home short. They don't know how Chano gets."

Caridad and Imperio remained on the sidewalk. Caridad buried her face in Imperio's shoulder. She couldn't stop crying. It was like a nervous breakdown. Imperio sort of put her hand on Caridad's head, but you could tell it wasn't easy for her. She knew Leticia was right, she knew that in if she'd been in her situation she'd have done the same, and sooner.

Finally, Leticia waved at Imperio and Caridad through the windshield without looking at them, and said, "Get in."

Neither one of them made a move. Then Raquel gently pushed them towards the door.

"Get in," Raquel said, "we're going to be late."

And they got in, quietly. Caridad stopped as if deciding where to sit, and of course, she sat in the front seat. We rode in silence towards the factory. Until Raquel spoke because she just couldn't help herself.

"In Cuba nobody fights over money any more," she said, "in Cuba nobody has any." And Caridad took in a deep sob.

The very next day Caridad paid up in dollar bills so wrinkled that they looked like she'd slept with them tight in her fist the whole night. And then it was all forgotten, for the moment.

You would think that women with those enormous problems wouldn't be so concerned with me. But they watch me like a *telenovela.*

There is one thing I have in common with all those long-suffering *telenovela* women that continue to capture my imagination: I never give up hope and I am always willing to take a chance. For a while I felt as blind as Rosalinda or as crippled as Ines in *Let No Man Put Asunder.* But I never gave up. Maybe I'll get somewhere as a fashion designer someday, and maybe I won't. I know I'm going to continue taking classes. I'm getting better. I got countless compliments on my wedding dress, which I designed all by myself. And who knows what's in my future? Maybe great success, maybe more mistakes. As the priest said in *A Long Walk To Love,* "The book of life is already written, all we do is turn the pages." I have to agree with him.

And my English is getting better all the time. I still can't read Barry's books, but sometimes I'll sit down and skip from page to page and I can understand the sentences, if not the story. Those stories are complicated! But I know someday I will. For now I'm happy that I can speak to people and understand what they say to me. My accent is very thick, so I have to concentrate hard to make myself understood. But it's an effort I'm only too happy to make. No one else in the van can say more than "thank you," and "bye-bye." It's their loss. English is such a beautiful language. They refuse to learn, it's almost as if learning English means that they are never going back home. As if they've given up. I don't know if I want to go back. Maybe for a visit, but I like it here.

I no longer feel as alone as I did back in Palmagria. All those poetry recitals, just me, alone, on a bare stage. The long, lonely walk to my wedding to Ernesto, the afternoons doing nails for the girls, feeling like an outsider in my own living room, the solitary years I spent locked up in my parent's house. I am no longer alone.

Barry was with me every step of the way as I prepared for our wedding. He took me to the beauty salon and read a newspaper while I had my hair and my nails done. What a luxury! I gave my hand to the girl and let her take care of me the way I used to take care of others. I told her I wanted perfect half-moons, but she said no one wears them like that anymore. Times have changed. She painted my nails an almost translucent pink. I have hands like a nun.

When I was ready, we practically ran back to the apartment like a couple of kids, my heart was pounding with joy. While I slipped into my wedding dress, Ernestico, Manolito and Barry sang *Las Mañanitas* to me. I was a little nervous, but the more they sang, the happier I got until I thought I would explode. It was so different from that other wedding day. Here in Union City, I have a family that supports me. I have a good feeling about this marriage. I really do.

Barry drove very slowly. I sat in the passenger seat, the boys rode in back. When the first police car passed us, sirens blaring, I jumped. Barry kept one hand on the wheel and with the other he took mine. We stayed like that as more police cars and ambulances passed us.

Above us the sky was full of smoke, but I kept my sights on a little piece of blue sky in the distance. New Jersey could burn to the ground. I didn't care. Palmagria could wash into the sea. It didn't matter. All that mattered was getting to the park. This was my wedding day; no amount of racial tension was going to ruin it.

As we drove, I counted my blessings. Who could have predicted that next week I would start my new job as supervisor. That I will, in fact, be in charge of the assembly line that attaches little heads to little plastic torsos. That I would be on the other side of the plastic curtain. And of course, I'll be making much more money. Yes, at last, I'll be able to afford that color television set the boys have always wanted! No more blurry, interrupted programs, no more pleading on my knees for the picture to stop rolling, or climbing to the roof in all sorts of weather to fix the antenna. And now that I've learned to drive, maybe I'll even buy my own car. Why not? Anything's possible.

The park was green, wide, and filled with friends. But Imperio and Caridad seemed so little and lost in all that green. Caridad, all alone without Salud, looked like she was about to fall over. And Imperio seemed tense, like she'd rather be anywhere else. So I asked them to stand next to me. They seemed a little stunned, which I enjoyed.

But none of that mattered anymore. At the party, Barry looked at me with so much love that his eyes were like fountains. I was in his arms and he twirled me around and around. Everywhere I looked I saw a smiles and laughter. The hall was full of people wishing me a happy future. There was music and beyond the music there were sirens and helicopters, fire and smoke. But none of that mattered either. Rosalinda may as well have been there, too. Her bandages gone, her eyes clear and bright with love for her Armando, and burning with the expectation of tomorrow, and that kiss.